AFTERSHOCK

TERRAN SCOUT FLEET
-BOOK FIVE-

JOSHUA DALZELLE

©2023
First Edition

PROLOGUE

"You read the brief I sent over?"

"I did. What a cluster fuck."

Admiral Marcus Webb leaned back in his seat looking at the holographic projection of NIS Director Jennifer Ward as she shuffled through stacks of actual printed hardcopies on her desk. She was on the planet Olympus, he was sitting aboard the UES Kentucky in orbit over Koliss-2, but the holographic images made possible through the hyperlink connection made it seem like they were in the same room together.

"How do you want to handle exchanging material and personnel?" he asked as she continued to paw through the pile of loose printouts.

"Special Agent Ackerman?" she asked. "I'll send a ship for him. I assume you'll be having your people look through the strike craft you captured?"

"They're already doing that," Webb admitted. "It's a non-invasive investigation. You'll get it in the same condition we did right down to the flash-frozen Cridal bodies still strapped into their seats."

"Delightful," she said. "How did that happen?"

"Hull breach. The group that executed the attack against the ship blew out power and life-support in a precision strike."

What Webb wasn't telling her was that the group who had shot up the Cridal attack craft had been a notorious mercenary crew with a human captain. He wasn't entirely certain of Jennifer Ward yet. The merc group that called itself Omega Force was still a political lightning rod that, like it or not, Webb had to tap dance around. Some recognized that their captain, Jason Burke, had been a man who was a victim of circumstance who had saved Earth on more than one occasion while another faction maintained that he was a dangerous rogue element who had put Earth at risk in the first place. The official policy stance toward the group remained fluid and depended entirely on which group held elected office at any given time.

It had been Omega Force that had disabled the Cridal ship and left it adrift for Webb's crews to recover. The small craft was proving to be a treasure trove of intel showing that the Cridal Cooperative appeared to be instrumental in a massive trafficking operation that spanned across much of the ConFed frontier regions. While this was despicable, it wasn't something Earth would have normally gotten involved in...at least until human colonists started disappearing. Now, it was a situation that had profound ramifications for Earth's continued membership within the Cridal Cooperative. Webb normally liked that his unit was always tasked with important missions that took them well beyond the borders of Earth's fledgling little star nation but, this time, he'd be just as happy to sit this one out. If he got it wrong the costs could be immense.

"You debriefed Agent Ackerman?" she finally asked.

"No, ma'am," Webb said. "He's not our asset. He did volunteer some information he thought would be critical for us to safely navigate the area but other than that he's been left alone."

"That's an appreciated bit of professional courtesy, Admiral," Ward said. "In return I will make Agent Ackerman's full report available to you since you will no doubt be tasked with a Scout Fleet mission soon enough. The word I'm getting from Earth is that the situation is...tense."

"And we would greatly appreciate that, Director," Webb said. "I'm prepping one of my best crews as we speak. The moment the president sends us a directive we'll be ready to launch."

"Hopefully they have better luck than our operatives did. Ackerman was one of the few to make it out alive."

Special Agent Bill Ackerman had been embedded in the Luuxir Border Region trafficking ring trying to find the source. Out of the two dozen or so agents deployed throughout the quadrant, he was one of only three survivors and the only one to come away with actionable intelligence. Webb was now keeping a watch on the young agent with an eye to poaching him for Scout Fleet later when things calmed down.

"That's unfortunate. Has the NIS thought about recruiting other species to gather intel? Humans are still rare enough outside of the Solar System that they automatically garner more attention than usual."

"Is that an offer to lend us your battlesynth?" Ward asked, sounding like she was only half-joking.

"He's not mine to lend. He serves at his own pleasure," Webb said.

"Of course. Please, tell Agent Ackerman we'll be sending a ship for him as soon as possible. Good luck, Admiral."

"To us all, Director Ward. Good day."

The hyperlink connection terminated, and the hologram of Director Ward slowly pixilated and dissolved in front of him. "What did you think, Reg?"

"She's not like other political appointees I've watched," Lieutenant Commander Reginald Weathers said, stepping out of the alcove he'd been observing from. On paper he was listed as Admiral Webb's chief aide but, in reality, he was the Scout Fleet commander's secret weapon. Weathers, who had advanced degrees in behavioral and forensic psychology, had the uncanny ability to read people and give Webb insights into their motivations and thought processes with an impressive degree of accuracy.

"How so?"

"She appears to be unguarded when talking to you," Weathers said. "She seems to be more mission- than career-oriented. Proceed as you normally would with an appointed director, but my gut feeling is that she will be an ally not a roadblock."

"Any chance she's fooled you?"

"Of course. I'm not the only one with my training, and it's hardly an exact science. I've always advised that you take my observations as just one data point as you make decisions."

"Fair enough," Webb said. "Go make sure our people haven't disturbed too much on that ship and let Mosler Station know we'll be coming down soon."

"Aye, sir."

Webb turned and looked out the window as the ship moved from a high parking orbit down to a lower, synchronous orbit that would allow them to offload personnel and cargo more quickly. The *Kentucky* had the ability to land if needed, but it was a huge pain in the ass, and it took hours and hours of precise maneuvering, so Webb preferred to drop her down, offload, and order her back up into high orbit where his other heavy-class ships sat in formation.

His stomach was in knots as he contemplated the mission tasking he was expecting from the president. Whatever they dug up would almost certainly have profound ramifications for Earth's relationship with the Cridal Cooperative. That also would mean that all the open contracts with the Cridal for ship building and weapons development could be affected, something Seeladas Dalton would not be happy about. Hopefully, the people in charge had some sort of plan for that in place before deciding to cut ties.

Standing to pour himself a drink, Webb reflected on how different his life had turned out compared to what he imagined when he had first applied to the US Naval Academy. Humans were now being abducted by aliens, and not just in cheesy movies. What was wilder was they were being abducted from other planets, not Earth.

"So much has changed just in my lifetime," he mused aloud. "Maybe we're not ready for all this."

But it was far too late to put that genie back in the bottle. Humanity had been thrust onto the galactic stage and, no matter what happened next, there would be no going back.

1

"How the hell is this my fault?"

"Everything is your fault! Especially this."

Marcos "Machine Gun" Angel, MG to his friends, was incensed. He and the rest of Scout Team Obsidian were in their own hangar, taking turns yelling at their team leader. Captain Jacob Brown tried to absorb and deflect the abuse, letting them get it out of their system, but he wasn't any happier about the situation than they were.

Obsidian had been on a four-month stand-down to let the team recover and train after a particularly rough mission to find some mech stolen off Earth. Now, not even a month in, they received an alert order placing the team on standby. That could possibly mean there was a pending readiness exercise coming their way but, more than likely, it meant Obsidian was about to be tasked with a mission.

"I just talked to flight ops. They're generating two ships," Ryan "Sully" Sullivan said from where he lounged on some stacked transit crates. He was one of two members of Obsidian who wasn't in the United Earth Marine Corps. Sully was the team's pilot and was an expert at flying damn near anything in the quadrant meant to fly, and even some things that weren't. He also did double duty as the engineer who kept the machinery in the sky.

"Two teams?" MG asked.

"The two ships being generated are *Corsair* and *Boneshaker*," Murph said. "So...still just us." Alonso "Murph" Murphy was a senior agent in the Naval Intelligence Section, but he had been permanently assigned to Scout Fleet, something he had mixed feelings about.

"*Boneshaker*?" MG asked, sitting up in alarm. "We aren't actually going to fly out on that piece of shit, are we, Cap?"

"She's been completely overhauled," Jacob reminded him. "All the patina and dilapidation are cosmetic now. She's practically a brand-new ship under the skin."

"I don't care." MG waved him off. "She's still a cramped, smelly pile of garbage."

Boneshaker was an older Eshquarian long-range combat shuttle the crew had stolen off the tarmac on Niceen-3 after the *Corsair* had been sabotaged. At the time, they had no way of knowing the ship belonged to a money-running crew working for Blazing Sun. Jacob and his team had jacked nearly six-hundred million credits from the syndicate's ruthless boss: Saditava Mok. In the end, they'd been able to keep the money, the ship and, most importantly, their lives in exchange for doing favors for Mok from time to time. Once Obsidian had come back in, Scout Fleet decided *Boneshaker* was a needed asset and had her torn down and rebuilt.

"I flew her last week," Sully said. "I think everyone will be pleasantly surprised."

"I can promise you I won't be," MG said. "So...any rumors as to where the asshole is sending us?"

"I believe that would be *Admiral* Asshole to you, Sergeant Marcos," Admiral Webb said as he walked across the floor. MG's eyes widened, and he tried to snap to attention, but the smooth plastic of the transit cases didn't have much purchase on the epoxy hangar floor and, when one went flying out from under him, he crashed to the ground.

"Sir!" he barked as he popped up. "I was not referring to you, of course. I meant our orders coming from Earth."

"You mean from the president?" Webb asked. MG looked trapped and turned to his teammates for help.

"Please," Murph whispered, "just shut the fuck up."

"I...well...no," MG stammered. "I meant asshole with all due respect, sir. I definitely wouldn't call him that to his face, if that helps."

"I expect so little of you, Sergeant, and yet somehow you manage to slide in under even that," Webb sighed.

"Yes, sir. Thank you, sir."

"At ease, you imbecile," Webb said. "I came personally to apologize for cutting your downtime short. Actually, that's not true. Given the nature of the threat we face, I couldn't give a flying fuck about you six sitting around the base for another month pretending to be training. Speak of six, where are Mettler and Tin Man?"

"On the way, sir," Jacob said. "I didn't give a hard showtime since I didn't know you'd be coming to brief us."

"This isn't your official brief. Just a heads up about what's likely coming." Webb walked over and sat on the crate MG had just vacated. "Consider this classified.

"We—and by we, I mean us and NIS—have been made aware that human colonists moving out to the frontier regions have been preyed upon by traffickers. The numbers are large enough that Earth has tasked Olympus with preparing a military response. As you all are well-aware, the Navy isn't really built to take the fight to disorganized, scattered criminal elements. They'd fly all over the quadrant never getting anybody to stand and fight.

"NIS embedded some agents within a number of the trafficking rings and found that the problem is far more widespread than we'd feared. The human colonists were never located, but what we're seeing indicates that likely millions of beings have been abducted and moved from around the quadrant."

There were some hisses of disbelief as that number sank in.

"Millions, sir?" Jacob asked. "How? How has this not made the Core Worlds come in and drop the hammer?"

"This part is highly classified. The ConFed is dead. Officially. The Core Worlds are negotiating a new treaty as Miressa and Khepri finalize the details of the new nation the Pillar Worlds are forming," Webb said. "We only know because of a well-placed source on Miressa Prime that has given us a heads up. By this time next month, all member worlds will be declared vassal states, but not member worlds of whatever this new nation is called. The ConFed fleet is already pulling back, and reserve units owned by individual member systems are being released to go back home."

"The quadrant is about to get a whole lot wilder," Murph said. Jacob looked over and saw his friend was ashen-faced and looked ill.

"To put it mildly," Webb agreed. "Very few know about this as word is being leaked out through diplomatic backchannels. What is likely to come out of this is a two-tier system in which the new nation still maintains its stranglehold on commerce, but they will no longer be responsible for maintaining the peace. Khepri will continue to provide centralized banking services while Miressa will still be the political center of the quadrant. What that means, however, is that regional conflicts will no longer be squashed by a ConFed battlefleet. They'll be allowed to spiral into full-blown wars."

"I feel like monitoring this situation is a more pressing issue, sir," Jacob said. "Definitely more in line with our capabilities. Can't NIS work the trafficking angle?"

"Normally, yes," Webb said. "The problem is that the trafficking operation has implications for our continued membership in the Cridal Cooperative. That's all I'll say on that until you get your official briefing, but we're all hands on deck right now with this."

"If Earth leaves the Cooperative, won't we be highly vulnerable?" Murph asked.

"That is the conventional wisdom, yes," Webb said evasively before looking up. "Nice of you two to join us."

"We were not aware our presence was mandatory," Tin Man said. "How are you today, Admiral?"

"Not bad all things considered," Webb said. "Captain Brown can fill you in on what you missed. For now, keep prepping for a long-duration mission without support. I'm going to head over and give Buzzkill the same pep talk. Hopefully, they won't be lounging around calling the commander in chief an asshole."

"Who called the president an asshole?" Mettler asked once Webb left the hangar.

"Take one guess," Sully said.

"I meant it in a positive way," MG protested.

"Let's get back to work," Jacob said. "You heard the man...long-duration, no support, so take everything you think we'll need. Tin Man, a moment please."

"Is this because Mettler and I were tardy?" Tin Man asked once they were away from the group.

"Huh? Oh, no. I don't give a shit about that," Jacob said. "You technically weren't even tardy. I need to know if your brethren have gotten any whispers about the ConFed collapsing and the military pulling back to the Pillar Worlds."

"We have been monitoring the situation," Tin Man admitted after a moment.

"You didn't think this was something we needed to know?" Jacob demanded.

"My conditions for operating within your team were never unfettered access to any and all information passed on to us through other battlesynth units," Tin Man reminded him. "There is a matter of trust and discretion that is expected of me. I would not knowingly lead you into harm, but I did not volunteer to be a source of intelligence for Earth."

"Fair enough, I guess. So, what is the situation you're monitoring?"

"Battlesynths on Khepri are all being deployed to protect vital infrastructure and critical personnel. The ConFed's main fleet is being recalled and divided among the Pillar Worlds according to importance. In the coming days an official announcement will be made that the ConFed Council is being dissolved and member worlds will now be self-determinant."

"Bleak," Jacob said. "Just like that?"

"The announcement will come after most systems have been made aware of the coming change through their diplomatic corps. It will be couched in terminology that will calm the masses, however. Rather than being told they're cut loose without protection, Miressa will say that they have selflessly decided to return sovereignty back to its member systems and vow to stop interfering in local affairs. It will be quite rousing."

"You're a cynic."

"You already knew this."

"That it?"

"More or less," Tin Man said. "There are some other details involving which battlesynth units are being sent to protect which targets, but that is not something I can discuss with you."

"How the hell do you guys even know all that?" Jacob asked.

"Battlesynths have developed their own underground intelligence network over the centuries. It was deemed vital that we have an overall understanding of the political landscape after some of the more draconian measures that have been attempted against us. My kind is used to protect some of the most sensitive people and locations in all the quadrant. We hear things."

"I won't press further. You know anything about a massive trafficking operation coming out of the frontier areas?"

"I have heard nothing about that. How widespread?"

"Apparently, millions missing so far including a large number of humans," Jacob said. "That's why we're saddling up. Reading between the lines, it sounds like it might have something to do with the Cridal."

"Fascinating," Tin Man said. "This will likely lead to a seismic political shake up of the Lower Orion Region that will coincide with the collapse of the ConFed. If the Avarian Empire wanted to come across the expanse and seize territory, now would be their opportunity."

"What the hell is the Avarian Empire?" Jacob asked, alarmed.

"It is not important right now," Tin Man said.

"Sure," Jacob said suspiciously. "Anyway... Recommendations?"

"The Cridal are not using government facilities and assets to move such a large number of beings," Tin Man said. "This would be a clandestine effort with multiple layers of protection to provide the people in charge with plausible deniability. We should look to places within this region that could support such a large-scale logistical operation and would not have a local government prone to interfering in private enterprise."

"Pinnacle Station?" Jacob asked.

"Too visible."

"It couldn't be the Ull again, could it?"

"Plausible, but highly unlikely," Tin Man said. "The Ull have become even more isolationist after the splinter faction working with Margaret Jansen almost dragged them into a war with Earth. For all their bluster about their superiority, the Ull leadership realized how close they came to total annihilation if Earth came at them with the backing of the Cridal."

"And the Ull wouldn't likely be willing to help facilitate a Cridal trafficking scheme," Jacob said. "At least not without playing both sides against each other for their gain."

"Correct again."

"So, again, I ask...any recommendations?"

"I am not familiar enough with this region of space yet," Tin Man admitted. "I rarely operated in this part of the galaxy and never this far down the spiral arm. My recommendation is that we wait to hear what your intelligence community has found, but my instincts also tell me that we should prepare for a covert campaign in a hostile land."

"So, we're taking *Boneshaker*?" Jacob asked, sighing.

"The *Corsair* is too notable in the places we will likely be going," Tin Man said. "For us to both complete our mission successfully and remain alive, we will need to be invisible."

"Blunt enough. I'll go get Sully prepping her."

Jacob's gut was telling him that something huge was happening.

The collapse of the ConFed and the subsequent propaganda campaign to try and convince the quadrant that it was no big deal was something that scared him deep down in his bones. For the first time since he'd joined the military, he felt like Earth could be at real risk. An irrational wave of anger at his father rose, which he pushed back down.

It was a ghost from his past, back when he believed the media lies about Jason Burke leading aliens back to Earth and letting them invade. He later found out that was all bullshit, but that conditioned response still reared its head from time to time, usually when he was afraid like he was now.

He flexed his prosthetic left hand into a fist, the Kheprian engineering so precise he couldn't hear the servos even at full power. Physically, the hand was probably better than the one a sadistic merc named Ma'hellich had sliced off, but it still wasn't *his* hand. He also had a new cybernetic left eye to go along with the new hand and a wicked scar that ran from his hairline down to his cheek. In reality, it was just dumb luck that Ma'hellich hadn't sliced the top of his head clean off, something he thought about often when he was alone in his house at night.

When the cybernetic prosthetics were first fitted, he reached out to an unlikely source for support and clarity: his father. Burke had been out getting his ass kicked by aliens and tossed into dire situations since before Jacob was born. He'd been hesitant to show any vulnerability to the man, but Burke had surprised him by being not only an understanding listener, but he offered some sage advice when Jacob had half-expected nothing more than a rant or lecture. He knew his father wasn't thrilled about him being in a forward recon unit like Scout Fleet, but he did an admirable job keeping it buttoned up and offering up what experience he had.

Jacob was about to turn back to rejoin his team when the general alert blared over the flightline PA.

"Inbound emergency flight...clear landing zone four-bravo and four-Charlie," the coordinator from Base Ops said calmly. "Inbound emergency flight...clear landing zone four-bravo and four-Charlie. All non-emergency personnel remain clear of the area."

"Captain! Just got off the horn with the admiral's office," Murph shouted. "They want us out at LZ Four-Bravo ASAP."

"What the hell is going on?" Jacob wondered as he jogged back to where his team was loading up into one of the dark gray open-cab flightline trucks.

2

"This was the emergency?"

"Trying to keep unauthorized eyes away, Captain," Reggie Weathers said.

Parked on the tarmac was one of the Navy's ubiquitous Madrid-class light duty courier ships. It was sitting quietly on its landing gear and appeared to be in pristine shape. The only way to know that something was amiss was that there were two full squads of Marines surrounding it.

"What's a regular Navy ship doing here?" MG asked.

"This ship is from the special detachment on Breaker's World," Reggie said.

"What are *we* doing here?" Murph asked.

"Observers," Reggie said, emphasizing the word. "The admiral wants you to have as much firsthand operational knowledge about what you're going up against as possible. An NIS trawler just arrived, and they have a team coming down to take charge of the investigation."

"NIS? On Mosler Station?" Mettler asked.

"This is more their jurisdiction than ours." Reggie shrugged. "One of our teams just happened to be who captured the ship, but we're turning it over to them. You'll be briefed further before you leave. This operation will be on many fronts, multiple departments. You won't be lone wolfing it out there."

"Heard that before," Sully muttered.

Jacob stood with his hands on his hips while the ship was secured, and the Marines boarded through one of the emergency hatches. Their posture indicated they weren't expecting any trouble aboard, so Jacob was a bit confused as to why they were even there in the first place. It was nearly twenty minutes before the ship's crew, humans wearing standard Navy uniforms, walked out and toward a waiting crew bus. Another thirty minutes after that, a group of twenty or so humans in civilian clothing were led out in restraints.

"Interesting," Murph muttered.

"Not as much as that," MG said, nodding to where the next group was being led out.

There were four Syllitr in restraints that were roughly dragged down the ramp and tossed onto the tarmac. Syllitr were the species from a world bearing the same name. It was a word that had many meanings in their native language, so they were known locally by a more common name: Cridal.

Syllitr was the seat of power for the Cridal Cooperative, a federation of worlds of which Earth was a full member. Now, four of their people were face down on the tarmac on a human military base. The humans who were cuffed had been moved around the far side of the ship where Jacob could no longer see them, and the Navy crew had been loaded into a crew bus and was driving off at a quick clip. As his eyes followed the bus, he saw the dark gray ground car of Admiral Webb approaching.

"Reg, what the hell is going on?"

"To be honest, I'm really not sure, Captain," Weathers said. "All I know is we were told a ship was coming in from Breaker's World and that the admiral wanted you and your team here as observers."

"So, you don't know anything about the Cridal face down on the pavement out there?" Murph asked.

"I know what you know."

Jacob snorted but said nothing. Reggie was too good to let on if he really knew anything or not. The Marines continued to separate and secure the two groups the admiral's vehicle pulled up near where the scout team was standing. Webb hopped out and waited while a middle-aged Sikh climbed out after him dressed in a sharp civilian suit. He walked with a pronounced limp as he walked after Webb.

"Commander Weathers, Captain Brown," Webb greeted his two officers. "Quite the sight, isn't it?"

"I suppose you could say that, sir," Jacob said carefully. "Who're the Cridal?"

"That's what my friend here is going to find out," Webb said, gesturing to the man next to him. "Gentleman, meet Mr. Salotra. He comes by way of the type of shadowy governmental office that has no official name."

"Captain Brown," Salotra said, pointedly staring at Jacob's prosthetic hand and eye. "You appear much as I envisioned. Your file photo doesn't do you justice."

"Thanks," Jacob said, not sure if he was being insulted or if Salotra was just trying to throw him off balance. If so, why?

"Here's the deal, boys and synths," Webb said. "The detachment on Breaker's World observed a freighter that had come into the system and took cargo from a few dozen shuttles off the surface. One of the shuttles had been flagged by NIS as possibly connected to the frontier trafficking operations I told you about earlier, so they intercepted it."

"When the Navy moved on the shuttle, the freighter tried to fire on it," Salotra took over the briefing. "They were out of range, and one of our cruisers began pursuit of the freighter, which meshed-out shortly after. The shuttle was taken without incident and, when it was boarded, there were the people you now see arrayed before you."

"A couple dozen humans in a shuttle?" Jacob asked. "I assume since they're restrained that we're not looking at a group of abductees?"

"We don't think so," Webb said. "NIS is coming to take them off our hands and provide us with any intel they extract. Mr. Salotra is here to take possession of the Cridal. Their mere presence is a political antimatter bomb just waiting to go off, hence why we cleared the flightline."

"Why let us see them at all, sir?" Murph asked.

"I need you to fully appreciate the stakes on this mission, Agent Murphy," Webb said. "If the Cridal are indeed facilitating a large-scale trafficking operation targeting humans the consequences of that will be...profound."

"We will isolate this information as best we can," Salotra said. "But I agreed that you needed to fully understand the ramifications of the Cridal running an operation against us and how critical it is that you make certain the intel you dig up and forward is accurate."

Jacob said nothing as he watched another flightline van pull up and collect the Cridal prisoners. Salotra nodded to them and walked off to join his people in the van. The Marines herded the human prisoners into yet another van. They weren't rough with them, but they weren't particularly gentle either.

"Thoughts, Captain?" Webb asked.

"Where's the shuttle? The one the Navy brought down?"

"On Breaker's World, sitting in one of our hangars under guard."

"Then, I guess we're heading to Breaker's World," Jacob said. "We'll fly out on *Boneshaker* this evening. Hopefully, by the time we get there, something actionable will have been pulled out of the prisoners."

"Commander Weathers will make sure you're kept current," Webb said. "We'll use Agent Murphy as our point of contact to maintain a strict chain of custody. All COMSEC protocols need to be strictly followed if you're taking the ship into unaffiliated space."

"Understood."

"You're also not authorized to pursue any leads you may kick up into Cridal space. At least not yet. For now, the president has made it clear that we are not to give any indication to the Cridal leadership that we suspect them of breaching the charter."

"Then, this is officially an investigation, sir?" Murph asked. "Not trying to shirk our duty, but we seem to be always working in this role, and it's not one we're suited for."

"But you've shown an aptitude for it, and you work fast," Reggie said. "More to the point, you're able to operate in hostile territory while the Naval Investigation Office can't."

"There's an interesting gap in capability and responsibility right now that keeps falling back on us," Webb admitted. "The NIO insists they're a law enforcement entity with no responsibility outside of Earth's territory. The NIS has agents trained in this sort of thing, but they don't have the infrastructure to deploy them rapidly around the galaxy to do their investigating, or so they claim. They embed agents in operations who take months to plan and execute. Scout Fleet is the only outfit that has covert ships and teams that are ready and able to move on a moment's notice."

"You're a victim of your own success." Reggie shrugged.

"Fantastic," Jacob said sourly. "And Obsidian gets tasked often because we already have one of those trained agents on the team."

"*Now* you're getting it," Reg said.

"I knew there was a reason I didn't like you," MG hissed at Murph.

"This can't be the same ship," MG said in awe.

Boneshaker had been rolled out of the hangar onto the active ramp and teams of techs were scurrying around her doing the final preparations for a long-duration mission. The dilapidated old Eshquarian combat shuttle still looked like she was only barely space worthy but, underneath, she'd been overhauled from the ground up including structural enhancements, a new state-of-the-art powerplant, and engines that made her faster than she had any right to be.

The living quarters and life support systems had all been upgraded as well to try and minimize the chance the crew would try to kill each other after more than a week aboard. Jacob was impressed with what Mosler Station's crews had been able to do while maintaining the patina on the outside that made *Boneshaker* practically invisible on any backwater world they might land on.

"Mission Support Services really outdid themselves," Sully said, practically bubbling as he gave them the tour. Obsidian's pilot was normally a stoic, reserved man with a dry sense of humor that hardly ever got rattled or over-excited. Apparently, the prosect of piloting the shuttle and not have it be a near-death experience brought out the child in him.

"Damn, new galley," Mettler said. "That'll be nice. What's the berthing situation?"

"Captain still gets his own quarters, so does the pilot," Sully said. "There are two more double rooms just forward of the cargo hold. Someone will get their own—"

"That'll be me," Murph said. "Rank has its privileges. Mettler and MG can share one." He looked terrible, and Jacob made a mental note to ask him later what was wrong.

"What about me?" Tin Man asked.

"You...need a rack?" Murph frowned.

"No."

"You see where I'm going with this, right?"

"While I do not technically require sleep or the privacy of quarters, I would at least appreciate being considered like I am a part of this team," Tin Man said. Jacob narrowed his eyes, not sure if the battlesynth was screwing with them or not.

"You're being serious?" he asked.

"Why would I not be?"

"Fine, you can bunk with me," Murph said, burping into his hand. "No loud music, no dirty laundry on the deck, and keep your shit off my rack."

"Thank you," Tin Man said, walking toward the flightdeck. He turned and winked at Jacob as he walked past. The human managed to keep a straight face as the others argued about whether they'd pissed off their teammate or not.

"Commander Sullivan!" a voice called up from the back. "You're all set. Fuel is topped off, and your munitions package is loaded. Spares are all in crates back here like you asked."

"Thanks, Brett," Sully called. "Go ahead and clear your people so I can do my final walkaround."

"Aye, sir!"

"Funny how much extraneous bullshit we have to do here just to get airborne because we have to follow Fleet procedures for everything," Jacob said. "When we're on-mission, we take off without even checking if the hatches are all shut."

"Keeps flight ops happy," Sully said. "If they're happy, I'm happy. I can't fuck with them too much or they make my life hell when it comes to annual recerts."

Jacob moved forward through the common area and to his cramped quarters that were just behind the flightdeck on the right. The shuttle only had a single main deck, and then engineering spaces below that were so cramped that you couldn't stand up straight while working in them. It was a pretty standard layout shared by most ships in the shuttle class, a catch-all category that included all ships smaller than a corvette but excluding specialized craft like gunships and couriers. *Boneshaker* was just under forty meters in length and was about average size for a long-range shuttle.

"Home sweet home," Jacob said, tossing his duffle onto the rack and looking over the refit. All the vertical surfaces had been covered in a soft faux suede material that was dark gray and had a nice smell to it. The rack had been elevated and mounted to the bulkhead to make room for storage drawers and the aft bulkhead wall lockers had all been upgraded. There was also a larger captain's safe where he would store mission essentials like hard currencies and tradable ingots. Next to the hatch there was a weapons rack where he could store and secure all his personal arms he brought along. Overall, he was impressed with what the engineers had done. The quarters could almost be called luxurious by military standards.

"We're good to go," Sully said from the doorway. "You ready to continue your training?"

"Now? Here?"

"Yeah...why? Is there some problem?"

"I'd rather work on it away from the prying eyes of the entire base," Jacob said.

"Stop being such a baby, Captain. Admiral Webb has decreed that all scout teams will have *at least* two qualified pilots. Since you're the only other officer in Obsidian, that means you. We're flying on a waiver since Tin Man can fly any ship in the galaxy if he needs to, but you are still on the hook." Sully made a shooing gesture toward the flightdeck.

"I'll ride shotgun, but I'm not taking her up to orbit," Jacob said. "I'm a Marine, this isn't what I signed up for."

"The Marines have pilots, too," Sully said.

"I *hate* flying the ship," Jacob complained as he closed the hatch to his quarters.

"Not as much as we hate you flying the ship, Cap," Mettler said as he walked by. "Didn't think it was possible to get motion sickness in a ship with artificial gravity, but you managed to pull it off."

"Is there some reason you're up here, Sergeant?"

"Murph is sick. Fever is over one-oh-two, and he's puking up everything I try to put in him."

"Damn," Jacob said. "We sure this isn't the brown bottle flu and you're covering for him? And don't give me that wounded look as if this sort of thing hasn't happened before."

"No, he's actually sick this time," Mettler assured him.

"I can't delay our launch, and I can't afford to be without him," Jacob said. "You have between here and Breaker's World to get him functional."

"Aye, Cap," Mettler said. "Just giving you a heads up."

Jacob walked up to the flightdeck and climbed into the pilot seat when Sully, already strapped into the copilot seat, pointed emphatically. He shrugged into the harness and tightened the straps as he looked over the ship's instruments. After seeing that she was up on her own power and the ground support crews had all cleared the area, he pressed a blue push-to-talk button on the left control stalk.

"Departure checklist," he said. "Standard flight mode."

The computer beeped twice in acknowledgement and, on the leftmost display, the checklist popped up while the rest of the flight instruments automatically reconfigured for flight mode.

"Using the checklist?" Sully asked. "See...we're already doing better than last time. Start reading them off."

"Powerplant to sixty percent," Jacob said.

"Check."

"External hatches and ports secured."

"Check."

"Engines from standby to run."

"Check."

They moved quickly through the twenty-nine-step checklist as per naval procedure, something they would never do in the field. Jacob wasn't against safety protocols as a matter of principle, but as a practical matter when you were on a mission and people were shooting at you there wasn't always time to do it by the book. In order to maintain some level of discipline, however, Admiral Webb had decreed that standard Naval flight procedures would be strictly adhered to on his base.

"Ship is ready," Sully said. "Do your thing."

"Mosler Station Departure Control, *Boneshaker* requesting clearance for up-lift on pad Eight-Alpha," Jacob called over the com.

"*Copy, Boneshaker. You are clear for up-lift, no restrictions. Climb out on course one-seven-oh for orbital insertion vector. Happy hunting.*"

"Copy departure course one-seven-oh for orbital insertion," Jacob said. "See you when we see you. *Boneshaker*, out." He took one last look at the ship's instruments before keying the intercom.

"We're cleared to launch. Standby for up-lift."

He fed power slowly to the drive to bring the ship up off her landing gear and settled into a hover five meters above the pad, pausing to retract the gear and do one last check of the ship. When no warning lights came up and the ship felt stable and settled, he swung her about to the south and throttled up to thirty percent power, raising the nose and followed the helpful guide arrows projected onto the canopy toward their orbital vector intercept.

Koliss-2 wasn't a heavily populated planet, and there wasn't a ton of traffic coming up and down from orbit like there was on a Tier-1 world, but they still had strict rules that the Navy base followed to the letter. Not making waves with the locals helped them blend in and remain hidden.

"That wasn't completely horrible," Sully remarked as he entered their slip-space profile for the flight to Breaker's World.

"Still hate flying these damn things," Jacob muttered.

"You're only half an hour or so away from handing off to the computer for the climb to orbit," Sully said. "We'll keep working on it."

"Can't wait."

3

Breaker's World was a crazy place.

It was a planet in the Lower Orion Region, which wasn't claimed by any government and didn't appear to have any sort of planetwide authority or charter, but still managed to remain relatively stable. There was a mix of the expected criminal factions along with legitimate enterprise, and they all seemed to coexist relatively peaceably.

The bored starport official didn't even look twice at the dilapidated Eshquarian combat shuttle, waiting for the expected bribe from Jacob, and then presenting them with a landing cert that wasn't actually backed by any governmental authority. It was one of the pitfalls of landing on the planet. Sometimes, you paid a scammer and ended up having to still pay the local crew that ran the starport.

"I can't believe the Navy has a permanent outpost here," Mettler said.

"I can't believe we didn't just land there," MG said. "Instead of paying bribes to the local mafia for the privilege of them not trying to steal our ship for the next six hours or so."

"It's not your money, so don't worry about it," Jacob said. "Let's go check that hangar space out, and then we can move on to check the shuttle over before NIS gets here to take it apart. Hopefully, we can get something useful. Be aware we're likely being watched while we're here even if we have no idea by whom. Let's try to keep our cover in place."

Their NIS contact had told them the ship the Navy had intercepted had been flying out of the starport they'd just landed at. When they'd checked the facility was listed as a commercial facility that specialized in scheduled maintenance and slip-drive alignments. On the surface, there was nothing there that screamed, "Hey! We're trafficking people over here!" It just looked like every other smalltime starport service center he'd been to while traveling around the galaxy.

"This is probably a waste of time, but what the hell," Mettler said. "Until NIS gives us our intel package and Mosler Station points us in a direction, we're sort of freewheeling it here."

"I'll take Tin Man and Sully with me. We need to find a group of workers taking a break somewhere around here," Jacob said. "Tin Man, can you fake an injury?"

"I beg your pardon?" The battlesynth sounded indignant.

"I need an excuse to approach an engineer or tech," Jacob said. "You're my ice breaker. I'm not saying actually disable yourself, just hold your left arm stiffly or something."

"I believe I can manage your request," Tin Man said.

"Why am I coming?" Sully asked.

"You mean besides your sunny disposition lately? I need you as a buffer between me and these starship techs. You speak their language, I don't."

"You're looking to find a gaggle of old gossips," MG said.

"We're guaranteed to have some around," Jacob said. "And they're the best source of information there is if you can sift through the bullshit. You know how I find out about all the stuff happening on Mosler Station? I talk to Marc."

"Marc? *My* Marc?" Sully asked.

"I didn't realize you were that close but, yeah, that's the guy. He's plugged into everything happening on the flightline, and he has a big mouth," Jacob said.

Marc Stiller was the crew chief for the *Corsair*. He was an enlisted spacer who was far too old for the specialist rank he wore, which indicated he'd been busted down a time or two. People tended to open up to him for some reason and told him things that they wouldn't if they knew he was an incorrigible gossip. Jacob had befriended him as a source of local intel, and the experience had opened his eyes to where potential secondary information sources might be when he was on a mission.

"What do you need us to do?" Mettler asked.

"Keep an eye on Murph and watch the ship. Shouldn't be anything too exciting," Jacob said. Murph was doing better, but whatever he'd picked up had kicked his ass, and he was still fuzzy-headed and weak. "We won't be too long."

The trio walked across the ramp toward where a cluster of repair hangars sat away from the row of rentable hangars on the other side of the admin complex. Jacob needed to find some people who lived there and worked at the depot fulltime to maximize his chances one of them noticed something strange. The lead was thin even by their standards, but it was either this or sit around waiting for the NIS to get their shit together and give them direction.

"Them," Sully said, nodding to a group of Eysups, their mottled red skin making them easy to identify.

"You sure?" They didn't look like ship techs or engineers to Jacob. If anything, they looked like a bunch of office workers having a smoke break.

"Positive," Sully said. "Let me talk first."

Jacob and Tin Man followed as Sully walked confidently up to the group. There were four of them and, now that he was closer, he could see that their clothing was all identical, meaning it was a uniform. The first Eysup to see them coming jumped and gaped at Tin Man first, but Jacob could see the recognition and fear on his face when he saw the two humans.

"Hello," Sully said as he approached. "My name is Ryan, I'm the pilot and engineer on that Eshquarian wreck that just landed."

"She did appear to be in a bad way," one of the Eysup spoke up. "You here needing service or looking to turn her in for scrap?"

"Not mine to give away, unfortunately," Sully said. "I'm actually here because you appear to be a scanning crew and my tall metal friend here is in need. His right arm—"

"Left arm," Jacob corrected.

"—left arm has been giving him trouble, and we thought that if we could see the joint, we would have a better idea of how to help."

"Scan a battlesynth? Isn't that illegal?"

"Not if I consent," Tin Man said. "Imaging the wrist and elbow joints will not break any laws unless you try to reverse engineer them from the data."

"We can pay, of course," Sully said.

"I've never seen one of your kind," the Eysup said. "I actually thought you were just a myth. We can do the scan over in the backshop. It would be much easier and safer than using one of the imagers designed for looking through starship hulls."

"Lead the way, my friend," Sully said.

Only the Eysup that had been speaking to them got out of his seat and led them back behind the hangar rows toward a group of low buildings that made up a small industrial park to support depot operations. The imaging backshop was staffed by a few more Eysups leading Jacob to believe it might have been a family operation. Breaker's World wasn't a place people tended to stay any longer than they had to.

"The smaller imager over here should do it. I assume you are resistant to radiation in the five hundred nanometer wavelength range?"

"I am," Tin Man said.

"This is a nice facility," Sully remarked as Tin Man was led to a table and shown how to lay his arm. The look he gave Jacob and Sully made it clear how little he thought of their plan so far.

"It's not terrible," the Eysup said. "We used to work at a depot up in the northern regions, but the storms that come in off the Nien Sea made life pretty miserable, so we moved our operation down here. Better class of customer operating out of the equatorial bases if you take my meaning."

"I'm not actually sure I do," Sully said. "We've never really been this far down the Orion Arm." The Eysup stopped and turned to look at them.

"You're human, are you not? Your kind flies through this system regularly."

"We weren't born on Sol-3," Jacob said. "We've actually never been to our homeworld."

"Is that what you're doing? Making a pilgrimage?" The answer seemed to satisfy Eysup as he continued strapping Tin Man's arm down to the table.

"Not exactly. We're something akin to bounty hunters or, more accurately, professional trackers. Someone had some family disappear, and they hired us to try and find them. The trail has them coming through Breaker's World at some point, but we're not sure where," Jacob said.

"I've not seen any groups of captives or anything like that come through here," the Eysup said.

"Captives?" Jacob asked. "Who said anything about captives? The people we're looking for were traveling in a group of colonists bound for the Concordian Cluster."

The Eysup paused and looked over at them.

"You think we're so stupid on this rock that we can't spot intelligence operatives?" he finally said. "You can dress up for the part and fly in on your beat-up looking ship, but you can't pass for the real thing to those who know what they're looking at.

"I knew the moment you walked up that you were here about your people being smuggled through here. You were fooling nobody."

As he was talking, he was backing up toward the door. Jacob had assumed it was just to put some distance between them because he was scared and realized his mistake too late. The Eysup leapt through the doorway and slammed the heavy alloy door behind him, locking it.

"This is going well," Tin Man said from where he was anchored to the table.

"Can you get yourself free?" Sully asked. Tin Man answered by standing up and snapping the alloy restraining clamps like they were made of balsa wood.

"Do we leave or wait here and see how it plays out?" Jacob asked.

"We are badly outnumbered," Tin Man said. "We need to get back to the ship immediately."

"Agreed," Jacob said, pulling his sidearm out from a concealed appendix holster. "Do it."

Tin Man walked up and kicked the door, firing his footpad repulsor just as he made contact and really leaning into it.

The heavy door held firm.

The frame did not.

The slab of alloy was sent caroming off the walls beyond, decapitating one Eysup and maiming three more in a group that had been approaching them. From what Jacob could tell, the one who saw through their cover wasn't among them. That meant he was probably still marshaling his forces to either come at them or hit the ship.

"*Boneshaker*, ground team," Jacob called over the secure com.

"Go, Captain," MG said.

"You're going to have inbound. Unknown number, probably all Eysups. Have her ready to fly and enable defensive countermeasures. Don't be too shy about it."

"We've got them huddled up near a side door of the hangar closest to us. They think we can't see them. Should I engage?"

"Not until they're an obvious threat. I can't confirm all are hostile." Jacob said.

"Copy."

The trio encountered no more resistance as they ran out of the backshop building and sprinted directly for the ship. Jacob was relying heavily on Tin Man's situational awareness and sensor suite to keep them from running into an ambush. The Eysups seemed eager but untrained. They probably really were a group simply plying their trade on Breaker's World and someone had paid them more money than they could refuse to keep an eye out for anyone too curious about trafficked beings.

As they ran, they heard the tail cannons of the ship give three short bursts. They were close enough to hear the screams of the Eysups as they rounded the corner. It looked like MG actually used a little discretion and opened up on the tarmac right in front of them when they tried to rush the ship. Most of the little red aliens were climbing to their feet, dazed and disoriented with dozens of shallow cuts from the flying pavement chips.

"There's our little buddy," Jacob pointed to a familiar Eysup struggling to get up. "Grab him, Tin Man."

"So, we're abducting people?" Sully asked.

"They shot at us first. Seems fair," Jacob said. "Get us airborne as soon as you get up front. Take us around to the Navy base as fast as she'll fly."

"Got it."

When they were within view of the ship, the rear ramp dropped, and Mettler was standing there with a carbine waving them on. Jacob let Sully and Tin Man board before leaping up the ramp and nodding to Mettler to close her up. Tin Man was securing the prisoner in the barred holding cell that folded out from the bulkhead as Jacob felt the engines throttling up and the ship lifting smoothly off the deck.

"You think the detachment commander will be pissed we're bringing a prisoner onto his base?" Mettler asked.

"No idea, but we don't answer to them," Jacob said. "This little bastard knows something, or at least knows who paid him and his crew to attack whoever came snooping around. Is Murph clear headed?"

"Eh," Mettler said, waving his hand to indicate it was iffy.

"Tin Man, you up to perform an interrogation?" Jacob asked.

"Why me, out of curiosity?"

"I assume you're trained and experienced in this sort of thing. I'm not. Murph is my only other guy who can do it. Having me go in there and just slap him around probably won't get us anything useful."

"I have extensive training in interrogations, psyops, and counter-psyops," Tin Man said. "I will talk to him when he wakes."

"Thanks," Jacob said. "Good job getting us clear out of there."

"We're fourteen hours from the Navy base," Sully said over the intercom.

"Fourteen hours?" Jacob asked. "You trying to save fuel?"

"I can only go so fast at this altitude. I can get there quicker with a suborbital flight, but we'll be visible to everyone."

"Fine. Keep us low for now. I need to let the detachment know we're inbound and request an NIS agent anyway."

"Looks like Breaker's World isn't a total bust," Mettler said.

"Maybe, maybe not," Jacob said, staring at their captive. Something gnawed at him, telling him this mission would test them in ways they'd never dreamed of. He hoped that it was wrong.

4

"Baker Station Approach, this is SF-Nine-One on final."

Sully was wearing his headset, so Jacob didn't hear the response, but from the look on his pilot's face, it wasn't what he wanted to hear.

"Then you can contact Fleet Ops and tell them why you are denying a ship with Alpha-One priority clearance to land. I'm sure they'll be fascinated by your explanation. I know my command will be."

"Nice to see the regular Navy is still operating at its usual level of bullshit," MG said from the hatchway.

"Pad Bravo One, copy," Sully said. "What a fucking asshole."

"It's not over yet," Jacob said, pointing to the center display where the ship's forward optics were trained on base. Two M811 ground transports were across the flightline toward their landing pad. "Looks like they're sending a welcoming party."

"You have got to be kidding me." Sully seethed. Of all the members of Obsidian, he had the lowest threshold for the bureaucratic bullshit and territorial pissing matches that were part and parcel of the military. "You want to contact Mosler Station? Let them know how we're being treated here?"

"Probably wouldn't be a bad idea to give the admiral a heads up in case this gets too out of hand," Jacob said. "Pull your velocity a bit. Let's see them commit to being morons before we pull the rug out from under them."

As Jacob was going through the hyperlink protocol to contact Mosler Station, Sully pulled power and decreased their approach speed. On the forward display, he saw two squads of Navy security forces—not Marines, interestingly enough—spill out of the transports and take up covered position behind the vehicles, concealing themselves from view.

"Captain," Reggie Weathers said over the superluminal com link. "Is this an emergency?"

"An annoyance," Jacob said. "Baker Station is expecting us, right?"

"Of course."

"Well, they've rolled out the welcome mat. Two squads of armed security forces on the pad deployed to ambush us after denying our clearance to land a couple of times," Jacob said. "Normally, I wouldn't bother you with the small stuff, but I'd rather not have to fight our way onto one of our own bases."

"I'll handle it," Reggie promised.

"I'll hold you to that if I get shot by these squids," Jacob said and terminated the link.

"Well?" Sully asked.

"Keep us slow, but take her in," Jacob said. "The Reginator is on the case."

Boneshaker continued her leisurely descent to Baker Station while the security forces on the ground maintained their concealed positions behind the unarmored transports. The closer they got, the more uncomfortable with the situation Jacob was. He knew that flight ops for the base would have reported their velocity drop to the boss, but they'd yet to contact them to see if there was a problem.

"Distance?" he asked.

"Twelve klicks," Sully said.

"Since they seem to like games, let's play," Jacob said. "Drop us to the deck and buzz the pad. Full power."

"You...you're serious?" Sully asked.

"Do it," Jacob said, tightening his straps. As Sully pushed the nose over and shoved the power up, Jacob punched-up Baker Station Approach Control. "Baker Station Approach, SF-Nine-One... we're detecting an armed and concealed force on our landing pad, likely hostile. We're taking defensive measures immediately. Standby."

There was silence over the com as *Boneshaker* leveled out at twenty-five meters altitude and roared toward the landing pad complex. Jacob noted that the new engines were smooth as silk as Sully pushed the shuttle supersonic in the dense, humid air.

"SF-Nine-One, abort! Abort now!" It was a new voice screaming over the com.

"Please, confirm that hostile forces on the ground are yours," Jacob said pleasantly, motioning to keep going.

"They are Navy personnel! Abort your attack *now!*"

"Very well," Jacob said. Sully smoothly pulled the ship into a vertical climb right before the landing pad, saving the security forces from being injured by a supersonic, low-level flyby. "Please, explain why you are setting up an ambush for a UEN ship on a scheduled flight, Approach."

"SF-Nine-One, you are instructed to land immediately," the original ground controller said calmly. "Please, comply without further incident. Baker Approach, out."

"In hindsight, that might not have been a great idea," Sully said.

"Sure, it was," Jacob said. "You established dominance."

"*I* did, huh? So, the plan is to leave me hanging out to dry?"

"More or less," Jacob said. "Don't worry, Reggie will have gotten it straightened out by the time we land. Probably."

"I suppose you thought that was funny, Captain Brown?"

The base commander, a Navy captain, stood in front of the rear ramp of the *Boneshaker*, and he was livid.

"Prudent, Captain," Jacob corrected. "We were ordered by our command to fly here in all haste and investigate a craft in your possession from a potentially hostile force. On approach, we observed two full squads of armed troops forming what could only be called an ambush. As team leader, I must always assume the worst."

"You arrogant Scout Fleet jokers think you can just do whatever you want, don't you?" the captain said. "This is *my* base. You don't just come flying in here and—"

"Let me stop you right there, sir," Jacob said, holding up his hand. "There seems to be a lot of subtext here I'm missing. I'm here to do my job, the same as you. If you are refusing us access to the shuttle, then we will be on our way. Time is very much a factor right now, sir." The captain was still an odd shade of red before he motioned to an officer standing behind him.

"This is Lieutenant Bauer," he finally said. "She will escort your team to examine the shuttle, and then back to your ship so you may depart."

Without another word, he walked back to his vehicle and left along with all the security forces, save for two who stood fast with Lieutenant Bauer.

"So fucking strange," MG muttered.

"I apologize for the theatrics, Captain Brown," Bauer said. She waved for them to follow her toward the hangars that were in two rows just south of the landing pad complex. Apparently, they were walking there as the base commander hadn't left them a vehicle.

"Care to shed a little light on that little episode?" Jacob asked. "I've seen some wild shit since I've been in the military, but that's gotta be up there."

"It wasn't personal, if that's what you're asking," she said uncomfortably. "Captain Allen has a bit of history with Admiral Webb. I think that might have clouded his judgment."

"If he thinks he's had problems with the admiral in the past, this little stunt won't help," Jacob said. "There's a lot of visibility on this mission and a lot of tense people watching us very closely...people with rank and position you don't want to annoy."

"I can only apologize, Captain."

"Wasn't your fault," Jacob said. "So, the shuttle has been stored securely without being molested?"

"Guarded around the clock, no one on base authorized to go inside the hangar. Access had to come down directly from Fleet Ops HQ," Bauer said. "We were told the NIS was sending a ship to collect it, then we were contacted again and told to expect a Scout Fleet team. Is there anything you can tell me about this ship?"

"What's your clearance level?" Jacob asked.

"SCI, level 4," she said.

"Were you involved in the operation to recover the ship?" Jacob asked. "Directly involved?"

"Why is that important?"

"I have to establish your need to know."

"I was on the team that brought the shuttle back to base," she said. "I also saw what was aboard it." Jacob thought about it for a moment. She seemed bright and observant, and he was authorized to clear her to see it. So long as they didn't divulge to her what they knew about the Cridal involvement, he wouldn't be looking down the business end of an official conduct review or a possible court martial afterwards.

"You can come in with us. Your escort needs to remain outside," he said after a moment's hesitation.

When the entry doors were unlocked by the sentries, and Jacob was able to step inside the hangar, what he saw wasn't what he expected. He'd assumed the shuttle would be Eshquarian or Aracorian since those were the two most-used types in the quadrant. Instead, he was looking at an older Bison-class heavy lift shuttle. The Bison was a human spacecraft built on Terranovus. They were no longer in active service with the Navy, but the civilian firms were still flying them. Sully whistled when he saw it.

"Old Bison. Block B ship from the looks of her. I can see why this is being kept a secret," he said. "I'll get the serial number so we can start backtracking her ownership history."

"I'll grab the flight logs," Mettler said. Since the death of Taylor Levin, Obsidian's former tech and his close friend, Mettler had taken it upon himself to fill the gap. For the things that were beyond his training, Tin Man was there to back him up.

"We have any restrictions on what we're allowed to do?" Jacob asked Lieutenant Bauer.

"You can't take anything with you," she said. "That's all I was told. All bits and pieces had to remain with the ship until NIS came to collect it."

"Got it," Jacob said. He motioned to Tin Man and walked up the boarding ramp. They walked through the large cargo bay and through the hatch into the engineering section. Inside, the walkway went straight through engineering into the midship service bays or there was a step set of stairs that went to the upper deck where the crew area was.

The Bison-class wasn't really designed for deep space service. Her slip-drive was underpowered, and the crew spaces were cramped and uncomfortable despite the enormity of its cargo bay. It was designed almost exclusively to service ships in orbit with the occasional dash to the outer system. Whoever had been flying the ship had brought it to Breaker's World for an ongoing operation, they hadn't been just passing through.

"Impressions?"

"This ship was meant to be left on this planet," Tin Man said. "I would not get too attached to the fact it is of human origin. It could have simply been conveniently available, or it could have been left on purpose as misdirection."

Jacob looked around skeptically. To leave the Bison on Breaker's World in the hopes some humans might stumble across it seemed unlikely. There was also the fact that it was captured trying to flee with Cridal aboard.

"We're not a forensic team, so pawing around through the crew quarters is pointless. Anything worth grabbing other than down-loading the flight logs and data recorders?" he asked.

"No dice, Cap," Mettler said as he walked down from the flight-deck. "Logs and FDRs were all nuked before they landed. Looks like the memory cores were physically destroyed."

"Well...this was a fun waste of time," Jacob sighed.

As they walked back through the cargo bay, he noticed something wedged behind one of the web seats mounted to the bulkhead on either side. He moved over and gave it a tug and found that it was a small pink notebook of the type you'd find in any department store. On a whim, he stuck it into his left thigh pocket despite Bauer's warning about taking anything and followed his teammates back down the boarding ramp.

"Get anything?" MG asked.

"Total bust," Mettler said. "Hopefully, Sully has some luck with tracking her history, but they destroyed all the data recorders."

"They had plenty of time to scrub it," Bauer apologized. "From the time we intercepted them to the time our Marines pulled them out, it was over two hours."

"The crew is already in custody back at Mosler Station waiting for an NIS pickup," Jacob said. "This was a longshot, but we're short on intel right now and just looking for a starting place."

"Wish we could have been more helpful...and hospitable," Bauer said.

"We'll be heading out now, Lieutenant," Jacob said. "Thanks for the help."

"Can I have a moment with you, Captain? Alone." Bauer asked as they were walking to the door.

"Certainly," he said, moving to block MG's suggestive leer from her view. "I'll meet you guys back at the ship. No fighting with the locals." When he turned back to Lieutenant Bauer, she held out a datacard for him.

"I take this as an incredible stroke of luck that you of all people showed up here to look this ship over," she said.

"What's this?" he asked, taking the card.

"My personal contact information, my service record, and a list of recommendations," she said. "I want out of here. This is a dead-end assignment, and my alternative is to find another special posting or go back to the regular fleet and spend my career playing politics aboard a starship, trying to scramble up the promotion ladder."

"You know I'm just a Marine captain, right?"

"But you have Admiral Webb's ear," she said. "Don't try to deny it, the stories of you and some of the shit you've gotten away with have spread far and wide throughout the Navy. I'd like an opportunity to serve in Scout Fleet, and I think you can make that happen. You can at least get me the audition, if not the role."

"What's in it for me?" Jacob asked.

"What do you want?" she asked suspiciously.

"Same thing every guy wants." Jacob smiled, pausing a moment. "Intel. That shuttle being here isn't just some random happenstance. Something is happening, or has happened on this planet, and you're someone who can pass on the occasional bit of information to make my life just that much easier. It would certainly be an enticement for me not to toss this card into the recycler once we leave."

"That's risky," she said. "I'm not asking you to do anything illegal...you are."

"There's a gray area here," Jacob said. "If you can get the information to me before it's officially classified, there's no problem. Besides, who is gonna tell?"

"I'll see what I can do," Bauer said. "But I can't promise anything."

"Likewise," Jacob said, twirling the card in his hand before slipping it into his pocket.

"So, it's like that?"

"It's like that. I'm aware of some of the rumors surrounding me and my team, but I can assure you Admiral Webb has a bullshit detector more finely tuned than any other flag officer I've dealt with. If I suddenly start trying to pitch him on hiring a lieutenant from a remote outpost I just visited, he's going to want to know why. I risk damaging what trust I have with him."

"That's fair," she conceded. "Like I said, I'll see what I can do."

By the time Jacob made it back to the *Boneshaker*, the engines were already humming, and the marker lights blinked, indicating she was ready for flight. As he expected, MG and Mettler were waiting for him on the back ramp, giggling like children.

"Well?" MG demanded. "Come on, Cap...spill it. What happened when we left?"

"In what fucking universe would I be sharing personal details of my life with you, MG?" Jacob asked. "Either way, you two can relax...it was an intel swap."

"That sounds ever dirtier for some reason," MG said, following into the ship as the ramp came up. "Come on, baby...let's swap intel."

"I'm just here to let you know that Sully backtracked the shuttle to a mining company operating in an unpopulated star system called LOR-773," Mettler said. "He has the course plugged into the computer already."

"Is everybody on board?" Mettler nodded. "Then, tell him to get us going," Jacob said. "I need to contact the boss."

They were able to lift off and clear the airspace before the commanding officer of Baker Station was able to screw with them any further. He'd seen some Fleet pissing matches that had gotten out of hand before but having armed troops lined up and waiting for them was a new one. Webb would either get a big laugh out of it or he'd have Captain Allen shipped back to Olympus in disgrace, trying to figure out where his career went.

"Standby for mesh-out," Sully said over the intercom before there was a slight shudder of the *Boneshaker* jumping into slip-space. Nice thing about Breaker's World was there was no minimum orbital altitude for mesh-out. As soon as you cleared the thermosphere, you could hit it.

Despite the bust on inspecting the shuttle, they now had a direction and a place to start. That made Jacob feel better since he hated idleness. They might be going in the wrong direction, but at least they were going somewhere.

5

"What a shithole."

"Yeah, I was expecting a little more," Jacob said. "Scans?"

"There are some automated systems still operating on both the planet and on some of the larger asteroids but, otherwise, the place is a ghost town," Sully said.

They'd arrived at LOR-773, also known as Site D for the McMillian/Shafer Mining Company. The company was a joint venture by a few companies on Earth that had lobbied the government to survey and begin resource mining unclaimed, unpopulated systems near Earth's expanding sphere of influence. With the shipyards over Terranovus becoming more efficient and orders for advanced starships stacking up, the need for raw materials was always at critical path. McMillian/Shaffer was one of a dozen slapdash operations scouring local space for asteroids rich in iron, nickel, or other needed minerals.

What they found when they meshed-in, however, was a mining operation without any people. Jacob had reached out to the company and confirmed that Site D was still active, and they fully expected a scheduled delivery within the next two months. He'd informed them of what they'd found and recommended they send some of their people and alert the UEAS that there was an extrasolar incident. He also made sure his own command knew about what they'd found. If Webb found out secondhand about a human settlement missing all the humans, he'd skin Jacob alive.

"The planet has stable gravity and acceptable atmospheric pressure, but the air is not breathable for humans," Tin Man said.

"Mostly methane," Mettler said, pointing to data graphic on LOR-733-4 on the screen.

"Then, the whole planet smells like a giant fart?" MG asked.

"That should make you feel right at home," Jacob remarked. "We can operate on the ground in enviro-suits, but let's not make the trip just to do it. Where was the main control center for this operation at?"

"The smallest of the three orbital platforms," Sully said, pointing to the icon on the screen for the installation. "This complex is huge, but there were only between twelve and fourteen hundred people here at any given time. The new *Nelson*-class heavy cruisers have a crew almost three times that size."

"Your point?" MG asked.

"My point is that let's not get too hung up on looking for some extinction level event here," Sully said. "Ghosting a thousand people wouldn't be that difficult, but would you really risk it to steal a worn out old surplus shuttle?"

"Still not seeing your point," MG said.

"But everyone being abducted in this trafficking operation makes even less sense," Jacob said, following Sully's line of reasoning. "They're peeling off huge numbers from refugee pipelines. Snagging a thousand or so skilled workers from a— Oh."

"What?" Mettler asked.

"The captain is thinking that the crews from a resource mining outpost might have been grabbed because of their skills," Tin Man said.

"Let's get to the command center and see what we see," Jacob said. "Hopefully, we don't trigger any automated defenses."

Sully took the *Boneshaker* in slow and steady. As they passed some of the derelict equipment, Jacob still couldn't detect any signs that there had been an attack here. Even if the outpost had no defensive weaponry to speak of, they still had some means with which to defend themselves. Instead, it just looked like everything was given the command to *stop*, and the people just up and left.

The command center itself was what Jacob expected. Designed with zero aesthetic sensibilities in mind, bulky, and beaten up by various impact marks and random discolorations. The automated airlock system immediately acknowledged their beacon and extended the cofferdam at Sully's command. All modern Terran ships used the Eshquarian-type airlock coupling since it was the most common in the region, thus it docked with their shuttle without issue.

"Data connection established," Sully said. "We're getting telemetry. Looks like the atmosphere inside the platform is stable and fresh so the enviro systems are all up and running still."

"MG, you're staying here to watch the ship with Sully. Everyone else who isn't a battlesynth, gear up assuming we could lose atmosphere at any minute. You don't have to wear the rebreathers, but I want you to have them on you." Jacob waited until the throng had cleared the flightdeck hatchway before stopping by his own quarters to grab a plasma rifle off the bulkhead rack and his tactical harness hanging in the alcove.

The team was quick and efficient in their preparations and within ten minutes they were all standing by the starboard airlock doing buddy checks on each other's gear. The indicators on the bulkhead were all green telling Jacob that the airlock collar had hard mechanical lock and the pressure on the other side was equalized and the air safe to breathe.

"If you need me, just shout," MG said. He didn't appear to be too upset he was being left behind, which was unusual for him.

"Keep the hatch closed but unlocked for now," Jacob said. "If I give the word, hit the emergency decouple and tell Sully to get clear."

"Will do."

"This is creepy," Mettler said.

"The background music still playing on the overheads is what's getting to me," Murph admitted. "Why the hell would they leave the music playing?"

They'd quickly moved through the bottom two decks and the strangeness of the whole thing was beginning to fray nerves. Even Tin Man wasn't immune as, inexplicably, he switched to full combat mode before moving up to the next deck. He offered no explanation why but took point from Jacob as they climbed the steep stairs.

It wasn't until they were halfway through clearing that floor that they found the first evidence that anyone had ever been there. Sitting in her chair, eyes wide and mouth open in shock, was the body of a human woman. There wasn't a lot of blood. Hardly any, in fact. The entry wound in her upper chest made Jacob think she'd been stabbed with something other than a knife at first.

"Cap, look," Murph said, pointing to the deck. Jacob bent and picked up two brass shell casings, 9mm.

"She was shot with a gun?" Mettler asked incredulously. "Like, an actual fucking gun?"

"Looks like," Jacob said. "Why isn't she...you know...smelling up the place?"

"Atmospheric handlers," Tin Man said. "Did you notice the food still on the tables in the galley? Dried but not decomposing. The excess moisture is constantly removed, as are airborne microbes."

"This is the director's office," Murph said from the hatchway. "Which would make her Janet Rushton, Site D operations director. At least according to the nameplate out here."

"Whoever killed her did it with a weapon from Earth, so it's a safe bet the person was human," Jacob said. He pointed up to the security camera in the corridor. "Let's head up to the control room and see if there's anything recorded."

Three more decks up they finally reached the main control room and discovered two more bodies. Both men in dark blue uniforms with matching logos and both armed with M21 bullpup carbines that Jacob had a passing familiarity with. There were more shell casings scattered around, but they were also 9mm and not the oddball 5.7x28mm round that the M21s used.

"They rushed the control room and capped the security guys," Murph said, looking at the bodies. "They used frangible ammo. Deadly, but they won't punch a hole through the hull or the windows."

"They couldn't afford modern weapons?" MG asked.

"These arms are still used on Earth," Jacob said. "They were issued for internal security since the UEAS doesn't usually authorize private firms to purchase anything more exotic like energy weapons."

"Then we're looking at an internal...something," Mettler said. "Still doesn't explain where everyone not perforated by 9mm rounds went."

"I will attempt to access the facility monitoring and security systems," Tin Man said. His arm cannons retracted, and his eyes returned to their normal color as he switched back out of combat mode.

"I'll get to work in the supervisor's office over here," Murph pointed to the open hatch for the office the on-shift ops boss would use.

Jacob let his people work while he walked around, taking in the scene. The platform they were currently on was small so the fact it only had two security troopers wasn't unusual. Someone aboard had popped the site boss, then came up and hit both guards before they could even get their hands on their weapons. Then, they disappeared with what appeared to be the rest of the Site D staff without bothering to scuttle any of the platforms or shut down the automated equipment. They didn't even collect the brass at the scene of three murders, so they obviously had very little fear of human authorities catching them.

To deepen the mystery, they had a shuttle that had originated from this mining site sitting in a hangar on Breaker's World that had been captured with both humans and Cridal aboard. Was this a part of the larger trafficking issue they were tasked with running down, or were they seeing what they wanted to see and connecting dots that weren't there?

"Obsidian actual, *Boneshaker*," Sully's voice came over the open team channel.

"Go, Sully," Jacob said.

"Jake, we have two ships that just meshed-in. Slip-drive signature indicates they're frigate class."

"Shit," Jacob said. "Not ours I'm assuming?"

"They're running silent, but the configuration doesn't match anything we have in service."

"Keep quiet and standby. I want to see who they are and why they're here."

"Copy," Sully said. "We're ready to make a fast exit if needed. They're loitering at the edge of the system right now, but it's unlikely they'll spot us docked to the platform until they get much closer. *Boneshaker*, out."

"Everybody catch that?" Jacob asked aloud.

"Yep. Working faster," Murph shouted from the office.

"Tin Man, does this installation have any defensive weapons?" Jacob asked. Tin Man turned to look at him.

"As a matter of fact, it does," he said. "Shall I begin the necessary steps to slave the defensive systems to our ship?"

"We can do that?" Jacob asked, surprised.

"Possibly," Tin Man said. "The system is networked together between all the various platforms throughout the system. I will just need to break in and add the *Boneshaker* as a new command node."

"Get on it," Jacob said. "You have the ship's command codes?"

"I do," Tin Man confirmed. "I will know within a minute or two if I am successful."

"Anything in there, Murph?" Jacob shouted.

"I think the attack originated up here not the other way around," Murph said, coming out of the hatchway. He held up a red cardboard box of 9mm frangible ammo. "There are fifteen missing from the box."

"So, they loaded up a mag in the office, came out and drilled these two," Jacob said. "Then went and hit the site boss. That tracks. Explains why there was no general alarm sounded at any point when they gunned down Janet two decks below."

"One of the shift bosses is our killer?" Mettler said. "That should be easy to narrow down if we can get a hold of the personnel files."

"Which I think I have in here." Murph held up a canvas tote bag he'd stuffed hard copy files and data cores into. "I broke the lock on the filing cabinet and just emptied it out. I'll sort through it later."

"I have been partially successful, Captain," Tin Man said. "I cannot completely control the defensive systems from our ship, but I can engage them in autonomous mode once we are safely out of range."

"Is there enough to take out a pair of frigates?"

"Not if they are expecting an attack."

"Better than nothing. I don't want them wiping out all the evidence before the Navy gets here," Jacob said, keying his mic. "*Boneshaker*, we're on our way back. Have a course plotted to try and get us away from the area without being spotted."

"Already laid in, Captain," Sully said. "I was anticipating the order. With all the active emission sources in the area, it won't be especially difficult."

"Okay, boys," Jacob grabbed one of the M21s off its dead owner and slung it over his shoulder, "let's get back to the ship."

"We are well outside the effective range of the installation defenses," Tin Man reported. "We are also receiving a live sensor feed, something I had not anticipated being able to do."

"It looks like the aggregate sensor feed is being broadcast all the time," Mettler said. "When you added the *Boneshaker* as a node, we were able to tap in."

The frigates came down quickly without any hesitation and deployed in a way that told Jacob they had either been there before or had detailed intel on the system. The ships had split up to maxi-mize their coverage but left themselves vulnerable in the process, which meant they expected no resistance to whatever it was they were there to do.

It seemed pretty clear they were there to do a final mop up after whatever the hell happened to depopulate Site D, but he had to be certain. He didn't want to do something he couldn't take back like opening fire on a pair of NIS ships that had been sent to investigate something his team had called in.

"Bogey One is heading for the Alpha Belt Processor Hub," Sully said. "Bogey Two is heading down to the command center we just left."

"Both still within range?" Jacob asked.

"Yeah, for whatever that's worth," Sully said. "If these ships have competent, alert crews, don't expect the defensive emplacements to make much of a dent."

It was another seven hours before one of the ships reached its target and made its intentions obvious. The frigate that had been closing on the massive ore processing platform that serviced the inner asteroid belt hit the platform with a high-power scan.

"They going to blow it up?" Jacob wondered. "Or are they looking for something?"

"I wonder what's so special about an ore processor," Murph said. "They went there first."

"They may start shooting," Sully pointed out. "The scan could be a precursor to scuttling the processor."

"Ah, right," Jacob said. "Activate defensive systems."

"Command sent," Sully said. "Now we see how competent these crews really are."

6

One of the frigates was disabled and burning in space within the first few moments of the engagement. The other was not.

"We're spotted," Sully said. "The crew going after the command center was a little quicker getting their countermeasures up."

The ship that had been attacking the ore processing platform had been taken completely by surprise, and the modest firepower of the defensive weapons scored almost thirty direct hits before the ship turned away and brought up their shields, or at least the sections of shielding that still worked.

The second ship hadn't been so easily entrapped. The instant it was hit with a targeting scan, it reacted with evasive maneuvers and brought up its defenses after only two low-power plasma shots burned the finish off their hull. After the near miss, it scanned the surrounding system and was able to spot the *Boneshaker* hiding in a Lagrange point equipment depot among all of the deactivated mining rigs.

"These guys are pretty good," Jacob said. "No way they should have been able to pick us out so quickly."

"Ideas?"

"Where is the next largest concentration of defensive weapons?" Jacob asked.

"Around something called the Quality Sort Terminal," Mettler said from the rear station. "It's actually the biggest structure in the system. It's in a heliocentric orbit trailing behind the third planet. There are around a dozen or so smaller structures flying in formation with it, but they're not labeled on this chart."

"Put defensive systems to standby and get us down there," Jacob said. "You can fly us there without them intercepting us, right?"

"Sure," Sully said. "But I see what you're planning and there are two problems. First, the defensive systems will still probably fire on us if we're in range. Second, this crew is pretty sharp and your trap pretty obvious. They're not going to fall for it."

"But they don't know that," Jacob said. Sully looked at him skeptically but brought them onto the new course without further argument.

The ship rocketed down toward the enormous construct that looked like where finished product was sent to be graded and prepped for shipment. As Jacob had hoped, the frigate adjusted course to pursue, leaving the command center untouched. But they were obviously holding back, using maybe a third of their ship's available engine power to chase them farther down into the system. Jacob was well-aware he wasn't a master strategist when it came to ship-to-ship combat, but even he could tell Sully was right: They weren't buying it.

"Anybody have any other good ideas?" he asked. "I don't want to flee the system and leave it to these assholes, but I'm not going to risk our lives and our mission in a fight we can't win."

"Glad to hear you say that," Sully said. "Because, as capable as she is after the refit, that's still a capital warship and this is still a shuttle."

"Come about and fly up to where the disabled frigate is still spinning in space," Tin Man said. "Make it clear we are about to attack the disabled ship."

"Given that they haven't bothered to go themselves to render aid, isn't that a bit of an idle threat?" Sully asked.

"The ship is disabled but in no immediate danger," Tin Man argued. "If that were to change it would force them to react. Once we are certain they will move to defend the other ship, we can then broadcast our demands. I would also suggest that you reach out to Mission Ops on Mosler Station and ask for an update for our fleet's arrival."

The frigate responded to their moves and angled about to pursue but again seemed in no hurry to actually catch them. It took Jacob a little time to put the pieces together, but he finally realized they were the ones being screwed with. The frigate had no idea who was flying the beat up old Eshquarian workhorse, so they were content to fly around, pretending to chase them while they called in additional forces.

"This is going nowhere," he said. "Let me talk to Umpire and see what they think."

Umpire was the callsign of Mission Ops back on Mosler Station. It was a desk manned around the clock, staffed by officers briefed on all ongoing Scout Fleet missions and could help a crew in the field with intel, pass things on to the regular fleet, or handle any of a thousand problems that might come up during a deployment. The procedure for making contact and authenticating a team in the field was brief and, within minutes, Jacob was talking to a live person back at his home base.

"Go for Umpire. Code in, please," a bored sounding voice said over the channel.

"Obsidian Actual, Sierra Seven Seven," Jacob said.

"Condition?"

"Bravo Tango Delta," Jacob said, letting them know that he was not under duress and that their threat level was moderate.

"What can I do for you, Captain Brown?"

Jacob quickly laid out the situation, starting with the arrival of the two frigates since Umpire would have already seen their preliminary field report on the decimated mining operation and the murdered employee aboard the command center.

"Please, advise on course of action," he said after giving Umpire the rundown on the situation. There seemed to be a stunned silence on the other end of the channel. Obsidian was notorious for operating under a communications blackout most of the time they were on-mission, and they never called in asking for direction.

"Standby, Captain."

Jacob leaned back against the bulkhead in the cramped com room, waiting as the officer manning the Mission Ops desk ran around like a wild person for someone authorized to make a decision. It was this sort of thing that was exactly why he never bothered checking in with them unless the situation were particularly dire or unusual.

"Captain Brown, this is Captain Bristow," a new voice said. Jacob's eyebrows went up a twitch. Captain Alan Bristow was in charge of Scout Fleet mission planning and execution. He was a direct report to Admiral Webb himself and was considered the obvious replacement for overall command when Webb decided to retire.

He also didn't like Jacob, or the mixed crew of Obsidian, and he wasn't shy about saying it to whoever would listen. If he ever took over Scout Fleet, the first people sent packing would be Jacob, Murph, and Tin Man, with the rest of Obsidian absorbed by the other teams. Despite all this, Jacob still had a grudging respect for Bristow's leadership ability and experience.

"Yes, sir," Jacob said crisply.

"Good work keeping out of reach of your bogeys," Bristow said. "Task Force Three-One is bearing down on your position and will mesh-in within the next seventeen hours. Ideally, we'd like your new friends to still be there. Any chance of keeping them occupied without getting yourselves killed?"

"I believe so, sir," Jacob said. "Right now, they're shadowing us well out of weapons range."

"Good, good," Bristow said, his voice muffled like he was doing something away from the microphone. "Standby, Captain."

"Yes, sir."

"We were able to have Fleet Ops get in touch with the taskforce flagship, the *Cincinnatus*. They've agreed to a slip-velocity increase that will put them in your system within...seven hours."

"That's good news, sir," Jacob said. "Would you like us to remain on-station and observe the engagement or turn it over to the Navy as soon as they show up?"

"Remain and observe, but do not participate," Bristow said.

"Understood, sir."

"Excellent. Umpire, out."

"Well?" Sully asked when Jacob walked back onto the flightdeck.

"Talked to Captain Bristow," Jacob said.

"He still hate us?" Mettler asked.

"Probably," Jacob said, "but it didn't come up this time. He wants us to dangle these assholes along for another seven hours or so. We have a Fleet taskforce on its way."

"Shouldn't be too hard," Sully said. "They're not trying to catch us. I'll start some randomized loops around all the mining platforms so we can maximize our cover."

"Do it," Jacob yawned. "Let's make sure we have two people up here at any given time. I don't want someone nodding off and that bastard sneak up and take a shot at us."

"How about those guys?" Mettler asked, pointing to the sensor display just before alarms started blaring. Nine more ships had just meshed-in, and none of their slip-drive signatures matched any UEN ship class. It looked like the enemy's reinforcements arrived first.

"Well...shit," Sully said.

The pursuing enemy frigate had closed the distance on them, still keeping out of weapons range, while nine newcomers deployed throughout the system in a loose blockade to keep the *Boneshaker* from trying to make a dash to the outer system. Jacob wasn't too concerned since his ship had the capability of meshing-out in from within the inner system and without needing to carry much relative velocity, but his pursuers wouldn't know that since that was a capability added by the engineers on Mosler Station. For right now, the enemy was operating under the assumption that the beat-up Eshquarian combat shuttle was exactly what she appeared to be.

"They'll start drawing the loop tighter now that they've surrounded us," Sully said. "Once those other ships begin to move down, our friend behind us will run us down and try for a capture."

"There's an idea," MG said.

"No...that was a statement," Sully said. "An idea is something else. But good try."

"What's the idea, MG?" Jacob asked before his weaponeer could respond to the insult.

"Let them capture us. How big of a crew will a frigate have? A few hundred, and less than a quarter of them fighters? Let's just fly right in there and fuck the place up."

"I like his idea," Tin Man declared.

"Of course, you do," Jacob said. "The problem, other than they might just shoot us down and not try for a capture, is that—"

"Here they come!" Sully shouted, shoving the power up. The pilot's situational awareness was just a touch faster than the computer and the alert sounded as the *Boneshaker*'s engines came to full power. Jacob looked at the tactical display and saw that the trailing frigate was accelerating hard and coming onto a direct intercept course.

"Can we outrun them?" Jacob asked.

"Eh...no," Sully said. "We accelerate faster, but that's a capital ship with a lot more engine power. They'll catch us eventually."

"We carrying anything heavy that could slow them down?" Mettler asked.

"Not really," Sully said. "Command doesn't want clandestine units flying around with ship busters or any heavy ordnance like that. We really don't have shit for expendable munitions to be honest. Just some medium range dual-stage missiles."

"The ships up top are moving down," Jacob said. "Are we boxed in?"

"Not yet," Sully said. "We need a bit more distance before we can mesh-out, though."

As Jacob was about to answer, the ship was rocked, and new alarms started blaring. The trailing ship had hit them with diffuse laser fire. Lasers weren't used much because they were easily handled by modern shielding, but they had some uses, warning shots being one of them.

"Are they broadcasting any demands?" he asked.

"Nothing yet," Mettler said. "Just chasing us and that last little love tap."

The next tap wasn't so loving. In an effort to get the room he needed to mesh-out without bringing them into weapons range of the ships ahead, Sully had cut their relative velocity a bit in a gamble to give them some room. His hope was that the ship behind was more interested in capturing them than going for a kill shot. Turns out it was something in between.

"Shit!" Sully shouted. "Brace! Brace! Brace!"

A perfectly aimed plasma cannon shot slammed into the starboard engine nacelle, destroying it completely. The computer automatically clamped the power feeds coming from the reactor and blew the damaged nacelle off the pylon with explosive charges before it could further damage the ship.

"Damage?" Jacob screamed over the blaring alarms. "Mettler, kill the sirens!"

"We're fucked," Sully said, defeated. "No grav-drive, no slip-drive. We still have reactive propulsion, but it's an underpowered emergency system. We're sitting ducks."

"It looks like we get to execute MG's plan after all," Tin Man said from where he loomed in the hatchway.

"Try not to sound too eager about this," Jacob said. "Everyone not made of metal probably won't survive this."

"Likely not," Tin Man agreed pleasantly.

"Incoming channel request," Mettler said. "It's unencrypted on the civil band."

"Put it on," Jacob said.

"It was a good showing, but I think we can all admit the fight is over," a voice said calmly in Jenovian Standard. "Please, shut down any offensive and defensive systems and prepare to be brought aboard. Any foolishness by your crew once aboard, and we will simply kill you all and jettison your corpses into space. This is not a negotiation. Comply or be destroyed."

"Channel closed," Mettler said.

"How far away is our fleet?" Jacob asked.

"Still over five hours out," Tin Man said.

"Sully?"

"She's dead, Jake," the pilot said. "No propulsion and an armament that wouldn't do much against a ship like that. At least not in a fair fight where they see it coming."

"Tin Man?" Jacob asked.

"There is nothing to be gained by wasting your lives," Tin Man said. "You are at a disadvantage right now. The smart thing will be to bide your time until you are in a position to change that."

"Boarding protocol," Jacob said, making his decision. "Purge all of it. Don't leave a fucking thing for them to find. Dump the mission files into the emergency beacon and launch it with a nine-hour delay."

While the frigate maneuvered for a grapple the crew of the *Boneshaker* went into action purging servers, com buffers, navigation computers...anything that would hold the least little scrap of useable intel was destroyed. He knew that by destroying the intel on the data cores he increased the likelihood he and his crew might be tortured, but Scout Fleet regulations were quite clear. It was the risk they all signed up for.

"We're on emergency backup power," Sully called from the flight-deck. "Reactor is completely shut down and weapons are safed."

"Are we arming up ourselves, Cap?" MG asked.

"No," Jacob said. "Tin Man is right. Going out in a blaze of glory is pointless. Let's work the situation and see if we can't bide our time until the odds are in our favor."

"You're the boss," MG said, clearly not happy with the answer.

The crew of the frigate was quick and efficient at grappling the *Boneshaker* and bringing her aboard. Jacob sat in the cargo hold on a crate when he felt the deck shake from the ship being set down, and then a loud knocking on the rear ramp. He nodded for Mettler to open them up, standing up and keeping his hands in front of him. When the ramp lowered, he was looking at the expected party of armed troopers aiming weapons at them. What he hadn't expected was the apparent leader of the little party.

"Who the fuck are you?" Jacob blurted.

"We can exchange names later," the human said. "For now, let's get the formalities of searching you and your ship out of the way. I appreciate you not forcing my hand by doing something completely foolish since it looks like you're not the people I thought you were. So, who are you with? NIS? NAVSOC? Scout Fleet?"

"Who did you think we were?" Jacob asked, ignoring the questions.

"All in due time...whoever you are," the man said, motioning his troopers forward. "Separate and secure them, but they are to be treated as guests not prisoners. Got it?"

"Got it," a voice came from the helmet of the lead trooper. The voice spoke in accented English. The more Jacob looked, the more he realized they all looked human underneath the tactical gear.

"This way, please," another trooper said, waving them toward another armored figure holding a scanner they would use to make sure nobody was carrying a holdout blaster or blade in their clothes.

"This is everyone?" the leader asked.

"All humans present and accounted for," Jacob said. The man narrowed his eyes a bit at that and moved to the team that was getting ready to board the ship, whispering something before leaving the hangar bay.

7

"There's nobody here, sir. There is some debris consistent with the class ship your crew was in, but analysis shows there's not enough to account for the entire vessel."

"And the beacon?" Admiral Webb asked over the hyperlink connection.

"Retrieved, sir," Captain Zell of the *Cincinnatus* said. "Intel is decrypting the files now. They had it set on a delay. It began broadcasting around twenty minutes after we meshed-in. Your crew was gone, as were the ships they reported engaged with including the damaged one."

"I would take it as a professional courtesy if you kept my office apprised of your investigation, Captain," Webb said. "Since you haven't found a debris field large enough to account for the *Boneshaker,* I will operate under the premise they are still alive."

"I will certainly keep you in the loop, Admiral," Zell promised. "When we access the files aboard the beacon, we will forward the raw data to you as it originated with your crew."

"That's appreciated, Captain," Webb said. "Mosler Station, out."

"Your thoughts, Admiral?" Reggie Weathers said.

"I wish I'd had them take the *Corsair*," Webb said, throwing his tablet down on his desk with disgust. "That old shuttle is—*was*—great for blending in, not so much for fighting and running."

"From the dispersion pattern in the preliminary report the *Cincinnatus* has already sent over it appears the shuttle had an engine failure, and it was jettisoned," Weathers said, reading from his own tablet. "No word yet if it was mechanical or if it took enemy fire."

"What did you think of Captain Bristow's report?" Webb asked.

"Seemed relatively straight forward," Weathers said. "I was more surprised that Captain Brown had called in while on-mission than anything else. He tends to like disappearing as soon as he leaves Koliss-2, and we don't hear from them again until the mission is complete or something has gone totally sideways."

"Is Buzzkill ready to deploy?"

"Standing by, sir."

"Get them out to this abandoned mining colony or whatever the hell it is. I want our own people putting eyes on this right now," Webb said. "We'll forward them anything we get of use in the files Obsidian dumped into that beacon. The fact it was on a timed broadcast delay indicates they were under duress when they disappeared from the system."

"And not under their own power if they left one of their engines behind," Weathers said.

"It's not looking good," Webb sighed. "The chances are high that the taskforce will find the *Boneshaker* crashed into a planet or asteroid. I know they're a resourceful crew, but everyone's luck runs out eventually."

———

"Interesting ship you've got."

The voice made Jacob sit up on the rack and turn toward the bars of his cell. They had been tossed in the ship's brig, but they had been given comfortable bedding and were being well-fed. All told it was probably in his top five times being held captive.

"Be it ever so humble," he said, spinning to face the human that had greeted them. "Thanks for blowing one of the engines off, by the way."

"I'll take your thanks at face value since were it not for my gunner's precise shot placement at taking out just an engine, we wouldn't be having this conversation at all."

"Fair point," Jacob conceded. "So, what do I call you?"

"Before all that, tell me about your unusual cargo," the man said. "Our people found an armory that definitely tells me you're part of the UEAS in some capacity, but they also found an inert battlesynth strapped to a pallet in your cargo bay."

"We found it," Jacob shrugged. "It was aboard the command center of that mining operation. Didn't appear to be damaged or shot up, just turned off somehow. Seemed something worth bringing along."

"Why strap it down?"

"In case someone in an unregistered warship blows one of our engines off. Keeps it from bouncing around."

"Funny. So, what secret division of our stalwart military do you belong to? I would have guessed NIS, but you don't quite fit the profile."

"*Our* military, huh? So, besides sharing a homeworld, where have you come from? Is the UEAS running entire covert fleets now?" Jacob asked.

"We've got a long flight. We can play this round and round game for a bit longer if it makes you feel better. Enjoy the cell, whoever you are."

"Will do," Jacob called to his retreating back.

He hadn't seen anyone but humans crewing the ship, so it was a safe assumption that this was a covert ship tied to the military. There were a few private military companies popping up here and there, but Jacob had never heard of them having whole squadrons of frigates. No way Earth would have approved something like that.

He settled back onto his rack to wait. They would be out of their cells soon enough, and then he could get some answers.

All his actuators gave a twitch as Tin Man came out of the self-maintenance cycle he'd put himself into prior to the *Boneshaker* being captured. As he'd hoped, he was still lying on the floor of the shuttle's cargo bay strapped to the pallet. The maintenance mode gave outsiders the impression that he was disabled or even dead but didn't fool anyone with any sort of familiarity with synths. It was a calculated risk he'd talked Captain Brown into taking, but now it appeared to have paid off.

The tiedown straps, while appearing substantial, had been sabotaged near the latching mechanisms so that they gave way easily and without too much sound when Tin Man flexed his extremities. They fell to the deck with a metallic clatter that was drowned out by the constant machinery noise within the frigate's hangar bay. He slowly climbed to his feet and scanned the area with his passive sensors. There was only one guard posted by the ship from the sounds he was detecting. Beyond that, it was difficult to determine how many others might be within the cavernous bay.

He grabbed one of the straps that had been holding him to the pallet, raised it about a meter off the deck, and let it fall with a metallic clatter. After getting no reaction he repeated the process raising it a bit. After two more repetitions, he heard the guard groan and shuffle toward the ramp leading up to the cargo bay. Tin Man concealed himself near the control panel, waiting for the inattentive guard to come all the way in.

"Anybody up here?" the timid question floated up through the open hatchway. Tin Man remained silent as footsteps slowly approached.

The guard appeared in the hatchway, his weapon slung behind him and his hands casually at his side. Tin Man was disgusted by his inattentiveness and demeanor but conceded it would help in his task that the human was so unprofessional. He struck fast, grabbing the guard by the front of his utilities and dragging him deeper into the cargo bay where they wouldn't be seen by anyone passing by.

"If you cry out, I will kill you. Nod if you understand," Tin Man said calmly. The man nodded, eyes wide and mouth hanging open. "Excellent. Where are the crew from this ship being held?"

"The brig, I think," the man said.

"I understand that. I am looking for an exact location."

"Deck four, section thirty-two."

"How do I gain access?" Tin Man asked.

"I won't tell you that," the human said, now showing a little bit of defiance. Tin Man approved.

"This is a human ship?" he asked. Now, the guard seemed torn on how he should answer.

"It's human-crewed," he said finally.

"If that is true, when I attempt to rescue my own human crew, I should not kill anyone aboard this ship?" Tin Man asked. That brought a spark of hope to the guard's eyes.

"Definitely! Definitely shouldn't kill anyone...starting with me."

"Have you ever heard of the Galvetic Empire?" Tin Man asked. The confused guard shook his head no. "It is the home of the infamous and widely feared Galvetic Legions. They are powerful, awesome warriors. If one of them had failed so spectacularly at his post as you have done today, they would have ended their own life in shame. Keep that in mind."

Without waiting for an answer Tin Man hit him in the head with a closed fist with just a touch over the amount of force he knew would render a human unconscious. The human crumpled into a heap, eyes rolling back in his head.

The fact they'd been captured by a human ship of unknown allegiance complicated Tin Man's task. Whoever had captured them had to be affiliated with Earth in some way, which meant the normal level of violence he would be comfortable with was no longer an acceptable option. He'd pledged his service to his Scout Fleet crewmates and killing off too many of their own kind would probably sour that relationship. Despite the harsh words he'd spoken to his lot mate, Lucky, in the past about his misplaced loyalty to humans, Tin Man had developed a strong affinity for the quirky, unpredictable creatures.

A direct rescue of his crewmates was impractical and likely doomed to fail without being able to use deadly force. Instead, he would try a more indirect method and began planning what route he would try to take to the ship's bridge.

Jacob sat up as his captor dragged a chair over to the bars of his cell and sat down. They both eyed each other without speaking for a few minutes.

"I imagine we've been trained by the same people in interrogation resistance," Jacob said. "You really want to waste time staring at each other?"

"Information on you was difficult to come by, Captain Jacob Brown," the man said. "Since Admiral Webb was able to peel Scout Fleet away from under the UEAS umbrella he's done a good job at cutting off the flow of information regarding his activities and personnel. People had some interesting things to say about you."

"All good I hope," Jacob yawned.

"Not particularly. But reading between the lines it's easy to see past the negative comments and see there's a real fear of you from people that might surprise you. Why do you think that is?"

"I'm a mean drunk. Makes cocktail parties awkward. Was this all you wanted to talk about?"

"What were you doing in LOR-773?" the man asked, sipping from a large mug.

"Not a chance in hell I start sharing information until I know exactly who you are," Jacob said, suddenly serious. "Even then, you'll have to convince me we're on the same side and that an intel exchange is in our mutual interest."

"I suppose it couldn't hurt to—" Alarms started blaring, red lights flashed along the corridor outside the cell, and Jacob heard security hatches slamming shut somewhere to his right. His captor pulled out a com unit and held it to his ear.

"Bad news?" Jacob asked. The man just sighed and put the com unit back in his pocket.

"Your inert battlesynth apparently just captured the bridge of my ship," he said. "Well played."

"It was his idea, actually," Jacob admitted. "He didn't kill anybody, did he?"

"No casualties," the man said. "He's sealed himself in, but my people said he went out of his way to not maim or kill."

"That's good," Jacob said, genuinely relieved.

"Fine. I will tell you everything and release your crew. Just call him off, please."

"You'll have to release us first before he agrees to anything. If you let us go you have my word, I'll order him to release your ship."

"Will it follow your orders?"

"I'll strongly suggest," Jacob said. "So far, he's been inclined to do as I ask, but I don't order him."

"Whatever...just call the son of a bitch off." The locks on the cell door clanged as they released, and the door retracted into the bulkhead.

Jacob stood up and stretched before walking slowly toward the opening, but his captor was still blocking the way.

"Don't do anything fucking stupid," he said.

"You want me to get your ship back for you or not?" Jacob asked. "I'll go lay back down and you can deal with Tin Man. He's not known for his patience, so I'd figure it out quickly. You assholes captured me...don't forget that."

"Let's go," the man said, waving a hand at the armed guards he had with him. "Release his crew. Take them to the mess deck and stay with them there. I'm taking Captain Brown to the bridge to negotiate with his battlesynth."

"Would you care for some constructive criticism?" Jacob asked as they walked out of the brig and into a narrow corridor.

"I'm listening."

"Stop thinking and talking about him like he's a piece of equipment or property," Jacob said. "Tin Man is an intelligent being, as unique as either you or me. They've been treated poorly as a species, and every one of them I've met takes great offense at the things you've been saying and how you're saying them."

"Noted."

He at least had the decency and intelligence to look genuinely sorry. As they walked out of security area, he hoped he'd truly understood what Jacob had been trying to tell him. If Tin Man wanted, he could tear the ship apart and kill everyone aboard.

8

It had been absurdly easy to find the bridge and subdue the crew.

Tin Man had served with humans for some time now and had grown to have a great respect for their courage and resourcefulness. He now amended his opinion as it seemed the members of Scout Fleet were not indicative of the species as a whole.

He had been spotted immediately leaving the hangar bay by the ship's automated security systems, but someone had overridden and silenced the alarm, apparently thinking it was a false alert. This let Tin Man make it all the way to the forward crew spaces before anyone bothered to challenge him. Most saw him, gaped at the unexpected sight, but proceeded past him without incident. It wasn't until he reached the bridge hatchway itself that he was challenged.

The guards were actually attentive and reacted quickly, but they were in a mindset to defend the space against fellow human interlopers that probably wouldn't be armed. One got off a snapshot that hit the deck a meter in front of him before Tin Man disabled both with carefully calibrated strikes to their craniums. Until he was certain these humans were the enemy, he would continue to work toward his objective while causing the least amount of harm possible. In truth, he rather enjoyed the challenge of taking over an entire ship without firing a single shot or killing anybody.

After overpowering the two guards he closed the blast doors to the bridge and initiated lockdown protocols while the rest of the bridge crew stared in horror, cowering in their seats. Going only by instinct he ripped open a panel in the bulkhead near the hatchway and disabled the actuators for the blast doors to ensure nobody outside could command them open.

"Who is in charge here?" he asked.

"You are?" someone at a forward station answered.

"Strong survival instinct," Tin Man noted. "That is an admirable trait...for some. Please, sound a general alarm and inform your commanding officer I have control of their vessel and want to negotiate."

The alarms blasted throughout the ship, and Tin Man watched over the station operators to make sure they didn't do something foolish that might lower their life expectancies dramatically. He was curious about this crew and the ship. They certainly didn't live up to the courage and professionalism Tin Man had seen from human crews on United Earth Navy ships. These seemed to be barely competent spacers pressed into military service.

"This is First Officer Brent Orso," a voice said over the intercom. "Who is this?"

"This is the person holding control of your ship. My demands are as follows: Release the crew from the captured shuttle, escort them safely to the bridge, and don't do something foolish like attempt to retake control through force. If you follow these instructions, I will surrender the bridge to the captain. Fuck with me, and I will kill everyone aboard."

"That would kill your friends, too," Orso pointed out.

"A sacrifice I am willing to make. Are you?"

"Standby."

Tin Man paced silently while he waited. The crew was nervous, but functional, and they appeared to be obeying his directive to not do anything stupid. He realized the fatal flaw in his plan was that the *Boneshaker* was too damaged to get away, but freeing Jacob and the others was still a crucial first step no matter what they did.

"Sir? Your friends have been released from the brig. A Captain Brown is on his way up here while the others are being taken to the aft mess deck," an operator said.

"How long until Captain Brown arrives?"

"A matter of a few minutes. This isn't a very big ship."

"How the hell does a battlesynth stroll all the way to your bridge without anybody noticing?" Jacob asked.

"It's a new crew," his captor said. "We're working out the kinks."

"Who are you people?"

"Just call off your—*the*—battlesynth, and then we can see where we go from there, okay?"

The trip to the bridge was quick and uneventful. Jacob marveled at how blasé the crew he encountered appeared to be in the midst of a hostile takeover of their vessel. They either had ice water in their veins and an unshakable trust in their commander or they were the most incompetent pack of slobs he'd ever seen.

"Intercom?" Jacob asked when they reached the sealed bridge.

"Right there," a guard indicated, pointing at an active panel near the hatchway. "It's a live channel to the bridge right now."

"Tin Man, this is Captain Brown," Jacob said after getting close enough to the panel that the small microphone icon turned green when it detected his presence. The uniquely human iconography on the panels was another interesting bit of information Jacob tucked away for later.

"I see you on the security feed, Captain. What would you like me to do?" Tin Man's voice came back.

"We're at a bit of a stalemate right now, but that can't go on for too much longer. Go ahead and open up the bridge and we'll try to find a peaceful solution to our little problem."

It took a few moments before the armored blast doors budged a crack, slammed shut again, and then smoothly opened fully. Jacob's captor charged past him and looked around.

"You're all okay?" he asked.

"No problems, sir. We've been treated well. He didn't hurt anybody and has been strangely courteous with his requests," one of the station operators said.

"Nicely done," Jacob said quietly to Tin Man as he passed and walked fully onto the bridge, turning to the ship security troopers. "I think you can go ahead and stay out there. Make no mistake that this ship is still under hostile control, and we will give it back to you when we see fit. As a show of good faith, I'll allow the doors to remain open so you can freely monitor the situation."

"Stand down," the man in charge said. "You couldn't take down a battlesynth with those weapons so don't even try. You'll end up killing half the bridge crew."

"Let's start at the beginning," Jacob said, slouching into one of the bridge seats and putting his feet up. "Who the hell are you?"

"You giving the orders now?"

"For the time being."

"My name is Glenn Mitchell. I'm what you might call a troubleshooter."

"Bullshit," Jacob scoffed. "A troubleshooter with a whole fleet of frigates?"

"It's not an exact title," Glenn said. "My point is that I'm not affiliated with the military or intelligence apparatus nor are any of the crews or ships I'm with at the moment."

"At the moment?"

"I'm in charge of this small force until our task is complete, then I'll leave."

"How vague," Jacob said. "Okay...so what's your task?"

"You first. Who are you guys, and who are you with?"

Jacob thought it over for a moment, and then shrugged. Their existence wasn't exactly classified.

"I'm United Earth Marine Corps Captain Jacob Brown, team

leader for Scout Team Obsidian," he said. "We operate under what's now known as Terran Scout Fleet which is a force answerable only to the president, although we are tangentially connected to the UEAS chain of command."

"And your mission?" Glenn asked. "What were you doing poking around an abandoned mining site?"

"The dead guards we found in the command center seem to indicate it wasn't exactly *abandoned*," Jacob said. "But, either way, I think you realized exactly what we were doing when you found out there were humans aboard that beat-up Eshquarian shuttle. We're likely looking for the same thing you are."

"We actually had no idea," Glenn said. "Your shuttle isn't exactly Fleet issue. Let me run this up to my superiors, and then we'll see where we stand. Can we maintain this ceasefire until I return?"

"Make it quick," Jacob said.

While Glenn slipped on a headset and began the process of contacting whoever the hell he reported to, the bridge crew seemed to think the tension of the situation had ended and began asking Tin Man ridiculous questions.

"Were you born or built?"

"Do you have a regular brain in your head?"

"Are you controlled remotely?"

Tin Man ignored them completely. It was only a few moments before Glenn tossed his headset onto the console and walked back over to where Jacob sat.

"You get this crew at a college freshman orientation?" Jacob asked.

"They're...green," Glenn said. "My employer has authorized me to share what I know pertaining to the McMillian-Shafer Mining Company anomaly at Site D. Any further cooperation would depend on you."

"On me?"

"My employer would entertain full cooperation as long as you are able to fully brief me on what Scout Fleet knows about the anomaly and what further actions you've been directed to take."

Jacob pretended to think it over. The truth was that Scout Fleet didn't know shit and NIS hasn't bothered to give them their primary intel package before they'd been forced to purge *Boneshaker*'s systems, including the slip-com nodes and hyperlink terminals. This was a good opportunity for them to get back on-mission...assuming they could find themselves another ship.

"Deal," he said. "Fair warning, we don't know much yet, but I'll give you what we have."

"Very well. Where would you like to start?"

"Lunch. I'm starving, and I'm sure my crew is, too. After that we can sit and put our cards on the table."

The food aboard the *Vega One*, as the ship was absurdly named, was subpar compared to what Jacob would have expected on a frigate-class vessel. That didn't slow down him or his crew in the least as they dove into the meal like a pack of starving wolves.

"Does our free exchange of information include finding out who you are and who you work for?" Jacob asked.

"I work for a private concern who would like to keep it private," Glenn said. "Through them, I'm funded and empowered to do off-the-books tasks...like tracking down where the hell thousands of people disappeared to from a commercial mining facility."

"Private?" Murph asked. "As in, non-governmental?"

"Very non-governmental," Glenn said. "I took the liberty of looking all of you up while you tried your best to empty the galley. Your team is credited with taking down the One World faction led by Margaret Jansen. Some rumors even have you being responsible for the death of NIS Director Michael Welford."

"Total bullshit!" MG said around a mouthful of a passable version of a Philly cheesesteak.

"Anyway...the people I work for watched the entire Jansen debacle, including her involvement in the second invasion of Earth, and decided that just another covert government force wasn't the answer," Glenn said. "They wanted something more agile and less susceptible to the high turnover rate that government positions have."

"Also, no pesky oversight," Jacob said. "That's gotta be nice."

"Tell me, Captain...what do you think might happen to Scout Fleet if Admiral Marcus Webb was no longer at the head of it? Perhaps the next president comes in and decides he's too rigid and replaces him with somebody like Jansen. How long until your secret military force ends up being used as a weapon against the people it was designed to protect?"

Jacob didn't like where the conversation was going, nor the implications of what Glenn was saying. Could Scout Fleet just become another One World with a different leader? Jansen's little empire began as a remote outpost on Terranovus. The freedom of movement and unlimited funds that Scout Fleet enjoyed would arguably be easier to operate a soft coup from than with what Jansen had started out with. For some reason, the thought made him look to Tin Man. The battlesynth was staring right at him, seeming to be aware of what he was thinking. He suppressed a shiver and turned back to Glenn.

"Were you looking only at the Site D anomaly, as you put it, or is there a wider scope to your investigation?"

"That is where it began because an entire mining operation disappearing and missing regular updates attracts a lot of attention in the corporate ecosphere," Glenn said. "As I dug deeper, I found reports of missing people—a lot of them—mostly concentrated along the colonial routes. Now that Earth is letting people apply to leave the planet there's been a steady stream of adventure and treasure seekers heading toward the frontier regions. Apparently, not all of them have made it."

"It would seem that we're looking into the same problem, but from different angles," Jacob said carefully. "Have you happened to connect any of the missing colonists to any galactic or regional powers?"

"The Ull?" Glenn asked.

"The Cridal," Jacob said, going for broke. He was given a lot of leeway and trust by his command in how he protected and used classified information. His instincts told him that he could trust Glenn Mitchell, but he needed to give the troubleshooter something to make him reciprocate that trust. At the mention of the Cridal Glenn's eyebrows slammed into his hairline and his eyes widened.

"This...changes a lot. I'm assuming what you're saying is—"

"Is exactly what you think I'm saying. We've intercepted Cridal operatives that appear to be working with, or even running completely, the trafficking rings preying on refugees and colonists. There are a lot of humans missing, but also other species. Taking in account all the different frontier regions we think they're operating out of we're looking at millions of beings taken."

"Why?" Glenn asked, looking sick.

"That's the fun part," Jacob said. "We have no fucking clue."

9

"What was your next move?"

"You mean before you and your fleet showed up, chased us around, and then disabled my ship?" Jacob asked. "We were actually waiting on the Navy. They were sending a full taskforce to take over the site and begin sweeping the area. We were trying to hold you down in the area until they got there."

"Sorry about that," Glenn said. "I suppose now that I've confirmed your identities I should go ahead and let you go."

"And do what?" Sully asked. "Unless you happen to have a spare Opsion-series Eshquarian shuttle engine lying around."

"Not that I'm aware of, but I'm not usually riding around on a capital ship to be honest," Glenn said. "You have a spare ship?"

"Strangely enough, we do," Jacob said. "If you let me contact my base, I can have it brought out to meet us."

"On one condition," Glenn said. "I come with you."

"Excuse me?" Sully asked.

"You heard me. I come with you, or I just drop you off at the next habitable planet we pass," Glenn said. "I can't properly dig down into it while I'm with this fleet of amateurs. If I'm with you I can move more freely and follow leads to places my employers would never agree to allow their shiny new ships to fly. They're probably not thrilled about the one you baited into a gun trap being all chewed up."

Jacob looked at him helplessly, aware the civilian operative had him dangling over a barrel. The looks on his crew's faces indicated they didn't care either way, just so long as they were able to get off the frigate and back on task.

"Son of a bitch," he hissed. "Agreed. I'm assuming you're at least good enough to not be a liability or you wouldn't be in the job you're in."

"How are you going to explain all of this to home base?" Mettler asked. The Marine had a glazed-over look now that he'd eaten enough for a family of five.

"I'm not," Jacob said. "I'm going to contact Umpire and declare an emergency and have the *Corsair* brought out and let them take the *Boneshaker* back to Mosler Station."

"How do we do that?" Glenn asked.

"I'll need ground power applied to our ship," Sully said before turning to Jacob. "You have the slip-com address memorized?"

"I do," Jacob said. "Good thing since we purged all the memory cores on the slip-com nodes."

"Then let's get to it," Glenn said, standing and motioning for the others to do the same. Jacob ignored the looks from his crew and followed the civilian troubleshooter out of the aft mess deck. He was as skeptical as they were about their new unwanted partner, but he didn't see any other way to get back on track in a timely manner. Just having the *Corsair* brought out wouldn't be enough. They needed his resources and information. Hopefully, he was as competent as he seemed to be.

"Didn't we just leave this party?" MG asked as the *Boneshaker* hit the landing pad with enough force to live up to her name.

"Sorry," Sully said. "Fucking thrusters are acting up, too."

They had touched down on Breaker's World again, this time on the other side of the planet from where they'd caused so much trouble before. It had taken the *Vega One* fourteen days to reach the planet and during that time the techs aboard had gotten the shuttle repaired well enough to attempt a planetary landing with decent odds of survival.

It had taken a few conversations and some serious fast talking on Jacob's part, but Scout Fleet had agreed to ferry the *Corsair* to the planet, and then come back for the *Boneshaker*. The first officer he'd talked to had flat out refused. It wasn't until it had gotten elevated all the way to Admiral Webb's office that things were put in motion, something Jacob was certain he would suffer for later. As Scout Fleet grew, the petty politics of the officers on base became more pronounced and distracting.

After securing the ship and collecting their gear, Jason had his crew muster in the cargo bay so they could perform an orderly exodus from their damaged ship.

"You might be interested in that landing spot over there," Tin Man said, pointing to an empty landing pad across the tarmac that had some old service carts sitting at the edge, rusting in the temperate climate and weeds growing up through the cracks in the tarmac. It obviously hadn't been used in some years.

"I would?" Jacob asked.

"It is the place where a badly damaged Jepsen DL7 gunship landed many years ago," Tin Man said. "It is where a young human named Jason Burke first stepped foot on a planet not orbiting a star named Sol. It is also the place where he met an engineer named Twingo, someone who would become one of his closest friends. This is where it all started for your father."

Nobody said a word after Tin Man's uncharacteristically solemn speech. Before he even realized he was doing it, Jacob was walking across the tarmac to the pad. He was trying to imagine a younger version of the man he knew, wide-eyed and likely scared shitless, walking around on this very spot as a psychotic synth plotted and schemed. He also imagined poor Twingo, a complete innocent dragged into a harrowing ordeal just because he'd been the one to answer the service ticket to come out and work on the ship that would one day be called the *Phoenix.*

He wasn't sure how long he'd been standing there when he heard footsteps behind him. There was no mistaking a battlesynth's footfalls with anything else, so he didn't bother turning to greet his crewmate. He wasn't certain if Tin Man considered him a friend, an ally, or none of the above. He'd come back to serve with Scout Fleet and seemed to have a definite affinity for Murph and simply tolerated the rest despite the fact he, and the members of his unit, had sworn a life oath to Jacob's family in repayment for what his father had done for them.

"It is somewhat difficult to imagine, is it not?" Tin Man said from just behind him. "Jason Burke was just a couple of years younger than you are now when Deetz found him."

"To me he hardly ever seemed like a real person," Jacob said, turning. "Earth's media treated him like some sort of Bond villain so yeah, it's tough to imagine him out here bumbling his way along and just trying to stay alive."

He looked out over the swaying grass beyond the starport and sighed.

"I wish I could have met him back then," he said.

"Not as much as he wishes he could have met you when you were young, I think," Tin Man said. "Not knowing of you and being gone while you were growing into adulthood is a heavy burden he carries with him. He carries it alone because he is afraid if he mentions it to you, it will appear as if he is blaming Taryn Brown. I never met your mother, but I know your father loved her very much."

The revelation came as a surprise to Jacob. He didn't meet his father until his mother had already passed away, so he never saw them together. It never occurred to him that his old man would be walking on eggshells around him while also carrying a load of guilt for things he had nothing to do with.

"Thanks for this, Tin Man," he finally said. "This...this helped."

"I am glad."

———

"Oh, baby...come to daddy."

"You fucking freak." MG sneered at Sully as the pilot rubbed the outer hull of the *Corsair*.

"That means nothing coming from someone like you," Sully said.

Jacob ignored them as he took his gear up to his quarters, a much more spacious stateroom than the cramped room behind the flight-deck he'd had on the *Boneshaker*. While he rankled at the delay the swap was causing, he was secretly delighted that they were getting back into the *Corsair*. The sleek ship was one of one. A complete ground-up custom built on Earth with the latest technology humans had at their disposal. Even though she was nearing ten years old, there weren't too many ships in her class as well-equipped or capable.

"Nice ship," Glenn remarked as he walked up the ramp. He traveled light, carrying what looked like a weapons case and a backpack on his shoulders.

"Lot more room than the shuttle, but not as much as one of your frigates," Jacob said. "Berthing is down below. Just grab any rack that's open."

"Weapons?" Glenn asked, lifting his case.

"We're a little looser than the regular Navy but, for now, I'd prefer if you stowed your personal weapons in the armory," Jacob said. "Not that we don't totally trust you, of course."

"Of course," Glenn said, setting the case on the deck and heading down the narrow steps to the lower deck and crew berthing.

Jacob finished putting his own gear away while the crew went about their tasks preparing the *Corsair* for departure. The sooner they left, the quicker they'd be back on task and the quicker the crew from Mosler Station could come and recover the *Boneshaker*. He was about to head up to the bridge when he saw the light above the com room lit indicating there was a high-priority message in the queue.

"You and your team have already lost a ship, and you've barely started," Admiral Webb's stern visage started when Jacob logged in and played the message.

"Not a promising start," he muttered.

"I'm cutting you some slack because NIS is playing their usual games and were late getting us the initial intel packet...*some* slack. You are hanging from a very thin thread right now. Pressure is coming down from the very tippy top on this one. While you've been bumbling around getting engines shot off one of my ships another two caravans have gone missing from the Pitedii Frontier Zone. That's over seven thousand human settlers, all from India, and their government is not taking it lightly. There are a lot of eyes on us right now so don't shit the bed, Captain."

Webb's face disappeared from the screen, leaving Jacob to stare at his own reflection. The admiral rarely directly talked to scout teams in the field lately, routing directives and information through Umpire instead. He also wasn't the type of leader to give that type of *motivational* speech. That he was resorting to using the crop on him, so to speak, told Jacob volumes about how much political pressure was being put on his boss from above.

"We're ready when you are, Jake," Sully said from the hatchway. "Everything good?"

"No...but when is it ever?" Jacob said. "Let's get her into space. We've got a lot of work to do."

———

"So...Glenn...what's your story?"

Glenn turned and saw the tall African American member of the crew, the one they called Murph, was looming in the hatchway, blocking his way out of crew berthing.

"My story?" he asked. "You asking where I grew up and who my mommy and daddy were?"

"I'm more curious about where you got your training and how you ended up being employed by a private company," Murph said. "Bit of an unusual arrangement."

Glenn knew that the man's name was Alonso Murphy, but other than the fact he was assigned to Terran Scout Fleet, he hadn't been able to find anything else out about the man. Home office suspected that he might have been an agent in the NIS but, in the wake of Director Welford's disappearance and the agency's restructuring, any record of Alonso Murphy had been scrubbed.

"Is this idle curiosity or a legit effort at pumping me for information?" he asked.

"I don't waste time on idle curiosity," Murph said. "Right now, I'm assessing a threat to my crew."

"A threat?"

"You heard me. You may have gotten yourself aboard this ship, but you are not a welcomed guest. If I think you're up to something or putting the crew or ship in danger, I'll cycle you through the airlock."

Glenn's instincts were to meet force with force, but his training told him that escalating a conflict on a ship full of alphas would only end badly. Mostly for him. Instead, he softened his posture and put his hands up placatingly.

"We all have secrets we can't divulge," he said. "But, for the moment, I think we have a common goal and a mutual interest in helping each other achieve it. Let's agree that we should all try to keep each other alive long enough to go our separate ways once that is done."

"Just keep that sentiment in mind," Murph said, turning to leave.

"Anything?" Jacob asked as Murph walked onto the bridge.

"Nah. He's a cool one," Murph said, slumping into the seat. "I got some good high-res images of him I'll send home to try and track down who the hell he is."

"You think he's playing straight with us?"

"He's using us as much as we're using him at the moment," Murph said. "Just remember that this dynamic is fluid and will change without warning. You go through our primary intel packet?"

"Yep."

"And?"

"It's thin, but your NIS pals were able to dig through the navigation logs on that ship they brought back to base and get us a destination: Proe-4." Jacob pulled up a star chart on his terminal. "It's a planet in an unclaimed system near the border of the Cridal Cooperative and the Saabror Protectorate."

"Why unclaimed?" Murph asked.

"Something about a buffer region along the Protectorate borders. It's part of an old treaty with the ConFed that they're apparently still honoring," Jacob said. "No advanced indigenous population but a geologically stable, life-sustaining world."

"Anything about those humans?"

"You can read it yourself," Jacob said. "All I'll say is that they were high-level supervisors and managers for a certain mining company you're probably familiar with."

"No way," Murph said. "That sure as hell isn't a coincidence."

"Read the file," Jacob urged. "Sully?"

"Meshing-out in twenty minutes," the pilot said. "Just under four days to the Proe System."

"Let's make sure we're ready when we get there. I want everyone to read the full intel file and program the computer to keep an eye on our guest at all times. I don't want him roaming around the ship freely," Jacob said. He'd been awake for over a full day now and, as it sometimes did, his prosthetic eye was beginning to give him a headache and blur his vision along the left side.

"Let the fun begin," he said. "I'll relieve you in a few hours, Sully."

10

"It isn't the worst place I've ever seen," MG said as they all got their first look at Proe-4.

"There are colonies all over the surface, but very little traffic in space," Murph said. "No capital ships at all. A couple older freighters with cold engines in high orbit."

"Let's take a closer look," Jacob said, turning to Glenn. "Anything to add here?"

"I've never even heard of this planet," he said. "There's nothing about it in our information."

Jacob wasn't sure he believed him but said nothing for the moment. Whatever there was to be found on Proe-4, it wasn't a trafficking operation that had taken millions of beings. He also expected that any outpost that was down there had been abandoned after one of their ships had been captured.

During the flight out the entire group, Glenn included, had pored through the material provided by the NIS and had several group brainstorming sessions trying to find a way to piece it all together. Despite the combined brain power, including the impressive mental horsepower of one battlesynth, they couldn't find a connecting thread among the disjointed reports they'd been given. The interrogators had pulled little useful information from their human captives, and the Cridal were off limits due to the terror the elected government still had at angering the Cooperative leadership.

The raw data from the interviews of the human captives, all high-level employees from the mining company, hinted at something big that needed large amounts of healthy, skilled labor. Their willingness to participate was not especially important. It was a tantalizing hint that wherever they were being taken, they were still alive, but it also could have been a ploy by a desperate person willing to say anything to save their own ass.

"We're being pinged by an automated traffic control system," Sully said. "Basic setup. *Old* setup. Just there to make sure nobody bumps into each other going in or out. I'll put us in a high parking orbit so we can get some eyes on the surface."

Proe-4 didn't have a lot of surface water, but it was still a green, lush world which meant there *was* water down there, just running where it couldn't be seen. The megaflora was breathtaking under the gaze of the *Corsair's* high-power optics. It also made spotting surface features damn near impossible. Even in the multi-spectral scans the data coming back was jumbled and the computer put up more apologies and errors than clear images of what was below the vegetation.

"Starports?" Mettler asked.

"Seven," Sully answered. "Two capable of supporting heavy lifters. That pair is clumped together near the equator where you'd expect."

"Nothing we're looking for would be operating out of a public starport," Jacob said. "Let's start the computer on pattern recognition and see if anything pops out that would indicate—"

"What is the make of the orbital traffic control system?" Glenn asked.

"Kheprian," Sully said. "Why?"

"You have any intrusion software that can access the data logs?"

"Worth a try," Jacob shrugged. "We have a listing of the C&C channel frequencies for the system?"

"It will not have remote access capability once deployed," Tin Man said. "No Kheprian automated systems do. System integrity and security is an obsession among their engineers."

"Suggestions?" Jacob asked.

"We must go to the surface and access the logs on the device itself."

"Is that even possible?" Mettler asked.

"On a highly populated Tier One or Two world? No chance," Glenn said. "But here? It's entirely possible we could get in, get the logs, and be gone before someone tried to stop us. It's probably the only chance we'll get of finding what we're looking for in a timely manner. Flying around scanning the jungles could take weeks we don't have."

"Agreed," Jacob said after a moment. "Let's find out which starport has the processing hardware for the OTC system and put her on the ground."

"How much for that guy?" Murph asked.

"Another few thousand," Jacob said. "The bribes out here are getting ridiculous. That's the fourth one I've had to pay off."

"The smaller ports tend to have more greedy little bureaucrats running around," Murph said. "On a more developed world, there's usually a guild in place managing all of it. We set?"

"Should be. I've been given assurances that our ship won't be searched and the security sweeps will skip this part of the starport tonight," Jacob said.

"Who're you taking?"

"You and MG. You can handle the technical part and that leaves Tin Man and Mettler to watch the ship and Sully's back."

"Glenn asked to come along," Murph pointed out.

"Good for him," Jacob said. "But he doesn't make decisions on this ship. Come on...we have about two hours, and then it gets dark here according the last little weasel I paid off."

"I'll go tell MG to get his shit together," Murph said, spitting on the tarmac before walking back up the ramp.

The squat, bunker-like building that housed the Kheprian OTC processing units stood alone in a fenced area away from the main terminal and hangar complex. There were the usual deterrents in place but, overall, the building had been left relatively unsecure. Jacob already had his gear down in the cargo bay and settled in to watch the target until dark.

"You been sitting out here the whole time, Cap?" MG asked, dropping his gear on the deck beside Jacob.

"Pretty much," Jacob said. "You ready?"

"Always," MG said, sliding his combat harness over his head and shifting to secure it in place over his soft armor. He did a quick self-test on his helmet but didn't put it on. Jacob noted that the weaponeer had actually picked a reasonable armament for the mission rather than just opting for the largest thing in the armory like he normally did.

"Damn," Murph said, yawning as he walked up to them. "Am I late?"

"Yes," MG said. "We've been waiting here for an hour."

"Whatever," Murph said. "Any activity?"

"The last patrol through this section was a bored pair of guards right before sundown," Jacob said. "They didn't seem to give a shit if they saw anything or not."

"I was up on the bridge just now," Murph said, securing his own gear. "It looks like one of the bribes paid off. No active monitoring detected around the building, although to be fair it seems to be in pretty poor repair so it may just be down."

"Let's get this done," Jacob said, sliding his own helmet on.

The walk to the building was uneventful, if somewhat gross. The short grasses between the tarmac and the building were hiding sopping wet, marshy ground that smelled like fresh decomposition. Jacob's helmet did an admirable job trying to filter out the smell, but it was fighting a losing battle.

"Smells like Sully's dirty underwear," MG said.

"I've told you to stay out of my underwear, you nasty little rat," Sully said over the team channel. Sully and Mettler were monitoring the mission from the *Corsair* while Tin Man was a short way away from the ship. He was both babysitting the unwanted guest as well as providing security for the ship.

"Fence is locked," Murph said. "Cap, you want to do the honors?"

Jacob looked and saw the lightweight security fence, not meant to keep out a determined intruder, was secured with a thick cable and a spherical lock that required a key. He commanded his prosthetic arm to full power and gripped the lock, squeezing with all his might. The powerful actuators whined slightly, and then the hardened ceramic shell of the lock cracked. He kept the pressure up, and the tough material shattered with a loud *pop* that echoed across the quiet tarmac.

"Damn. I need to get one of those," MG said as Jacob easily ripped the rest of the lock apart and slid the cable through the loops to open the gate.

"No problem," he said. "When we get back to the ship remind me to chop your arm off."

The trio slipped in and closed the gate behind them. There was no way to hide the fact the lock had been destroyed, but they'd be long gone before anyone came snooping around. The door to the building had a more formidable lock, but one of the officials they'd bribed had given them a code that would let them in without sending a general alert to the starport operations center.

"Here goes nothing," he said, punching in the eleven-digit code, concentrating on the alien icons.

The door opened with a dull thump as the electromagnets let go, and they could just make out the dim, red light beyond. Murph gave them a thumbs up and motioned for MG to cover the door as he opened it. MG nodded, and Murph swung it open quickly so the Marine could race in, sweeping the small vestibule beyond.

"Clear," he said.

Jacob went second, his weapon lowered but ready. Beyond the vestibule was a metal walkway that took them out over a large sunken area that was packed with standard Kheprian equipment racks of the kind you'd see throughout the galactic quadrant.

"Was there a leak?" MG asked, nodding to the floor below.

"Coolant baths," Murph said. "Most of the equipment is submerged in that and the racks you see on those little islands are interfaces for the individual components. If you need to repair or swap something, you need to raise the submerged rack from the pool."

"Seems needlessly complicated," Jacob said.

"What's easier to maintain, a recirculating pool of fluid or kilometers of lines, fittings, disconnects, and all the other stuff you'd have to build into every enclosed box?" Murph asked. "This fluid is cooled and filtered constantly, and it protects the gear inside."

"Where do we need to go?" Jacob asked.

"Main terminal," Murph said, pointing straight ahead. "It will be that way if this is still laid out the same way it was built."

They continued over the equipment pit toward the bank of blinking terminals along the far wall. Jacob marveled at how much gear it took to run an orbital traffic control system even in a star system where there was no traffic to speak of. He couldn't imagine what it took to manage all the ships around someplace like Miressa Prime.

"Did you pay someone to leave this terminal unlocked?" Murph asked.

"I did not," Jacob said, keeping watch toward the entry door they came in through. "You mean it's completely unsecure?"

"I'm looking at an interface screen with no prompt for credentials," Murph said. "Let's see what happens when I try to download the logs."

He winced as he slid in a standard data card, waiting for an alarm to go off. When it didn't, he shrugged and began working through the menus to find the inbound and outbound traffic logs. Jacob's heart sank as he watched the vast amount of data scroll across the display as it loaded onto Murph's card. For some reason, he thought there would only be a few entries and they'd be able to easily pick out the ship they were looking for and see where it had been flying to on the planet.

"Cap, you read me?" Mettler's voice came over the channel.

"Got you," Jacob said.

"Our guest is gone. No idea where he went, but he's definitely not aboard or in the vicinity. Tin Man is widening his search but he's in the wind."

"Son of a bitch!" Jacob said. "MG, go back across and cover the door. If Glenn pops his head in, take it off."

"Copy that," MG said, jogging back across the walkway.

"No warnings first?" Murph asked, not looking up from the terminal.

"Fuck him. He was told to stay put, and he snuck off. We have to assume anything he's up to is hostile."

"You don't have to try so hard to convince me. I'd have left him behind on Breaker's World. He's hardly been living up to his end of the bargain so far with the information he brought to the table."

"What do you think he's up to?" Jacob asked after a few minutes.

"Crossing Tin Man by sneaking off like that?" Murph snorted. "Seems like an overly complicated suicide attempt because the battlesynth *will* find him."

11

Getting off the *Corsair* hadn't been terribly difficult, but it took longer than he would have liked thanks to that damnable battlesynth patrolling outside. The two crewmen left aboard were sharp, but Glenn had been trained by some of the best and slipped by them with ease.

The starport was eerily quiet. He knew that Captain Brown had paid a handsome bribe—far too much in his opinion—to make sure security would make themselves scarce, but there was hardly any exterior lighting and no sounds of ships coming and going. He glanced toward the bunker that held the planet's only OTC system that the rest of the scout team was pillaging and saw that the door was still closed. If all went well, he'd be back aboard the ship before the team extracting the traffic data were done.

"Every administrative building on every planet has the same lack of imagination," he muttered.

The starport terminal complex was laid out in the expected way with a processing building and a separate admin building that was outside of the security zone. On a planet like Proe-4, the security zone was a bit of a misnomer. At some point, they must have found that the high fences were just in their way and removed entire sections of them allowing Glenn easy access to the offices.

He was able to gain entry into the building easily enough, but he couldn't be sure if there had been a silent alarm tripped or not so he would have to work quickly. It took just a moment to find the office he was looking for: base logistics manager. It was called something different here, but his implant assured him the title was the same.

"Give me what I need," he whispered as he found the data port built into the desk and plugged his specialized intrusion unit into. The adaptive AI on the small device made quick work of the corporate-level security codes and gave Glenn full access to the terminal. Once in, it took less than a minute to find the files he was looking for and dump them into the device's memory. He grabbed a few more promising things for good measure, and then ordered the device to back him out and erase any evidence he'd been there.

With efficiency born of experience he put the office back exactly as he found it and turned to leave. The last thing he saw before losing consciousness were bright red glowing eyes and an alloy fist coming at his face.

———

"What was he doing?" Jacob asked, staring down at the restrained troubleshooter as Mettler worked on the horrific contusion and cut on his face. "How hard did you hit him?"

"I hit him with sufficient force to subdue him," Tin Man said stiffly. "I did not know if he had any enhancements that would protect him. As it turns out, he does not. He broke into the office complex near the terminal and was downloading files from a logistics manager using this." He handed Jacob a nondescript black box with a few leads dangling from it terminating in the most commonly used data connectors in the region.

"What is it?" Jacob asked.

"It appears to be a Kheprian device used primarily for corporate espionage," Tin Man said. "They are sold throughout the quadrant, but they are not cheap, nor are they easy to find. They are technically illegal to own on Khepri itself."

"Your homeworld likes to build a lot of sneaky and destructive shit they just let loose in the galaxy, don't they?" MG asked. When everyone else stared at him with their mouths hanging open the Marine rushed ahead. "What I mean is—"

"I understood what you meant, MG," Tin Man said. "I took no offense, though you would not be mistaken if you included my kind in your comment."

"Mettler?" Jacob asked, wanting to smooth over the awkward moment.

"Seems to be okay," the medic said. "I'll wake him up in a bit."

"Should we try to see what's in that device?" MG asked.

"You will not be able to crack the encryption," Tin Man said. "The AI at its core will thwart any effort to access the data."

"What about your stuff?" Jacob asked Murph.

"Computer is parsing the data now," Murph said. "We punched in the parameters for the captured ship so we should know soon where it's been on the planet."

"What is the meaning of this?" Glenn slurred. Everyone looked down at him, nobody made any move to help him or take off the restraints.

"You're in no position to be asking anything," Jacob said. "What were you doing with this over in the admin buildings?" He waved the Kheprian espionage device in front of him.

"You have your mission, I have mine," he said evasively.

"Not good enough. Either we get some real answers, or you can remain here as a permanent resident...or until you can talk your mysterious employers into coming to get you," Jacob said. "At this point you're nothing but an unwanted liability."

"What do you want?"

"I want to know who you're working for, what you're looking for, and why you're playing games with us like you are."

Their captive just stared at him. Not a glare, not pleading...no emotion whatsoever. It was honestly more chilling to Jacob than if he had blustered or pled to be let go.

"I work for a group that calls itself the Collective," he finally said. "They're mostly industry magnates, thought leaders, or financial oligarchs. They realized early on that while space presents huge opportunities, it also comes with unparalleled risks and dangers and the stakes are so much higher than they had been when they competed against each other on Earth.

"The One World incident and the full truth of how that came about scared them. Some of the Collective members were actually involved in helping build the first outpost on Terranovus. When Jansen went bad so spectacularly, they realized they needed something with more permanence than an elected government to handle problems like her should they arise again."

"You're talking about a shadow government," Murph said. "The subversion of the rightfully elected government to make sure your bosses can keep the money train rolling, right?"

"Essentially." Glenn shrugged. "How is this different than simply bribing politicians and doing what they wanted through that?"

"Let's table the philosophical talk for now," Jacob said. "What's this Collective's stake in missing miners?"

"One of the members' last names is Shafer. She's quite keen on finding out who depopulated one of her more lucrative spec sites."

"That fleet you showed up in?" Murph asked.

"Theirs," Glenn confirmed. "It's a fairly new venture, hence the crews' lack of...experience, let's say."

"Bumbling amateurs would be more accurate, but sure," Jacob said. "That satisfies the who—for now at least—so now tell us the what. You went through a lot of trouble to sneak into that building. Why?"

Glenn clammed up again, seeming to be involved in some internal struggle to decide how much he should, or could, share.

"I needed specific manifest data," he said. "Not just what ships came and landed on the planet. I needed to know if anything was off-loaded or loaded when the ships were on the ground at any of the public ports."

"What's their name?" Jacob asked after a moment.

"I'm sorry?"

"The name. Who is it you were sent to find?"

"I don't think I—"

"Cut the shit. You weren't sent to find out where the people at the mining site went. The government is already dumping massive amounts of resources and manpower into that. You're looking for one person. Who was at Site D that was related to Shafer?"

"Not bad, Captain," Glenn said grudgingly, apparently not seeing any way out. "It's actually two people: Janet Rushton and her daughter, Gabrielle. Janet is the daughter of Lydia Shafer."

"Holy shit," Murph muttered.

"What?" Glenn asked.

"We found Janet Rushton in her office on the command platform. She'd been shot in the head," Jacob said. "We searched the whole thing and didn't see anyone else other than two dead guards in the command center itself."

"I thought you said you only found two guards," Glenn said, now agitated.

"I did," Jacob said. "But I didn't say that was all we found. There was a dead woman in an office with Janet Rushton's name on the door. We took images and DNA samples if you have a way to confirm her identity."

"I've...met her," Glenn said. "I can confirm her identity. You're certain Gabrielle wasn't aboard? She's an eleven-year-old girl."

"She was not aboard the platform," Tin Man said. "I checked on internal sensors for any additional biotics or remains when we took the command center."

"So, she's still alive," Glenn breathed.

"Well...she wasn't there," Jacob corrected. "That's not the same thing. Mettler, go ahead and let him up."

"Thanks," Glenn said, rubbing his wrists after Mettler pulled the restraints off.

"You realize you could have just told us that you were hired by some rich person to get their family back, right?" Jacob asked.

"Not quite that easy when you're dealing with these people," Glenn said. "Just the fact that Janet and Gabrielle had gone missing, likely abducted, was something the Shafer family wanted to keep a tight lid on. Don't ask me to explain it...something about the intersection of politics, corporate elites, and old money."

"We need to pool what limited information we have," Jacob said. "How soon can you—"

"I don't think our friend's little stunt went without notice," Murph said, nodding to the monitor that he'd set to show the exterior sensor feed. While they were still some distance away, a group of armed beings were definitely making their way toward the *Corsair*, and they seemed to have come from the direction of the starport terminal complex.

"I honestly thought we'd be gone by now," Glenn said. "Hadn't counted on getting punched in the face by a battlesynth."

"Almost nobody ever does," MG said. "We gonna smoke these guys?"

"No, dipshit," Murph said, turning to Jacob. "Right?"

"We're not here to pick fights with the locals," Jacob said, hitting the intercom. "Sully?"

"I see them. Ready to leave when you give me the word."

"Get us out of here. Take us out to the south and find an open patch of sky to fly circles until we dig through this data."

The engines spooled up even before Jacob took his finger off the intercom button. As he expected, the soft pangs of small arms fire hitting the ship's belly as they flew off could be heard, but nothing that was any real threat to the *Corsair*. Sully sent them rocketing to the south, flying low and without any transponders squawking so they could just disappear into the night.

"We're clear," Sully said. "Doesn't look like they have anything on the ground to launch after us, but I'm going to keep us low and fast for a bit longer."

"That gives us a little time," Jacob said, tossing the device he'd been holding back to Glenn. "I need answers, and the sooner the better. I'm going to report in."

"Captain, I'd take it as a professional courtesy if you kept the names of my objective out of any official reports," Glenn said.

"Asking a lot considering you've done nothing but lie to me since I agreed to take you along," Jacob snorted. "But, for now, I'll keep this quiet unless directly asked. I can't promise that will always be the case."

"Fair enough."

12

"This better be good," Webb growled.

"Apologies for waking you, sir," Reggie Weathers said, his tone of voice making it clear he actually relished waking his boss at 0330 hours.

"What is it?"

"You said you wanted to be alerted the instant—"

"Get to the point, Reg, or I'm going back to sleep."

"Buzzkill has reported in. What they found was rather interesting," Weathers said. "The Navy's taskforce has been performing the cleanup operation at LOR-773 for the last few days. The Navy is doing its usual job of being thorough, if somewhat mechanical."

"What's that supposed to mean?" Webb asked irritably.

"Buzzkill moved into an observation position in the outer system. They were able to identify two Cridal ships doing the same that the taskforce has apparently not detected. So far, the enemy ships are just sitting quiet, and they have no indication a larger force is accompanying them."

"We're officially calling the Cridal ships the enemy now?"

"Must have been a slip of the tongue, sir," Weathers said. "Either way, they're asking what to do. They have no direct line of communication to the taskforce other than us informing Fleet Ops that they're in the area."

"I'm on my way up," Webb said. "Have all the data ready for me."

"Of course, Admiral."

Webb swung out of bed and grabbed his utility top. He'd been sleeping in the operations center since Obsidian had lost a ship and gone dark and Buzzkill started recon of the depopulated mining site. He'd been doing this job for some time now and his gut was telling him that something seismic was on the verge of happening, and he wanted to be near Scout Fleet's nerve center when it did.

He was out of his quarters in the lower levels of the Operations Center and on a lift up to the Hive, as the operators called the expansive room, in less than five minutes. When he stormed into the dim, dome-shaped room all heads swiveled over to him for a moment, and then went back to their tasks. The Hive represented a new concept in mission planning and management. From the single room, an on-site commander could monitor all their teams in the field and have incoming, real-time intel filtered and fed to them so they could make decisions quickly.

The room was equipped with an untold number of holographic generators that could put high-definition displays or even three-dimensional models anywhere in the room that Webb wanted. He walked to the center of the room and climbed up on the raised dais where his workstation was.

"Talk to me," he said when Weathers came up. "Have we positively identified the Cridal ships by type and origin?"

"Type, yes. Origin, no," Weathers said. "They're a newer class of recon trawler designed and built on Earth specifically for the Cridal fleet. It's not a ship we have in service with our own Navy."

"Do we know if they arrived after Obsidian got themselves captured, or have they been there watching the entire time?" Webb asked.

"Thermal analysis shows the slip-drive emitters still shedding residual heat indicating they arrived sometime after Obsidian disappeared, but before the taskforce arrived," Weathers stabbed at his tablet and a rotating model of the ship in question appeared before them. "This is the actual ship, not just a stock model the computer had. As you can see, sir, there's some damage along the port flank that looks fresh. It's definitely something that would have been repaired if the ship had been in port prior to this mission."

"How close is Buzzkill?" Webb asked.

"Not very. Maybe seven hundred klicks away from the nearest."

Webb punched up the stats for Buzzkill's ship, the *Abigail*. She wasn't a full custom job like the *Corsair* was, but she still packed a punch. She was a highly modified Aracorian high-speed courier that had been beefed up and kitted out with enough weapons she almost qualified to be called a gunship. She should be more than a match for an already-damaged recon trawler...if they could get close.

"Tell Captain May I want that ship," Webb said. "Take it intact. Crew alive preferably. Get word to Fleet Ops that we'll be conducting combat operations in the area and to not interfere. I don't need one of our destroyers wading into this and shooting my team out of the sky by mistake."

Weathers quickly passed on his orders to the waiting operators in the room and set things in motion. Webb didn't throw his scout teams into direct action lightly. Obsidian was the odd outlier because of their team makeup. Brown, Tin Man, and Murphy were especially capable of violence, not to mention that little psychopath weaponeer they had, Sergeant Marcos. Buzzkill was more like his other teams. While highly trained and capable, they tended to stick more to Scout Fleet doctrine on their missions and preferred to observe and report rather than close and kill.

The target was critical, however, so he had to trust that his people knew how to handle themselves. In the last four days he'd had three calls with the president himself asking for status updates. The Cridal connection to all the human colonists disappearing had the political class completely spooked. Most of Earth's leadership had never been off the planet, much less traveled outside of the Solar System. In a lot of ways, they still thought of the burgeoning little empire they were leading as a poor lost puppy that would die in the cold without the Cridal Cooperative's charity when the truth was that the Cridal were the ones who were watching Earth surge ahead, leaving them behind.

Could that really have anything to do with the Cridal being involved in tens of thousands of human colonists disappearing? Webb doubted it, but he also couldn't completely discount it.

"Buzzkill has sent confirmation, Admiral...they're engaging," Weathers said.

"Here we go," Webb muttered to himself.

"Have we been spotted?" Captain Al May asked.

The small trawler dead ahead of them was about a third again as large as the *Abigail*. It had taken them the better part of a full day to maneuver directly behind their engine baffles and begin their approach. As they closed to within optimum weapons range, the ship began maneuvering as if preparing to reposition. Or flee.

"Don't think so. They've not run up the powerplant and they're still running cold engines. If they think they can run from us like that they're in for a shock," the pilot said. "We still a go? Four minutes to attack threshold."

"Let's go get 'em," May said.

A few moments later the *Abigail* roared to life. The pre-programmed scripts the pilot had set up specifically for this attack brought all the offensive and defensive systems online, targeted the ship ahead, and brought the powerplant to full power. The instant it did, the *Abigail* lit up like a beacon on their target's sensors.

Now, the enemy ship had a choice; continue to play dead, run for it knowing there was a whole taskforce down in the system, or turn and fight. In the face of three poor options, the other ship's captain hesitated. It was this split instant of indecision that May had counted on. It let the *Abigail* close the gap quickly, putting them so close that by the time he authorized weapons fire there was little the trawler crew could do but brace for it.

"Firing!" the pilot called. The twin forward quad-cannons opened up, brilliant blue plasma lancing out and hitting all along the target's twin engine nacelles. In less than a minute, the engagement was over. The ship was rotating uncontrolled in space as a few hull punctures vented atmosphere and spun it about on tiny crystalline jets of vapor.

"Cridal ship, standby and prepare to be boarded," May said into the com over the proximity frequency. "Any attempt to escape or engage your weapons will result in your immediate destruction."

"They're not powering up weapons," the pilot said. "Want me to call in the cavalry?"

"Yeah, tell them to come get these guys," May said. "We still have that other Cridal ship?"

"Disappeared when we fired engines. No mesh-out signature anywhere, but they're no longer appearing on sensors."

"Keep an eye on these assholes. I'll call this in to Umpire and let them know the Navy will be taking possession of their prize. They'll have to try and wrestle it away from them or the NIS."

As May punched in the code to talk to Mosler Station he thought about the ramifications of what they'd just been ordered to do. There was no doubt that the crew aboard that ship was on a slip-com channel back to Syllitr, the Cridal homeworld. That meant the political timebomb that Admiral Webb had warned him about, the one that was ticking but nobody knew what the timer read, was about to go off. His orders had been to take the crew alive and there was no way to do that *and* keep them from using their com systems. Slip-com was a technology that was immune to jamming or interference so all he could do was sit and wait while they explained to the Cooperative government how an Earth vessel had just shot their engines out.

"Fleet boys are sending up a cruiser to take these guys off our hands," the pilot told him. "Seems they got word already to be expecting a call from us." May just gave him a thumbs up as he listened to Umpire over his headset.

"You want us to do *what?*" he asked.

"There are human remains aboard a platform down at the mining site. You will go down, collect them, and ferry them to Outpost Cornwall," the Umpire coordinator said. "The Navy is being informed now to give you free access."

"Any reason you're turning my ship into a coroner's wagon when there are over a dozen regular fleet ships hovering around down below us?"

"It's a chain of custody issue, Captain," a new voice broke into the line. One he recognized immediately. "We'd rather the body be loaded onto your ship and delivered directly to the NIS to ensure there is no chance of tampering or loss. It's not the most glamorous job, but it's the one you're being given."

"Understood, sir," May said, not wanting to argue further with the Big Boss himself. Admiral Webb was as fair a commanding officer as he'd ever had, but he didn't like being questioned once he gave an order. It might take that dipshit Brown half a dozen times to learn that lesson, but May prided himself on being a quicker study than his Obsidian counterpart.

"Get it done, Captain. Umpire out," the original coordinator said before signing off. It sounded like that asshole, Bristow. He'd already made his mind up that if Webb retired and that sack of douche took over Scout Fleet, he'd put his transfer request in immediately. Detachment or planetside life might be dull, but it was better than being dead because some moron ordered you onto a suicide mission to make himself look better.

"As soon as the cruiser gets up here to recover these guys, we need to head down to the platform marked on the display as Command One," May told the pilot. "We're apparently now a morgue service."

"Huh?"

"Gotta pick up a dead body and take it to some secret squirrel NIS outpost."

"And that's the best use of our time?" the pilot asked in disgust. "So, once again Obsidian comes in, guns just fucking blazing, has a grand ol' time trashing the place...and now we get to ferry the bodies back and forth?"

"I don't think it's quite that cut and dry this time," May said. "Captain Brown is always saying he's a victim of circumstance. This time he might actually be right."

The pilot muttered something and punched in the com address for the local taskforce network. Terran forces were all using the new hyperlink technology that allowed for multiplexing rather than single point-to-point communication like slip-com. May half-listened as he coordinated getting the *Abigail* down to the command platform and retrieving their corpse while he kept a sharp eye on the sensors to make sure their second bogey didn't come sneaking up on them to return the favor.

"Look at the bright side," he said once his pilot had finished talking to the taskforce. "We get the same special duty pay as Obsidian without getting shot at so much."

"Yeah...those guys have all the fun."

13

Jacob was not having fun.

"Who the fuck is shooting at us now?!"

"I think it's just some locals," MG shouted back. "They're not very good at— *Oww!* Bastards!"

Jacob peeked up over the edge of the ditch he'd dove into for cover and saw that MG had taken a shot to the shoulder. The pauldron of his light armor was smoking and singed, but the weaponeer was still moving and appeared more pissed than hurt.

They'd pulled a location where the ship they'd been tracking had landed on the planet dozens of times and when they'd arrived discovered a hastily abandoned base. Sticking to protocol, Jacob had Sully drop him, MG and Tin Man on the ground for a quick recon before risking the *Corsair* by putting her on the ground. The ship had barely cleared their line of sight when they started taking fire from two different hillsides surrounding the small base.

"Tin Man?" Jacob called.

"Four hostiles to the southwest. Three on the northern hill," Tin

Man reported. "Their weapons are antiquated but still pose a threat to you and MG. Shall I take the group currently setting up a mortar?"

"Yeah...why don't you go ahead and take care of that," Jacob said, rolling his eyes. Tin Man rocketed off toward the four-man group on his repulsor jets, arcing up and away from the base. "MG, we need to get the group to the north."

"I'm injured."

"Shut the hell up and get ready to run. When I open fire, move toward that building behind you." Jacob didn't wait for a response. He popped up and opened fire on the hillside sending dozens of plasma bolts into where he thought they were hunkered down at. MG sprinted across the tarmac and made it to cover safely, but he had no lane to lay down suppressing fire so Jacob could move.

"Standby, Cap. I'll move around to where I can get a shot on them," he said.

"No time. Hang on." Jacob opened up again on the hillside and leapt up out of the ditch, accelerating across the smooth tarmac as hard as he could. Thanks to his genetic gifts, he blazed across the open area faster than any other human could manage, save for one.

"How bad's the shoulder?" he asked as he slid to stop beside his teammate.

"Didn't go through the armor. Just burned like hell. What's the plan?"

"Let's move toward the back at an angle away from them," Jacob said. "They'll be covering the closest avenues that give us an open shot. Since we're carrying the wrong weapons, we'll need to get close."

"Yeah, I wouldn't mind having one of those sweet Galvetic rail-guns right about now," MG agreed.

Jacob led them down between the massive concrete buildings in a northeasterly direction, taking them away from the shooters on the hillside.

"All four shooters on this hill are subdued," Tin Man reported over the team channel.

"Subdued?" Jacob asked, looking at MG in confusion.

"They are human."

"Oh. Well...damn," Jacob sighed. "That means the other three probably are as well."

"I will move that way to make sure they do not flee," Tin Man said. "Continue your approach as you are."

"What the hell are humans doing here?" MG asked.

"We're about to find out," Jacob said.

They made it to the end of the row of buildings and found that they butted right up against the hill their shooters were on. Now that he was looking up, he was having second thoughts about a two-man assault on a fortified location nearly two-hundred and fifty meters up a hill where they'd be exposed the whole time.

"Tin Man, this hill is going to be tough to take with just the two of us," he said into the com. "What's your read?"

"You will want to hold off on a frontal assault, Captain," Tin Man said. "Things have become more complicated."

"Elaborate."

"The embankment your shooters were taking cover behind conceals the entrance to a cave. I detect many more humans inside. Some of them quite small."

"Children?" MG asked.

"Really? What the hell else would they be?" Jacob asked. "Can you make contact, Tin Man? Try to let them know we're a human crew and not here to harm them?"

"Standby."

Tin Man thought about the problem for a moment before deciding on a course of action. He was quite curious why there appeared to be a colony of wild humans living in the hills when there were perfectly serviceable buildings down below. In his experience humans could be irrational at times, especially in large numbers, but he hadn't met one yet he would consider genuinely stupid.

The group defending the cave opening appeared to not have

anything more than basic small arms, but it wouldn't take much to rig the entrance with explosives, and Tin Man wasn't impervious despite what his new teammates seemed to think. He scanned the entrance to the cave as best he could before he moved cautiously forward again.

The small fireteam was wholly focused on trying to reacquire Captain Brown and MG so they were taken completely by surprise when Tin Man opened up with his arm cannons. The shots slammed into the rock to their left, causing them to spin about in a panic and letting Tin Man know they were not professional soldiers.

"Please, remain calm," he said in English. "Put down your weapons, and I guarantee your safety. We are a scout team from the United Earth Armed Forces, and we may be able to assist you."

"Shoot it! It's up above us!" a human shouted in the same language, but with a heavy accent Tin Man couldn't place. Some more wildly placed shots hit the rock and scrub around where Tin Man was crouched. He ignored it and studied the weapons they were firing. They were low-power carbines made by the Eshquarians that shipboard security forces favored. They were effective at close range but lacked the power to punch through bulkheads or hull plating. The particular model had been out of production since before the ConFed had invaded the Eshquarian Empire so whoever these humans swiped them from, they weren't exactly on the cutting edge.

"I will give you one more chance to surrender," Tin Man said, amplifying his voice. "Only one."

"We will never—" Tin Man leapt off the ledge, firing his repulsors just enough to cushion his impact as he landed right in front of the three-man squad. Before they could adjust to the sudden change in the engagement, the battlesynth walked right into the middle of the group and yanked their weapons from their hands, tossing them over the embankment. The three men stood in stunned silence as their weapons clattered down the hillside.

"Now," he said pleasantly. "Are you ready to talk like civilized beings?"

"Yeah, we can talk. Right, guys?"

"Oh, yeah, definitely ready to talk."

The third member of the party said nothing. He was still gaping at Tin Man in horror.

"Come up, Captain," Tin Man transmitted over the team channel. "Cave entrance has been secured."

"The son of a bitch threw a gun at me!"

"I don't think it was on purpose," Jacob said as he and MG hiked up the hill.

They'd moved out of cover when they saw Tin Man jump down onto the embankment, then three plasma carbines were tossed over the edge seconds later. One of them came close to hitting MG square in the head.

"But you can't prove it," MG insisted. "Shouldn't you write him up or something?"

"I've been in charge of Obsidian since Commander Mosler was killed, and I've never written anybody up despite the fact none of you *ever* fucking listen or do what you're told half the time," Jacob said. "So, now you want me to start issuing paperwork? On the only team member we have that isn't actually in the UEAS?"

"That's why I said *or something*," MG said. "You're the officer here...do officer shit."

"Just keep walking," Jacob growled.

When they cleared the edge of the embankment, he saw Tin Man standing casually to the side talking to three men in clothing that had definitely seen better days. Jacob took note that the battlesynth had stood down from combat mode, his arm cannons retracted and his eyes their normal color.

"Captain Brown, this is John Pruett," Tin Man said, motioning to the tallest of the three. "He is in charge of the settlement here."

"Settlement," John snorted. "We're a refugee camp made up of a handful of escapees. We're barely alive out here."

"Mr. Pruett my name is Jacob Brown, I'm a captain in the United

Earth Marine Corps. I'm sorry if our appearance out here startled you." Jacob held his hand out, and John Pruett took it, if hesitantly.

"I suppose we appreciate you not killing us all," he said. "We weren't sure who you might be thanks to this tall guy here with the glowing red eyes. We figured the element of surprise was best."

"Sound strategy when you might be outgunned." Jacob nodded. "Can you give me a quick rundown on what you're doing here and how many of you there are?"

"We were employes and their families of the McMillian-Shafer company," John said, confirming what Jacob had already suspected. "We were loaded onto transport ships from our jobsite. They claimed there was an emergency, and we had to evacuate. Before we realized what was happening, they gassed us, and we woke up here in those buildings below. There were some other humans there as well as a few pens full of other species. I realized pretty quick something was up and was able to get myself and a few dozen out of the building, but we had no idea where we were. Still don't, actually. All we know is that we're not within a three-day hike of any settlement in any direction."

"You're correct about that," Jacob said. "You'd need to walk at least a couple weeks to get to the closest bit of civilization. You're on the planet Proe-4. Ever heard of it?"

"Nope. But that's not my specialty. I'm an engineer on a separator crew. I don't have anything to do with flying ships or nothing like that."

"Did you witness this base being abandoned?"

"Oh, yeah," John said. "Hard to miss it. They brought down three large cargo haulers back-to-back-to-back. They'd load one up, and another would come in right after. Lucky for us it was a rush job so most of the food and water was left behind although most of us are sick of the rations they left."

"Okay, John, here's what we're going to do," Jacob said. "First, go ahead and send some people to retrieve your mortar team on the other hillside. Next, I'm going to bring my ship down, and I'll need to debrief you and any others in your group you think may have pertinent information about who took you and why. Then, we'll call in for a pickup, and the Navy will bring a ship to get all of you off this planet and back home."

"Now you're talking, my young friend," John said with a big smile. "That makes me twice as happy that you didn't kill us by mistake."

"You and me both."

It took a bit to get the group calmed and organized, but Jacob convinced the people in the cave that the buildings below were indeed abandoned and would be a safer place for them to stay. They'd apparently already lost two of their group to venomous bites from the local wildlife but had been more afraid of their abductors coming back, so they remained hidden in the hillsides.

Sully brought the *Corsair* down onto the landing pad far enough away from the buildings that there was a bit of a defensive buffer. Jacob didn't think Pruett was lying about who they were, but he wasn't about to risk the safety of his ship and crew on that assumption. He also let Pruett and the two other people he brought with him to talk to Jacob use the facilities aboard the *Corsair* to clean up and get a proper meal.

"Thanks, Captain...needed that."

"No problem. I talked to my command, and they have a Navy cruiser on its way as fast as she'll fly," Jacob said. "It will still be some days out, but you're all going home. I'll leave com gear so you can talk them in."

"Thank God," the woman who had come with them breathed. Jacob knew her name was Jackie and that she had been appointed to look after the children in the group, but she didn't say much.

"This is Alvin Curtis, Captain," John said, nodding to the third of the group. "He's the only member of our little band on the command platform when it all went down."

"I suspect your story is the one I want then, Mr. Curtis," Jacob said, motioning them all to seats in the galley. "What was your job at Site D?"

"Logistics coordinator and fleet operations manager," Curtis said. "I was a direct report to Janet Rushton." Jacob noticed Glenn give a slight twitch at Janet's name.

"Just tell me what happened in your own words, sir," Jacob said. Curtis took a moment to collect his thoughts before starting.

"We had a supply ship come into the system off-schedule one day. It was early on first shift, and I had just walked into the control room. I noticed the ship but didn't bother asking about it. There was starting to be a lot of random traffic in and out of Site D since we'd discovered heavy nickel deposits in Belt A, as well as large quantities of rare earth elements on one of the rocky worlds. Lots of VIPs and government types coming in and out.

"Things got weird when the small cargo hauler flew directly to the command platform, something that was highly unusual since most cargo traffic went to the logistics hub only. I asked about it, but the on-shift site manager told me it was a surprise for Janet, so I thought nothing of it and left to go back to my office."

Curtis paused and took a drink from the water glass Mettler had put in front of him and stared off into space for a moment.

"My office was right next to Janet's. I heard a group walk into her office, then heard her yelling. It was something like 'No way in hell is this happening!' and then there was some more arguing. She was pretty shaken up after that. It was the next morning when someone charged into my office dressed in all-black tactical gear and ordered me onto the floor. I was put in restraints, and then I was hauled down to the cargo ship and strapped into a seat."

"Was the crew human?" Jacob asked.

"Some," Curtis said. "Others were Syllitr."

"You're sure about that?" Glenn asked.

"Certain. I was on Syllitr for two months during a consultation with the Cridal on Site D. They wanted to see if there was any feasibility of a joint operation, but it was determined that the site wasn't sufficiently surveyed to bother with two independent operations mining the belts."

Jason and Murph looked at each other. There was little chance that the Cridal government hosting a mining company from Earth that was then depopulated by a joint Cridal/Human operation was a coincidence.

"Do you know who arranged the conference on Syllitr?" Murph asked.

"The one who set up the whole thing was Kobvir Glecsh, the Chief of Staff to Prime Minister Dalton," Curtis said. "But beyond the opening comments we never saw him. We dealt almost entirely with the minister of expansion and her staff."

"On it," Murph said, heading toward the com room. This was the first name they had to go on, and Mosler Station would want it ASAP.

"It seems we can tie Janet's killer to someone she knew," Glenn said.

"Percy Walker," Curtis said.

"Excuse me?" Jacob said.

"Sorry, Captain...it slipped my mind. Percy Walker was there. He's the site survey director for corporate. I saw him when they were dragging me out."

"Was Walker there at the conference with the Cridal?" Glenn asked.

"Oh, yes," Curtis nodded. "He was a VIP attendee. There were maybe thirty or forty of us there from two different mining companies. Director Walker was there on behalf of McMillian/Shafer to try and establish relationships within the Cridal government."

"So, there's no denying the Cridal are involved at this point," Jacob sighed. "Fuck."

"Indeed, Captain," Curtis said. When Jacob looked at him quizzically, he went on. "As an executive level employee that works outside of the Solar System, I make it a point to stay current on quadrant politics. The slow-motion collapse of the ConFed, for example. Now we have what appears to be at least a faction within the Cridal Coop-

erative helping execute operations with the help of corporate operatives. Times are about to become interesting."

"Understatement of the century," Jacob said as Murph walked
back in, nodding to him that he'd gotten through to Mosler Station.

"Mr. Curtis, did you notice if Janet Rushton's daughter was with
her that day?" Glenn asked.

"Gabby?" John Pruett spoke up. "She was at the site?"

"She was," Curtis said sadly. "I didn't see or hear her in the office
area, but I know she was on the command platform staying with
Janet in her quarters."

"She's not in your group?" Glenn pressed.

"No, sir. She may have been in one of the other pens inside those
buildings, but she wasn't one of those who escaped with us," Curtis
said.

"Last question, and then I'll let you get back to your people,"
Jacob said. "I don't suppose you have any idea where they took everybody after evacuating this base?"

"I can't swear to this, but there was a lot of talk about a world
called Dorshone," Pruett said as the other two nodded.

"Dorshone?" Jacob asked. "That doesn't even sound like a planet
name."

"It does," Tin Man said. "That name is not the one it is given in
the ConFed Navigational Registry."

"Where's it at?"

"Within the Saabror Protectorate."

"Well...that's not good," Murph said.

14

"Dorshone?" Webb asked.

"It's also known as Dorst-5. It's within the Saabror Protectorate," Weathers said.

"Oh," Webb said, spinning in his chair to look at the three-dimensional holographic depiction of the galactic quadrant. It was currently zoomed in to the mid/lower Orion region showing all of human and Cridal space right to where Seeladas Dalton's crumbling cooperative met the border of the Eshquarian Empire. Along an area of space that bordered both was a region with red warning lines through it. The Saabror Protectorate. It was a multi-species nation that was hyper-aggressive to outsiders violating their borders and seemed to hold a special level of contempt for the Eshquarians and the ConFed.

It was largely unknown save for long-range observation and was a strict no-go zone for any Earth vessels or personnel. Earth was a small regional power of the type the Protectorate liked to make examples of.

"What else did you guys get from the survivors, Captain?" he asked.

"This wasn't random, and it was well-organized," Jacob Brown's voice came from the overhead speakers. "It's impossible to deny that the Cridal aren't instrumental in this, but the Saabror connection is still unclear. We're not sure if they're just using a planet there for a safe harbor they know we'll avoid or if it's more than that."

"Tell me about this Glenn Mitchell," Webb said.

"He's honest...at least he's not lying with what he's willing to tell me at all," Jacob said. "But he's definitely holding something back. He's been given a specific task that nests inside this mission to find the missing human settlers and miners, but we're not sure what yet. So far, he's been as asset."

"I don't need to tell you to keep an eye on him," Webb said. "I don't want to be naming the next Scout Fleet base Brown Station."

"Understood, sir."

"Right now, you're still on-mission, Captain. While I technically can't authorize you to breach Saabror space, I understand that sometimes scout teams don't always check for clearance before pursuing a target. It's part of the leeway that's built-in to this unit."

"Understood, sir," Jacob repeated. "Obsidian, out."

"I'll make sure the com buffers are purged, sir," Weathers said. "The last bit was a little on the nose."

"That's what I keep you around for," Webb said. "Is the *Kentucky* ready to fly?"

"She always is. Do you have a specific destination in mind?"

"Earth. I need to speak with the president. The Cridal connection has just crossed a threshold many of us were hoping it wouldn't but, now that it has, I'll need to do my best to convince him to lean on Dalton's government to give us access to her chief of staff."

"This...should be handled through official channels, sir," Weather said carefully.

"Scout Fleet exists outside of official channels for a reason, Reg," Webb said. "This information is too volatile to trust all the hands it would have to pass through on the way up. I need to hand it directly to him in its unedited, unredacted form."

"They'll come after you with everything they have," Weathers warned, referring to the political class that roamed the halls of power, each looking for a chance to move up the ladder, even if that ladder was made from knives they'd stuck in the backs of their colleagues.

"Doesn't matter. I owe the people taken nothing less," Webb said. "Please, make the arrangements. I want to be heading to orbit within the hour."

"I'll handle it, sir."

"Oh...and please have Umpire operations relocated to the *Kentucky* for the time being. Have any personnel you need for that ready to go."

"I was sort of hoping he'd tell us to come home," Murph admitted. "The Saabror Protectorate isn't known for being welcoming to uninvited guests."

"This is what we all signed up for, right? Fun, adventure...travel to exotic new places, meet interesting new people. Kill them." MG leaned back and shrugged. "It's all the same to me."

"I have operated extensively within the Saabror Protectorate when I was still an active asset in the Kheprian military," Tin Man said. "While it is dangerous, I feel your people have overstated that danger somewhat. There are open lines of trade, even immigration into and out of the Protectorate. If we adhere to certain protocols, we should be relatively safe."

"How relatively?" Glenn Mitchell asked.

"As safe as you ever are on a Scout Fleet mission," Tin Man said.

"I was actually hoping for a little better odds this time around," Mettler sighed.

"Sully?"

"It's in the nav computer, surprisingly," Sully said. "Seven-day flight."

"Let's get to it," Jacob said. "I'm going to take one more look around and give our survivors some final instructions, and then we're out."

By the time he walked off the back ramp, the engines of the *Corsair* were rumbling to life, steaming and hissing in the cool evening air. He saw Alvin Curtis standing by an open door of the building they'd relocated all the survivors to and waved, jogging over to him.

"You have everything you need, Captain?" Curtis asked.

"Wish I could stay until the Navy gets here to pick you all up," Jacob said. "But we might have a chance to find the others alive, so we have to fly fast."

"Is there? A chance?"

"The *Corsair* is a lot faster than the cargo ships they'd have used to remove the people. It could be close, but they'll still beat us to Dorshone."

"Hope you're able to run them down, Captain," Curtis said, sticking out his hand.

"Get your people back home, and then retire to some nice, quiet part of Earth," Jacob said, shaking the proffered hand.

He took the time to walk through the cavernous building, nodding and smiling to the scared, disoriented people. They'd pulled some gear out of the *Corsair* to make sure they could talk to any incoming Navy ships as well as defend themselves a little better than with just the peashooters they originally had.

His thoughts were still on the survivors as he trudged back to the ship. Leaving them behind was a risk, but they were a small group with competent leadership, and there was still a larger group being held captive that needed their help. While the math was simple, it didn't mean he felt any better about having to pick one group over another. If locals or this trafficking ring showed back up in any real numbers, the people on Proe-4 were well and truly screwed.

The crew must have been impatient since as soon as the ramp was halfway closed, Jacob felt the ship lift from the landing pad and accelerate to the south toward the equator. He did a quick inspection of the cargo tie-downs before going into the ship and toward his quarters, wanting nothing more than a few hours of sleep.

"Navy is less than three days out, Cap," Murph said as he walked through the galley. "They're sending a cruiser and a destroyer escort just in case."

"Good," Jacob said. "That should make anyone think twice about hitting the cruiser during the recovery operation. How's our guest?"

"Asleep already," Murph said. "He wants to contact his people but agreed to wait until we were in slip-space and things settled down."

"Accommodating," Jacob said. "Send Mettler up to keep Sully company on the bridge when you see him, and then I'll take next shift."

"Will do."

Jacob walked into his quarters and began tossing his gear on the rack. He grabbed a pair of pants off the back of his chair that he'd worn earlier and stopped as something fell out of the pocket. He frowned, looking at the small, leather-bound paper book that was lying on the deck.

"What the hell?"

He picked it up, turning it over in his hand before he remembered he'd grabbed it off the ship they'd been sent to inspect. It had been wedged down between the webbed seats and the bulkhead. He pulled the elastic strap off and opened it up, nearly choking when he saw what was inside the cover.

The personal journal of Gabby Rushton. KEEP OUT!

"Holy fucking shit," he whispered, reading the words again and taking in all the little doodles of flowers, a tree, and what might have been a horse under it. He sat down in the chair, reading through the entries. He felt a little grubby reading the personal thoughts of a young girl like he was some sort of voyeur, but the chance to get even a sliver of a lead inside that they could use.

Most of it was what would be expected, but at the halfway point young Gabrielle began chronicling her trip with her mother to Site D. It was obvious that accompanying her mother on a work trip was completely against her wishes but, apparently, her parents had insisted.

The platform I'll be living on with Mom is a nightmare. Everyone is old. Nobody smiles. Most of them smell bad. Dad tells me this will be the learning experience of a lifetime, but I know I'm stuck here so he won't be bothered with me while Mom is away.

"Sounds like a blast," Jacob muttered, flipping through more pages. Most of the entries were a lot of the same. Just a young girl venting about how the universe was conspiring to make her life as miserable as possible. A name on one of the later pages caught his eye.

Percy Walker came back to Site Dumbass today. Mom doesn't like him, but I do. He always brings me something and has the best stories about his travels outside of the Solar System. At least he gets to travel to new planets and see aliens instead of sitting here...staring at rocks floating by. He and Mom were arguing about something. Sounded serious. Percy accused her of being shortsighted and said that somebody named Saber (I think?) was dying and that they'd get what they needed one way or another. Sounded really dramatic. Mom said he was disgusting and that she was going to report him if he brought it up again.

The rest of the entry had nothing to do with the interaction, but it was enough. It was pretty obvious that *Saber* was really *Saabror* given what they'd figured out so far. What did it mean that they were dying? The way a nation usually died involved some sort of natural or economic calamity, but what did that have to do with trafficking millions of beings? What was the end game? Trafficking was lucrative, but not for legitimate governments on a large scale it wasn't.

"Anything interesting?"

"Other than me almost shitting my pants from you sneaking into my quarters without me hearing you?" Jacob asked, turning to look at Tin Man. He tossed the journal to the battlesynth. "See for yourself. Doesn't get interesting until about halfway through."

Tin Man read the journal with the speed and efficiency he did everything with. Jacob knew that the battlesynth would now be able to recall every aspect of the small book when asked meaning there was no longer a risk of losing it.

"Percy Walker insisting that the Saabror Protectorate is dying is rather fascinating," he remarked.

"And bullshit," Jacob snorted. "Any sort of economic collapse from a bordering power would have been in all the intel reports."

"So, you say," Tin Man said. "But how many have been caught off guard by the ConFed dissolving? How many still aren't even aware that is what happened?"

"Fair point," Jacob conceded. "So, what would a dying Saabror Protectorate want with a mining site that was barely out of the prospecting phase?"

"Is that a question you need answered for your mission...or for yourself?"

"What's that supposed to mean?"

"Admiral Webb is a skilled warrior and a surprisingly wise leader considering he is not even a full century old yet," Tin Man said. "He has a term he likes to use. Mission creep."

"I know it," Jacob said, annoyed.

"Since I have joined Obsidian there have been multiple instances where you had met mission objectives, yet still you pursued," Tin Man went on. "You show compulsive tendencies that cause you to continue well beyond the scope of your orders. While you always ask your teammates if they are willing, I feel you are also well-aware that their loyalty to you and to each other prevents them from backing out."

Jacob said nothing, not liking the turn the conversation had taken. He felt what the battlesynth had said was wildly unfair, but not altogether untrue. Perhaps the mission to find the *Eagle's Talon* had been the beginning of his compulsive behavior. After locating the ship he'd taken it upon himself to capture it as well. Then, he went after rogue intelligence agent Elton Hollick and took it upon himself to bring down Margaret Jansen's One World faction with the help of his father's mercenary crew.

In every one of those instances, he had met his mission objectives, but time-critical events were happening that meant by the time NAVSOC got the proper personnel in place, the targets would have already been gone. Was he just reckless? A loose cannon with a hero complex? An immature man with daddy issues trying to live up to his father's reputation?

"My comments were only to help you frame your own thoughts, Captain," Tin Man said. "Your actions have always been selfless and were a credit to your species and to your family. I only want you to keep in mind that you cannot win every single fight on your own."

"I think I get what you're saying," Jacob said. "Thanks."

"Get some rest. I will relieve Sully for a time and ensure Glenn Mitchell is continually observed."

"Thanks again," Jacob yawned. "A couple of hours, and I'll be ready to go."

He was asleep on his rack before he even got his boots off, his mind troubled with all the ramifications of what they were uncovering, big and small.

15

The flight to Earth had been short thanks to the captain of the *Kentucky* flogging his engines at Webb's request. The ship should have been decommissioned already and a new, modern ship replacing her, but Webb had used his influence to have her refitted for a third time rather than put in the boneyard with the rest of the obsolete hulks in the Olympus System.

His shuttle had been given priority status, and he was walking across the ramp in Zurich, Switzerland. It was the current temporary capital of the Unified Earth government, recently moved from Washington DC due to the perception that America was assuming full control of everything outside the orbit of Earth. Since the United States was still a country, the agreement was that a city would be picked that wasn't currently a national capital until a permanent location could be chosen.

Where this became even more confusing was that Scout Fleet, technically outside of the UEAS chain of command, reported directly to the president of the United States. He, in turn, sat on a council of five leaders that were supposed to be working together to guide humanity into this new age.

The whole thing made Webb glad that he was on Mosler Station

and not in Zurich or DC. The growing pains of building a fully integrated one-world government were proving to be titanic. In the
meantime, the nations of Earth had assumed roles they were already
suited for. Thus, the Americans had been tasked with building and
organizing the vast space-going military they were building given that
they had fielded the most expansive seagoing Navy on Earth. Webb
couldn't wait to see how the president would react when he dropped
a bomb in his lap that had profound ramifications for all of humanity
going forward.

"He will see you now, Admiral," an aide said before Webb and
Weathers were even fully through security.

"Thank you," Webb said as Weathers took a seat in the large
lobby. He was escorted through one more security scanner before
being allowed into the office. The president was pacing in front of the
floor-to-ceiling windows when he walked in.

"Good afternoon, Mr. President. It's a pleasure to see you, sir."

"Have a seat, Admiral. You may as well be comfortable while you
ruin my year."

President Harold Weinhaus looked as if he'd aged a decade since
last Webb had seen him. Webb felt for the man. While he was living
in glorious obscurity on Koliss-2, Harold Weinhaus was meeting the
storm head-on. The political and societal upheaval on Earth wasn't
insignificant as it began to really sink in for the average earthling that
this wasn't going away.

Aliens were real. Intergalactic dangers were real. Even as most
would rather stuff that genie back into the bottle, there was no going
back. On top of trying to manage a fledgling galactic power, leaders
like Weinhaus were trying to ease the average citizen into the
new era.

"I wish I could laugh, Mr. President, but by the time I'm finished, I
feel you'll wish you never let me into your office."

Weinhaus groaned and sat down behind his desk. It was a plain,
simple desk. Much different than the one he sat behind when he was
in Washington DC.

"Hit me," he said.

So, Webb did.

For the next three hours, the admiral briefed the president on what they were learning about a massive trafficking operation that had collected tens of thousands of human settlers and deep space laborers. He gave him the unvarnished truth that it appeared certain the Cridal Cooperative government, or at least a faction of it, was at the center of facilitating the individual trafficking rings.

From the Omega Force operation that Webb had assisted on the cleanup of the Luuxir Border Region trafficking operation to Scout Team Obsidian's discover of the McMillian/Shafer Mining Corporation site being depopulated, the overall picture coming together was an unpleasant one.

"My God," Weinhaus exhaled. "Dalton?"

"I've found no direct involvement with her personally, but her chief of staff is certainly a high-ranking player," Webb said. "The raw data is on that card I gave you earlier. I understand the implications of what this could mean, sir. It's why as of right now, you're the only person outside of my inner circle who knows the full picture. I've not yet exchanged this intel with my NIS counterpart."

"As always, Admiral, your discretion is highly appreciated. What you've given me is an armed nuclear bomb with a faulty trigger. It might never go off, or it could kill us all right now."

"How will you proceed, sir?"

"I have no choice but to confront the Cridal directly. We will demand to speak to Kobvir Glecsh and have him explain why he features so prominently in an operation that is abducting humans," Weinhaus said. "I will inform Dalton's ambassador through our diplomatic corps, and then a mission will be sent to Syllitr."

"Which gives Glecsh ample warning to flee...if he's even still there," Webb said.

"You have an alternative?"

"I do not, sir. Diplomatic protocols must be followed, of course. I was just lamenting the fact there is no simple solution to getting a hold of him to question."

"I can't authorize a covert operation to the Cridal homeworld. As it is we'll be tap dancing to keep us out of a war once the general assembly catches wind of this. There are enough nativists in the body that will use this as political fuel to try and halt our expansion. They want to get rid of Terranovus and Olympus, fortify the solar system, and post a keep out sign on Pluto." Weinhaus leaned back, rubbing his eyes.

"Lot of isolationists out there, sir. The Galvetics refer to them as prey," Webb said. "An isolated Earth with no allies is nothing but a target for the predators out there like the Ull. At least before we became too much for them."

"I know that. You know that. But the average citizen these people are pandering to have no idea there's no going back," Weinhaus said. "Either way, that's a political fight for the assembly. My job is a lot simpler and more unpleasant. I need to go to the Unified Council and tell them why I'm sending Terran ships to Syllitr with the intent of accusing our benefactors of being slavers. So, that should be fun."

"I have my best team still in pursuit from the McMillian-Shafer site, sir," Webb said. "I will be sure that your updates are immediate."

"At least I have you, Admiral," Weinhaus said. "Cutting you away from the regular military and having you operate independently was one of my better moves. But be warned; I only have two more years left, and then I will be out. Whoever replaces me may not recognize the benefit of a Scout Fleet that reports directly to them."

"Or worse, they will see us as their own private spec ops asset and deploy us in a tactical capacity," Webb said. "I'll be burying a lot of good people if that happens."

"And on that cheerful note, I must conclude this exceedingly unpleasant meeting," Weinhaus said. "My schedule is somewhat inflexible. Normally, I'd offer you a drink, Admiral, but with the news you've just dumped on me, I'm not certain you deserve it."

"Then, a raincheck until I bring better news, Mr. President," Webb said, rising and shaking Weinhaus's hand.

"Get back to work, Admiral," Weinhaus said. "You always do good work, but I need you to do it faster this time. I don't need to tell you that things are tense here already in the uncertainty of what comes next without the ConFed running the show. News that our Cridal benefactors have betrayed us won't do much to make it any better."

"I don't envy you, sir," Webb said. "My people will dig to the bottom."

"Who is Gabrielle Rushton's father?" Murph asked as he put aside the journal.

"Douglas Rushton. *Senator* Douglas Rushton," Jacob said, handing over a tablet with the senator's bio. "Ah, wait. The senator is her stepfather. Doesn't list her biological father. Must be some nobody or Janet never knew who he was."

"Between her stepfather and her grandmother, I can see how the girl has a hired gun like Glenn Mitchell tracking her down," Murph said. "Lotta juice in that family."

They were lounging on the bridge while going over the intel and trying to connect more dots while they had the watch. So far, they hadn't turned up anything new in the mountain of data they'd collected so far.

"I still feel like Mitchell is going to be nothing but a liability," Jacob said. "So far, he hasn't done anything that makes me want to maroon him on an alien planet, but I just have this tickle in the back of my head that's still telling me not to trust him."

"I'm not saying your gut is always wrong, but— What the hell is that tone?"

"Incoming hyperlink request," Jacob said, moving over to the com station. He saw who it was from and motioned to Murph to seal the bridge before accepting the channel request. A few seconds later, a holographic projection of Admiral Webb sitting at his desk on the UES Kentucky swirled to life.

"Gentlemen," Webb greeted them. "Are we secure?"

"Bridge is sealed, sir," Jacob said. "We're secure, and we're the only two here."

"Perfect," Webb leaned back. "I'm on my way back to Mosler

Station and got a preliminary report from the NIS regarding Janet Rushton's autopsy."

"Must be interesting if you're calling us, sir," Murph said.

"The gunshot wounds happened postmortem," he said. "It was also done well after the two guards in the command center were shot and by a different gun."

"What the hell?" Jacob asked.

"She had a cocktail of drugs in her system that caused her death," Webb said. "The body was then shot many days later."

"This doesn't make much sense," Murph said. "Unless someone just shot the body randomly because it wasn't obeying orders to get out of the office or something."

"What were the drugs meant to do?" Jacob asked.

"The pathologists and toxicologists working on the case think the cocktail was meant to put Janet into a pliable state."

"Truth serum?" Murph asked skeptically.

"No...more like a compliance serum," Webb said. "Under their influence, she would have been easier to convince to do things she normally wouldn't, but the effect would have only been temporary."

"But long enough to do something like order the station defenses shut down and for people to begin an orderly evacuation into the ships that just arrived?" Jacob asked.

"But they miscalculated," Webb said. "Janet had an adverse reaction and her heart stopped. Then someone came behind days later and shot her. You wouldn't have known the difference since you're not trained coroners. For you, the obvious answer was the one right in front of you."

"Then, we're back to who the hell shot her and why," Jacob said. "This is feeling like the whole thing was staged, like someone wanted to make sure we assumed she was killed when the guards were... assuming the little scene was meant for us at all."

"Assuming that," Webb agreed. "That's the latest intel on our end. The official report will come to you through the usual channels."

"Understood, sir," Jacob said. "We're close to mesh-in near our next target. We'll pass along anything we get."

"Do that. *Kentucky*, out."

Jacob and Murph were silent for a moment, trying to put this new piece into their incomplete puzzle. The postmortem gunshots had to be to keep anyone from poking around too much and discovering the drugs in her system, but why?

Tin Man's words came back to him as he struggled to work in this new bit of information. Did it really matter? As far as he could tell the news that Janet Rushton died from what amounted to lethal injection rather than a 9mm bullet was immaterial when it came to locating the missing humans and seeing who had them. It was as likely Rushton was killed for some reason that had nothing to do with the trafficking operation, so was this another rabbit hole he was about to get sucked down?

"Want my advice?" Murph asked.

"Shoot."

"Let's just focus on finding the people. I'm just as curious as you probably are about this new wrinkle with Rushton's death, but I don't think that will help us in the short term."

"Strangely enough, I was just thinking the same thing," Jacob said. "We'll look at the official report from the NIS and see if there's something more in there but, for now, we're one hundred percent on finding the abductees."

"Would one of you care to unlock the bridge hatch? Or did you want to go ahead and attempt mesh-in?" Sully's voice came over the intercom.

Murph got up and opened the hatch, letting the annoyed pilot onto the bridge.

"What were you two weirdos doing up here?" he asked, sniffing suspiciously.

"I'll go get the rest of the team up and ready," Murph said.

"I've got us coming in well outside the normal navigable areas of the system," Sully said, sliding into his seat. "It means a longer ride down toward the planet, but a lot less chance of an incident."

"I'm all for erring on the side of caution in this case," Jacob agreed. "Not gonna lie...flying into a Protectorate system already has me on edge."

"Me, too," Sully said. "I'll keep the weapons and countermeasures powered down, so we don't come in waving a big red flag, but I'll have them primed and ready."

Jacob just nodded and looked up at the mission clock. Just over half an hour until they popped in. He went over to the security station and pulled up a personnel tracker display to make sure his people were out of their racks and getting ready. When he did, he could swear he saw two icons representing Glenn Mitchell. When he tried to look closer, one of them flickered and disappeared, leaving only the one that showed the civilian in berthing where he belonged.

"What the hell?" he muttered. He tried to scroll back the security feed, but it only showed the single icon in berthing. Had it been a glitch or was he seeing things? He had been up for quite a long time. Maybe his mind was playing tricks on him.

"Tin Man, please confirm where our passenger is," he said into the intercom.

"In berthing organizing his equipment."

"Has he been moving around much during the flight?"

"Not that I have seen on my patrol, nor have I found any evidence he had left berthing. Is there a problem, Captain?"

"I don't think so. Maybe a glitch with the internal sensors," Jacob said.

"Copy."

Sully gave him a look but said nothing. Jacob tried a few more times to repeat the internal sensor anomaly but after three attempts decided that it just wasn't there. He locked out the security terminal and went back over to the command chair as Sully prepped for mesh-in.

Unlike the smaller combat ships they'd used like *Boneshaker*, *Corsair* had a more traditional bridge layout. There was a recessed pit where the pilot and copilot sat. On the starboard side there was a seat for the team leader that had monitors feeding them information, and then on the port side there were two stations for sensors and tactical systems.

Jacob rarely used the command seat. It was where Ezra Mosler had sat and, to him, the seat still felt like it belonged to the late commander. Mosler and Webb had pulled Jacob out of the academy to join Scout Fleet after Jacob had royally screwed up as a cadet. He'd used the genetic gifts he'd inherited from his father to try and win in a combat exercise and footage of him running through the woods at night at over twenty-five miles per hour in full gear was caught by a high-flying drone. In order to keep him out of some mad scientist's lab, then-Captain Webb had Jacob's record sealed and him fast-tracked into the Marine Corps, and then directly into NAVSOC.

He smiled to himself thinking how petulant and bitter he'd been about taking a commission into the Marines. Before that he'd had aspirations of walking the bridge of a mighty warship in the Navy, traveling between the stars and seeing strange, exotic new places…all from the comfort of starship. Being a Marine and getting down and dirty had been the very last thing on his mind. In his youthful arrogance, he felt it beneath him. He remembered whining that it wasn't fair and how the Navy was missing out on just how special he really was. Now, looking back, he realized how lucky he was that anyone had wanted him at all.

Life has a way of humbling you. Quickly, he thought, flexing this synthetic left hand.

"Standby for mesh-in," Sully announced over the intercom.

There was a slight judder felt through the deck as the *Corsair* popped back out into real-space. Jacob watched intently as the sensors populated the threat board and analyzed all the in-system traffic. Sully's hands remained near the slip-drive controls to execute an emergency mesh-out if Jacob called an abort.

"What the…"

"Captain?" Sully asked tensely.

"Stand down slip-drive," Jacob said before hitting the intercom. "Murph and Tin Man to the bridge."

Sully secured the slip-drive, brought up the main engines, and then brought the tactical picture over in front of him where he could see it for himself. His eyes narrowed in confusion, but he said nothing.

"What's up?" Murph asked as he walked in.

"Hell if I know," Jacob said. "But it looks like we've flown into one of the most disorganized boneyards in the galaxy."

"What the fuck are you jabbering about?" Murph asked, leaning over to look at the display and frowning in confusion. "Huh. I guess I see your point."

There were multiple formations out in the system made up of row after row of what appeared to be unpowered derelict starships. What made this strange was the haphazard nature of the formations along with the ships themselves not looking old or damaged enough to be retired from service. The computer struggled to age the ships exactly because there were shipbuilders in the Protectorate they didn't have a full dataset for, but the estimates still put them at only a few years old at best.

"Tin Man?" Jacob asked.

"An unexpected anomaly. I cannot say for certain this is not related to the trafficking activity, but it seems unlikely," the battlesynth said. "None of these ships are showing any damage that would indicate piracy. There is also no obvious damage to suggest they all suffered from catastrophic system failure. I would suggest we fly near the closest formation to this position and take a high-res scan."

"Sully, get us moving," Jacob said. "What do you all make of the traffic near the planet that *is* flying?"

"Seems normal," Sully said. "Nothing that would tell me there is something happening on the planet other than normal commerce."

"There!" Murph almost shouted, bringing up a zoomed image of a freighter in orbit over the planet. "This is one of the ships that was on the sensor data we pulled off the Site D computers."

"You're sure?"

"Positive. They're even flying the same transponder codes."

To keep the *Corsair*'s cover, they were flying codes that had them registered on Niceen-3. The planet known as the Gateway to the Reaches was a criminal stronghold that not even the mighty ConFed battlefleet was able to subdue. While the codes pinged them as likely smugglers or worse, most planets wouldn't bother harassing a ship so small. It also made local thugs think twice before challenging them. They wouldn't know if the *Corsair* belonged to one of the ruthless cartels that came from the Caspian Reaches, so they'd usually just let them pass.

"Let's still do the flyby, but I want to get close to that ship down there," Jacob said. "Get the team ready for a boarding action." Murph's eyebrows shot up, but he just nodded and walked out.

"You are sure—"

"I'm sure I'm going to be ready for anything once we get down there. Nothing more," Jacob said.

"Very well," Tin Man said, falling silent.

16

"Lot of ships from ConFed— Sorry, *former* ConFed shipyards," Murph said. "We have ships from the Aracorian yards and a no-shit Miressan cruiser. All in pristine condition."

"But those are the minority," Tin Man pointed out. "Most are ships that come from the Aulogus Region. It is considered the industrial heart of the Protectorate and has seven major shipyards supported by mining and manufacturing."

"Feel free to jump in with any knowledge we don't have," Jacob said sourly. "You know...since you're an expert on the region, and we've never been here."

"I will do my best to guide you," Tin Man said. Jacob just rolled his eyes.

The *Corsair* had buzzed the closest holding formation at high speed, letting the sensors soak it all in while Sully steered them for one of the abductor's ships in orbit around Dorshone. Now, the crew pawed through the data they'd collected while they approached the planet.

"We're twelve minutes from orbit, everybody," Sully called. "I'll insert us into high orbit so we can scan the surface and the traffic, then I'll push us down into a transfer orbit that will take us close to the ship."

"Sounds good," Jacob said. "Everybody ready?" He eyed Glenn Mitchell, who looked almost bored by the whole thing, before turning back to the main display.

"Sure," MG said with a yawn. He was already decked out in an EVA combat suit since he was on the boarding team if it came to that. Jacob had his with him on the bridge, and Tin Man didn't require any special equipment.

The first high-altitude pass gave them a clear look at the freighter. She was under power and appeared to be functioning normally, flying a provisional beacon that identified her as being from Pinnacle Station, but not affiliated with any nation or star system. Many places wouldn't let ships near a planet flying a provisional beacon, but Dorshone appeared to be letting them navigate freely.

"So, it's just the one?" Murph asked.

"Looks like," Sully said. "They might have hidden the others out in those parking formations."

"We can't do a more targeted scan of those formations without being too obvious," Mettler said.

"What's the declared population of this planet?" Glenn spoke up.

"Hang on," Mettler said, spinning back to his terminal. "Information on the Protectorate is sketchy, but the Zadra Network has it at... four point eight billion. But keep in mind that was from a census that's over twenty years old. Why?"

"Look at the nightside when we fly over," Glenn said. "Does it look like a planet with nearly five billion people on it?"

When the *Corsair* crossed over the terminator again, they all took a closer look at the nightside of Dorshone. It was dark. Too dark for a planet with advanced cities and infrastructure.

"Do a surface scan when we hit the dayside," Jacob said. "Look specifically for thermal blooms and energy signatures."

The *Corsair* swung around one more time at her current orbit and Sully rolled the ship so the high-res sensor array on the belly was aimed at the surface. The ship recorded the pass and began to spit out the data. What they saw was even more confusing than the dark cities on the other side.

"There are no hazard warnings being broadcast. Atmosphere is reading as safe. Where the hell is everybody?" Mettler asked.

"The power grid looks to be running at maybe fifteen percent capacity," Jacob pointed to another stat on the display. "There are entire cities with no thermal activity at all."

"It's a damn ghost planet," MG said, sounding spooked.

"That last scan caught their attention," Sully said, pointing to his headset. "Orbital control is asking what our problem is."

"Tell them we're looking for our partners that said they were coming here but never came back," Jacob said. "Give them the registry for the ship we inspected on Breaker's World."

"Clever." Murph nodded. Sully continued his conversation for a moment before nodding his head.

"They bought it. That ship has been here multiple times, though they wouldn't give me an exact number. They're confirming it left," he said. "They're not saying we have to leave. Seems they just sort of lost interest. Do you want to do another full-planet scan?"

"Let's shelve this for now," Jacob said. "Go ahead and begin walking us toward our target. We focus on getting answers from this ship, then we can speculate about migration patterns within the Saabror Protectorate."

Over the next three hours, the *Corsair* bumped down through the prescribed transfer orbits to make it look like they were getting ready to make landfall. The ship had power to spare to perform a more extreme maneuver and intercept the freighter without trouble, but that would give away the game.

When they were an hour away Jacob went down to the forward EVA bay with MG and Tin Man. The tactical suits the humans wore were a compromise between protecting them in the vacuum of space and allowing them to be combat effective once aboard another ship, but they didn't do either job particularly well in Jacob's opinion.

Once Jacob and MG were sealed into their matte black suits, and they'd both double-checked each other the order was given to seal off the bay and pump it down. The atmosphere was evacuated at a controlled rate to make sure that if there were any issues with the suits, they had time to halt the procedure and pump the room back up.

"Com check," Jacob said.

"Tin Man."

"MG."

"We copy," Sully said. "Am I good?"

"Loud and clear. We're good to go," Jacob said.

All Scout Fleet teams trained extensively for EVA operations. When the teams were first proposed by Webb and Mosler they had envisioned that there would be a lot of EVA operations. As forward recon units Webb had thought they would be required to investigate ship wreckage or, as they were about to do now, board hostile vessels.

Despite exhaustive, brutal training regimen the Scout Fleet trainers put them through, Jacob was never comfortable getting out of the ship while it was still in space. He leaned against the bulkhead and focused on his breathing, calming himself. The lights inside the bay cut out, and the hatch was outlined in red, indicating they were within fifteen minutes.

"I'll lead," MG said. "I know you like going first, Cap, but since I'm carrying the breacher I'd rather be the first to hit the hull."

"Be my guest," Jacob said after a moment of thought. When he'd first been put in charge of Obsidian, he'd been self-conscious and obsessed with trying to show his team he was the type of officer that led from the front. He'd always tried to be the first through the hatch. Now, after a bit of maturing and experience, he was comfortable letting his guys do their job and realized that more often than not he was in their way when he'd insisted on charging in ahead of them.

The lights around the hatch began blinking amber, telling them to standby. A second later the hatch slid silently open, and the static barrier dropped, letting the last few molecules of air escape out into space. MG moved forward and grabbed the handles, peering out, and then motioning down. Jacob moved up and could see that their target's running lights were visible below the *Corsair*, maybe five hundred meters away.

"Good luck, guys," Sully said right before the lights turned green, and MG shoved himself through the hatch.

Jacob went second, Tin Man last. As soon as he cleared the hatchway Jacob's suit locked onto the pre-programmed target, a ventral maintenance airlock near the aft section, and fired his jets automatically to get him going in the right direction. The holographic display in his helmet highlighted MG in front of him with a green bracket since he couldn't see the black suit in space.

They'd timed the jump for the nightside though they'd still show up on active scans if the freighter crew fired up their sensors. Their suits were using hyperlink coms so they were flying in with zero emissions to give them away. That meant Tin Man had to keep com silence until they were inside the ship since there was no practical way to fit him with hyperlink short of making him wear a helmet.

"Contact," MG called. "Breacher is on. Standby by for— Fuck!" There was a flash of light, and then atmosphere started billowing out of the ship.

"MG!" Jacob called.

"Hatch was rigged! It blew as soon as the breacher made maglock!"

"You good?"

"I'm good, I'm good," MG said, already calming down.

"Engines are warming up on that ship, Captain," Sully said. "You need to get aboard or get clear."

"Tin Man! Get in there!" Jacob ordered over normal coms. The battlesynth went zipping by, his foot repulsors glowing as he aimed precisely for the open hatch still spewing out atmosphere. Jacob commanded his suit to full speed and flew off after him, his arc jets glowing dimly in the dark.

"Tin Man is in. No resistance," Tin Man called.

"MG, going in."

"I'm at the hatch," Jacob said as he floated through feet first and was grabbed by the ship's artificial gravity. As soon as he was in MG smacked the control for the emergency aerostatic barrier. The shield shimmered to life and the rushing air stopped immediately.

"No contact," Tin Man said. "Holding at first junction."

"Copy," Jacob said. He pulled the two release cords simultaneously to detach the maneuvering jets from his harness and pulled his weapon around while MG shed his EVA gear as well. They moved out through the open hatchway into the dim corridor and looked at each other in confusion.

"No alarms?" MG asked. "They didn't even lock down internal hatches?"

"Just once on this mission I'd like something to not be so fucking weird," Jacob grumbled. "Coming to you, Tin Man. We're pressing to the bridge."

The first resistance they hit came when two junctions later when they passed the crew common areas. Seven armed crewmembers had fortified their position and had a clear lane of fire that forced the trio to duck into a small galley. They'd been engaged with standard plasma weapons a shipboard security force would carry but nothing too heavy.

There were a few poorly placed pot shots hitting the hatchway meant to keep them in the galley. That meant there was probably backup heading their way. MG pulled a grenade out and handed it to Jacob, smiling.

Jacob tried to look at the throw he'd have to make before passing the grenade over to Tin Man. "Think you can hit them without exposing yourself?"

"You cannot?" Tin Man asked.

"It's the suit," Jacob said. "Limits my range of motion but, otherwise, I could totally make that throw blind around a corner."

"Sure, you could," MG muttered as Tin Man took the grenade, backed up to the hatch and threw it without even looking. The weapon clinked off the bulkhead and dropped behind the hasty barricade the crew had erected, detonating with a harsh *wump*.

"Okay...that was pretty fucking rad," MG said. Tin Man winked at him and walked out the hatch, his arm cannons up and ready.

"Let's go," Jacob said. "How're we looking, *Corsair*?"

"Engines are still coming up on your ship," Mettler said. "No distress signals have been sent so the locals are ignoring us. Sully wants to move off a bit, so we don't look so suspicious."

"Go ahead," Jacob said. "We're committed to taking the bridge or die trying at this point."

"I feel like I'm going to regret you saying that, Cap," MG said.

They followed Tin Man down the smoky corridor, their self-contained rebreathers and sealed helmets keeping out the noxious fumes as the ship's automated damage control systems extinguished the fires the grenade started and began evacuating the smoke.

"The bridge is one deck below us," Tin Man said.

"Fastest route?" Jacob asked.

"Maintenance access crawlway two sections up," Tin Man said. "I will not fit, however, so you will need to gain access to the bridge, and then open the security hatch."

They made their way up to the section where the crawlway access hatch was without meeting any further resistance. The ship either wasn't carrying a full crew complement or they were setting up a hell of an ambush for them somewhere up ahead. His question was answered a moment later while MG was working on the access hatch.

"Captain, you've got three large shuttles coming up from the surface heading your way," Mettler said over the team channel. "They're definitely on a direct intercept course, and they're coming fast."

"That would be our missing crew," Jacob said. "Any way you can slow them down without directly engaging?"

"Sully said he'll do his best. *Corsair*, out."

"Holy shit," MG said after he got the hatch off. "Will *we* fit in there? What the hell species crews this ship?"

"We'll have to dump some gear, but it's doable," Jacob said as he unhooked his tactical harness and removed his rebreather and body armor. The helmet umbilical detached and automatically switched to stand-alone operation. It would still give him full communications and would actively filter his incoming air, but it would no longer be a closed-loop system that would keep everything out. MG covered him as he did, then took his turn once Jacob retrieved his weapon.

"You drop down to the junction directly below us, then move forward two sections," Tin Man said. "There will be a hatch that will open up onto the bridge."

"How the hell do you know all that?" MG asked. Tin Man pointed to the bulkhead where there was a diagram attached near the access panel with a map of the maintenance crawlways. "Lucky guess."

"Give me three minutes, and then a diversion at the security hatch would be appreciated," Jacob said. "No unnecessary risks, though. Who knows what sort of anti-intrusion systems there are built into the bridge access hatchway."

"I will handle it."

Jacob slid through the hole in the bulkhead and was relieved to see the tunnel was larger than the hatch, but not by much. He moved down the ladder quickly to clear the way for MG. The grunting and cursing told him his teammate was on the way. MG wasn't as tall as Jacob, but he was built like a fire hydrant and wider at the shoulders.

He got to the junction, checked the diagram on the crawlway bulkhead, and then started moving forward through the crossing tunnel, now making better progress going horizontally instead of vertically. He passed countless access hatches and panels that would let maintainers get to critical components and locations within the ship on his way to the bridge.

"What's that glow?" MG asked.

"That would be active shielding over the hatch for the bridge," Jacob sighed. "Of course."

"We probably should have expected that," MG said. As they got closer, they could see that the shielding was installed in such a way that it only protected the hatch itself and the release fasteners. The surrounding decking was clear.

"Breaching charge?" Jacob asked.

"Left it with my armor."

"Grenades?"

"Same."

"Anything?"

"Nope."

"Damn," Jacob said. He looked back behind them, and then forward again. "Move back to that large hatch on the port side and start working on the fasteners."

"What insane idea do you have?" MG asked.

"Remember that crazy ass NavSpec operator that we trained with last year?" Jacob asked. NavSpec was the uninspired name for one of the tactical group that fell under the NAVSOC umbrella Scout Fleet used to be a part of.

"The weird dude with seven fingers?"

"Yeah, that one. He showed me how to overload an M7," Jacob said. "Basically, makes it a plasma grenade with a moderate yield."

"You realize stupid shit like that is why he had seven fingers, right?" MG asked.

"Just get back there and get started," Jacob said, pulling the powerpack from his weapon and reconfiguring it so the safety systems were bypassed. Once he was certain he'd done it correctly, he jammed the powerpack back in and set the selector to full. This would charge the firing chamber to its limit and was designed for short-duration use when maximum firepower was needed.

With the safety limits bypassed, the system would charge until it ruptured. Once it really started to whine and get hot, he put it on the deck next to the active shielding over the bridge hatch and scrambled back to where MG was waiting by the open panel.

"We're not going to fit in there," MG said.

"Swing it open and use it as a shield," Jacob said. "The helmets should keep our eyes and ears safe, but the explosion is...energetic. It's also a little unpredictable."

"This is so stu—" the M7 plasma carbine exploding drowned out whatever else MG was going to say.

The blast pressurized the tunnel and pushed the pair back the way they came, the helmet cutting off their audio completely as they bounced down the crawlway. One thing Jacob hadn't thought of was the explosion consuming all the oxygen in the crawlway. Without their rebreathers they were quickly out of oxygenated air. The last thing he remembered before losing consciousness was trying to look and see if MG had survived the tumble they'd taken, but the blackness overtook him before he could turn.

17

Tin Man stood before the hatchway, arm cannons deployed and ready to open fire on the armored hatch to draw attention away from his two teammates. Right before he fired, a blast from somewhere ahead of him shook the deck and alarms started blaring. The lights flickered and went out and his sensors told him that entire systems had just gone offline.

The locks on the hatch let go with a *clang* now that power was removed, and it swung open a bit, letting out a noxious smoke. Tin Man grabbed the edge of the hatch and yanked open the multi-ton chunk of alloy. His multispectral vision could see there was a gaping, shredded hole in the ceiling and that everyone that had been on the bridge, twelve beings total, had been tossed around like ragdolls in a tempest.

Some were very obviously not alive, others were moving slowly and moaning, clutching their ears. What concerned Tin Man most, however, was that the ship appeared to have lost attitude control. It was in a slow tumble along the orbital trajectory, but none of the displays on the bridge were working so he could verify their course and speed.

"What the— Oh, shit!"

Tin Man's head snapped over, and he saw a shocked human standing in the hatchway, a sidearm held loosely at his side. He looked at Tin Man and raised the pistol.

"I would not do that," Tin Man said, raising his own arm with the cannons still deployed. "Who are you, and what is your function aboard this ship?"

"I'm...I'm Jorge Espinoza. Engineer." He tossed the pistol away to the other side of the bridge.

"Are you trained in giving medical aid?"

"Of course...all crew are."

"Then, tend to your comrades," Tin Man pointed to the bridge crew, some of them humans as well.

"We have medics aboard right now," Jorge said. "I was sent up to see what happened to the bridge. We were all told to remain in our work centers when the hull breach alarm sounded."

"You may notify them that their services are needed," Tin Man said. "Do you know what I am?"

"Something scary?"

"Close enough. Bearing that in mind, inform your crewmates that any attempt to do anything other than render emergency aid will result in the deaths of everyone aboard...starting with you. Am I understood?"

"I'll make the call."

Tin Man watched as the man scrambled from the bridge to a com panel that was just outside the hatchway. He listened to everything the terrified man was saying as he continued to scan the room, hoping that his teammates hadn't been on the bridge when the explosion had occurred.

"Tin Man, do you copy?" Commander Sullivan's voice came over the com.

"I copy."

"What the hell happened over there? The ship looked like she was getting ready to break orbit then the engines shut down and now she's in an uncontrolled tumble. Is everyone okay?"

"There has been an explosion on the bridge that likely took our helm and engine control momentarily," Tin Man said. "I currently do not know where Captain Brown and Sergeant Marcos are. I will continue searching while the crew tries to re-establish control."

"Fantastic, but you have another problem. Shuttles carrying the original crew are still coming in case Jake didn't pass that onto you. They're approaching from your aft and matching the tumble to dock."

"Is there anything you can do?"

"I'm going to drop in behind them," Sully said. "I'm hesitant to open fire on them right now, but maybe I can give them something else to worry about."

"Very good, Commander. I will be in touch. Do what you have to do," Tin Man said. He turned to Jorge, who had come back in and was rolling a survivor onto their back.

"Is there an auxiliary helm where this ship may be controlled from?" he asked.

"It's in engineering," Jorge said carefully. "The chief engineer and one other are already down there trying to stabilize our flight."

"Are your medical personnel on their way?"

"Seconds away," Jorge said, sighing and leaning back on his heels. "Carla didn't make it. Why have you done this?"

"We are investigating the abduction and trafficking of many thousands of humans, among others," Tin Man said. "This ship has been identified as being part of a fleet that attacked a human mining operation."

"Trafficking?!" Jorge asked. "What? We were transporting...son of a bitch."

"What?"

"As far as we were aware, this was a simple passenger transport mission. Move the people from a mining operation that was shutting down, bring them here."

Tin Man said nothing. He found it highly unlikely that the crew aboard this ship didn't realize the people in their holds were captives. Jorge Espinoza didn't look like a warrior, and he wouldn't be the first person Tin Man had dealt with who would lie to save themselves.

The medics arrived a moment later, and after gaping at Tin Man, they went to work on the wounded. One of the bodies, though badly damaged, was obviously a Cridal, further cementing the connection to the Cooperative. He stepped back and let the crew work, still scanning for his teammates but unable to physically go look for them. As he pondered his next action, he listened to one of the medics speak to Jorge.

"Sorry, Captain, I couldn't—"

Tin Man snapped around just as Jorge shoved the medic out of the way and pulled a large-bore plasma pistol from his waistband, aiming it directly at him. He telegraphed his trigger squeeze, and Tin Man, likely moving far faster than Jorge thought him capable of, dove into a forward roll and punched the human in the left knee, shattering the joint and taking him down with a shriek of agony.

"I warned you not to do anything stupid," Tin Man remarked, grabbing the large pistol and disabling it by snapping it in half. "By the way, this would have barely discolored my armor plating."

"Captain!" the medic shouted, looking at Tin Man like she was unsure what to do.

"You," Tin Man pointed at her. "How many are left aboard this vessel?"

"Sixteen total," she stammered. "It's a skeleton crew while everyone else was on the surface on R&R."

"Where is auxiliary helm control?"

"One deck down, two sections aft," she said, not looking at Jorge —Captain Espinoza—as he hissed at her to be silent. "There's another station in the engine room."

"What was your cargo?" Tin Man asked.

"Miners from LOR-773," she said, tears now running down her cheeks. "They were being...relocated."

"Why?"

"I don't know," she cried. "We were paid to move the people, nothing more."

"Who are you people?"

"I don't understand—"

"Who do you work for?" Tin Man snapped, knowing his was running out of time.

"It's a private company. It's—"

"Shut your fucking mouth, you idiot!" Jorge said, finding his voice. Tin Man stomped on his foot, crushing all the bones flat. The scream that came from the captain was long and piercing. Tin Man usually didn't go in for torturing or abusing detainees and helpless foes, but he made an exception for traffickers and certain types of smugglers.

"Please, continue," he said once Jorge quieted down to a soft whimper.

"The ships belong to a private company called WBB Logistics," she said in a rush. "We're all freelancers hired to crew ships on a rotating basis. We were brought aboard under a com blackout and told we were flying to LOR-773. Halfway there we dropped out of slip-space and picked up a mercenary crew along with some of these guys"—she gestured to the Cridal on the deck—"and then went to the pickup. It wasn't until when we were flying away that some of us realized these weren't really passengers, but prisoners. That's all I know...I swear!"

"Please, make sure your captain does not die," Tin Man said. "Do not make me kill any more of you." He walked off the bridge as there was nothing else he could do from there. Before he could search for his companions, he needed to stabilize the ship's flight as well as find a way to repel the crew that was coming up to take the ship back. They would certainly have their armed mercenaries with them. Tin Man almost felt sorry for them.

Almost.

"That was a little more energetic than I expected," Jacob groaned. His helmet had finally rebooted, and the flashing lights of his holographic display had roused him back to consciousness.

"I hope you die of ass cancer," MG said.

"Excuse me?"

"I'm concussed, Captain. I can't be responsible for what comes out of my mouth...you bag of shit."

"Anything broken?" Jacob asked.

"Nah. Just banged my head and bruised my right side, but I'm good to go. You?" MG asked.

"Pretty much the same. Think my coms are down." Jason tried to raise Tin Man and the *Corsair* but was getting nothing.

"My helmet is completely dead. No targeting system, no coms. Nada."

"Let's get the hell out of this tunnel," Jacob said. "Knowing Tin Man, he's already subdued the ship and is flying it back to human space by himself."

The large panel they'd used as a shield had been so badly deformed by the blast that it was jammed in place, so they had to backtrack and found an exit hatch that put them on the deck above the bridge. When MG got the panel off the amount of smoke that rolled in let them know that the damage from their handiwork was more widespread than they'd intended.

Jacob was sore and stiff as he pulled himself out of the small hatch and drew his sidearm. The weapon had survived their tumble, so he was at least armed with something. He looked at the map placard above the hatch and saw that they needed to go aft, and then down a starboard ladderwell to get to the bridge. MG checked his own weapons, and then nodded he was ready to go.

"Do you know how to do that overload trick with that M201 pistol you're carrying?" he asked.

"Nope," Jacob lied. "Just the rifle."

He couldn't see MG's face, but he could tell from the silence that the sergeant didn't believe him. In hindsight, using his primary weapon as an improvised explosive inside of an enclosed tunnel wasn't the best idea he'd ever had.

They backtracked to where they left their gear, which was miraculously still there, and then went on toward the bridge. The closer they got, the more acrid smoke hung in the air. With his combat harness back on, the computer interfaced with his neural link and dosed him with a mild painkiller and a partial nanobot booster to start repairing his injuries.

"Ah...sweet, sweet narcotics," MG said after he donned his own gear.

"Don't dope yourself up too much," Jacob said. "We still need to... well I'm not sure what we're doing at this point, but we're going to be professional about it."

"I can see why they made you an officer."

"Thanks."

"Wasn't a compliment."

The bridge was a slaughterhouse. Jacob winced as he looked around. The bomb he'd set off had created a downward blast into the space that had flung the crew around, smashing them into bulkheads and terminals. If the overloaded weapon hadn't blown the hatch out of the tunnel so cleanly and given the force of the blast somewhere to go, Jacob and MG would most certainly be dead. He made a mental note to be far more careful with that little trick in the future.

"Who are you?" a woman who was apparently a medic asked. She knelt on the deck and tending to a man with a ruined leg.

"That's not a simple answer. We're with a tall metal biped," Jason said. "Probably has glowing red eyes."

"It's gone. Went down to the auxiliary helm control to try and stabilize our flight after an explosion took out bridge control," she said, wiping her brow wearily.

Jacob walked around the bridge while MG covered the medics working on what few wounded were left. The blood stains on the floor indicated at least four had already been taken off the bridge, hopefully to the infirmary. He was startled by a sharp double-beep that told him the backup coms embedded within his tactical gear had finally booted and took over for the fried set in his helmet.

"*Corsair*, Obsidian Actual," he said once hyperlink was up. "Status."

"Where the hell have you been?!" Mettler's relieved voice came back. "We're trailing above and behind you around two thousand klicks out. The ship you're aboard has started maneuvering erratically so it's made it difficult for the incoming shuttles to dock, but they're still closing."

"Standby," Jacob said, switching to regular coms. "Tin Man?"

"Captain. It is a relief to hear your voice," the battlesynth answered.

"Approaching shuttles," Jacob said.

"Still closing," Tin Man said. "They are the crew for this ship that had been down on the planet when an alert went out after we breached the hull. I am attempting to keep them off without the need to have Sully splash them."

"Open the hangar bay and evacuate the atmosphere," Jacob said. "I'm betting a bunch of people on the surface for R&R won't be carrying enough EVA gear for everyone. Let them in, and then close the bay doors."

"Clever," Tin Man said after a moment. "Let me disable the remote access modes so that they cannot use an override, and then I will comply. I will stabilize our flight, and then lock down the helm so I can meet our guests at the hangar bay."

"Excellent," Jacob said and switched back to the *Corsair*. "Tell Sully we're going to let them aboard and trap them in the hangar bay. Once they're in bring the ship in and dock her to one of the ventral airlocks."

"Copy."

"Obsidian Actual, out," Jacob said, turning to MG. "We've got incoming. Head down to the hangar bay control room and give Tin Man a hand."

"Will do," MG said, walking off the bridge with a mock salute. "Stay safe. Don't blow up any more of your guns."

"Shuttles are making their final approach, Captain," Tin Man said. "Just so you know, the man on the bridge with the injured leg is Jorge Espinoza. He is the captain of this ship. We will want to make certain he does not try to end his own life."

"Got it," Jacob said, looking at where the medic was working. "I'll make sure."

18

Kobvir Glecsh was living under a level of stress that was starting to negatively affect his health.

The Cridal Cooperative Executive Chief of Staff had been living a double life for so long that he wasn't sure who he really was anymore. At one time, he considered himself a loyal and steadfast servant of the Dalton family and the empire they had built. He'd served Crisstof Dalton, had tried to advise his First Son Steader Dalton, and was now one of Seeladas Dalton's most trusted advisors.

But that's not all he was. Or wasn't.

He wasn't actually Syllitr. It was a secret that nobody still alive knew about. Crisstof had Kobvir's appearance surgically altered to make him appear Syllitr to a cursory examination so he could operate more freely as his fixer on a planet where outsiders weren't particularly welcome. Kobvir Glecsh was actually a Musa-bi. He was from a world deep within the Saabror Protectorate, and he still had ties to that place.

When those ties had been pulled, his split loyalties became a liability. What he was being asked to do would almost certainly make the Cooperative the target of some very powerful players, but if he didn't do it, they would just find someone else and have him executed for treason. He'd even thought about approaching Seeladas at first. Explaining the whole thing to her and seeing what she could do about his predicament, but she'd not been herself lately. Her expanding empire was showing the first stress cracks as it grew too much, too quickly, and she wasn't handling it well.

"Once you started taking humans you set off a chain of events that will see us burn," he said to the Musa-bi sitting across from him. "You wanted them because they're clever and breed quickly. I'm telling you they're *too* clever, and they're not like the Verans. They keep track of individuals. Nasty, brutish, violent creatures."

"And yet you fear them so," his companion laughed. "We needed a keystone species. You're the one who suggested them."

"I didn't know you were going to take so damn many!" Kobvir snarled. "A few colonist ships here and there, not entire settlements and corporate mining sites."

"Relax. They'll never find their missing people and will eventually write them off as unexplained disappearances. You'll be rewarded as will the Cooperative. You're going to be a hero to Seeladas Dalton...relax and enjoy it."

Kobvir wasn't so sure. He'd taken an extended leave of absence claiming a family emergency prior to his operation in the Luuxir Border Region completely crumbling. The plan had been to return to Syllitr and resume his duties, but one of his loyal aides had told him that Seeladas was demanding he be found and brought in. That didn't sound like he was about to be welcomed with open arms. Her office was being tight-lipped about why, but there was some chatter about his use of Cridal military assets in an operation involving the Eshquarians.

He figured he had another day, two at the most, before he had to make contact directly and see if he could read the situation. Did the prime minister's office know everything? Or was he just going to be scolded in the usual way for using Cooperative assets for side projects?

"Either way, I will need to leave shortly so I can at least— What's wrong?"

"One of our ships in orbit sent out a distress alert," the other Musa-bi said. "It's the single human freighter we had left."

"Is it an emergency?" Kobvir asked.

"I don't think so, and yet some instinct is screaming at me that something has gone terribly wrong."

"You're probably just overthinking things. It happens as you get to the closing stages of an operation."

"Perhaps, but perhaps not. Either way you should leave immediately. You being caught on this planet is the last thing we can afford right now."

"That one seems really surprised," MG remarked.

"How can you tell?" Tin Man asked.

"See the look on his face?" MG asked as a Cridal trooper was thrashing on the deck of the hangar bay, eyes bulging from their skull in the near-total vacuum, mouth gaping like a fish.

"I am beginning to think that Commander Sullivan was correct. There is something wrong with you."

The shuttles, like most, were equipped with aerostatic barriers on the hatchways. They wouldn't keep anything more substantial than small dust particles or sand out, but they made sure outside contaminants or airborne pathogens didn't make it into the interior of the craft. The first trooper out the hatch found out the hard way there wasn't any atmosphere on the other side. Now all three shuttles were sealed tight, and the com panel was lighting up with channel requests from the flight crews demanding answers.

"How do you want to handle this?" MG asked.

"For now, we are handling it," Tin Man said. "The crew is safely contained, the shuttles have no armament, and even if they tried to ram their way out, they would not compromise this ship."

"I dunno," MG said, peering through the window. "They're not going to just sit there helpless for too long. They'll either do something really smart we haven't thought of, or something really stupid that will kill all of us."

"Perhaps," Tin Man conceded. "You have a suggestion?"

"One of us goes out and slaps some mines on the portholes, and then we open the com channels to negotiate. Then, we'll be able to dictate terms since we can threaten them with explosive decompression."

"We don't have any mines."

"Our grenades have different modes," MG said, shaking his combat harness. "One of them is remote detonation. I can set them off from in here, and they have an adhesive spot on the base."

"It disturbs me that your plan is not only clever and effective but also humane."

"How is that disturbing?"

"Because you are not usually clever or humane, which makes me think you are up to something," Tin Man said.

"Quit being a bitch and go put these grenades on the shuttles," MG said. "Then the real fun can start."

Tin Man took the grenades from MG and cycled himself through the airlock. The passengers in the shuttle were looking wild-eyed through the portholes and forward canopies as the battlesynth walked toward them. He could see them shouting and waving their hands.

He calmly walked from ship to ship and affixed grenades to the canopies and one of the cabin portholes on each before rejoining MG in the control room. The crews aboard the shuttles looked to be even more agitated now, but there was nothing they could do as they stared at the small munitions with the blinking green lights.

"I'm connected to all of them," MG said. "I'm not going to batch fire them so that way we can blow them individually. It'll let us play them off each other."

"To what purpose?"

"It's fun?"

"I will handle the negotiations," Tin Man forcefully pushed MG away from the com panel and slaved all the channels together before transmitting.

"As you have surmised, those are explosive devices attached to your ships. They are there to ensure you do not attempt anything foolish. If you do, we will remove your ability to breathe. Attempt to call for aid, we will detonate the devices on all three ships. Please, select a single person to negotiate on your behalf."

"This is First Officer Diaz," a voice with a soft Latin American accent came over the speakers. "Who am I speaking to?"

"You are speaking to the one holding the detonator and thus your lives in his hand," Tin Man said. "We have Captain Espinoza in our custody and full control of this vessel. Your presence is not needed, but I am not one who kills needlessly."

"What do you want?" Diaz asked.

"For now, for you to remain where you are," Tin Man said. "Do not try anything that would make me question the wisdom of leaving you alive."

"You need to work on your threats and insults," MG said. "It should be more natural sounding. Just tell them if they do something stupid, you'll fucking kill them all."

"I have been doing this for many centuries," Tin Man said. "I do not need advice from a fucking half-wit like you."

"That was better."

Apparently, Diaz wasn't content to just sit tight. Not five minutes after Tin Man's ultimatum there was movement near the aft end of the leftmost shuttle as two troopers in EVA suits were trying to sneak around toward the portside airlock. Tin Man cycled himself through the control room airlock and walked calmly over to them, shooting each with a single blast from his arm cannons.

"Sergeant Marcos, please restore atmospheric pressure in the hangar bay. Set to a barometric altitude of eight thousand meters," he said over the com.

"Why would— Ah! Got it. Restoring atmosphere to eight-k," MG said, spinning the dial on the environmental controls.

The pressure came back up quickly, and MG gave Tin Man a

thumbs up through the window when the instruments told him target pressure had been reached. The battlesynth nodded and banged his fists together twice, the signal for MG to blow the charges. He selected the batch-fire icon for all the charges on his forearm display and triggered the munitions.

The grenades all detonated, blowing out the portholes and punching holes in the forward canopies, letting the shuttles' atmosphere billow out in a rush of vapor. The rapid decompression wasn't fatal, but it was agonizing for the shuttle occupants. They writhed and screamed until finally going still due to the lowered oxygen concentration.

Once it was clear they were all incapacitated, MG checked his suit's seals and joined Tin Man in the hangar. They went from ship to ship making sure there were no fakers before calling it in to Captain Brown.

"How many were there total?" Jacob asked after MG reported in.

"Sixty-two including the flight crews," MG said. "Looks like the full crew compliment including a handful of security troopers. Most are human. Couple Cridal mixed in but no other species."

"That's too many to easily restrain or move," Jacob said. "I really don't want to kill them, but I'm not— Standby, MG." There was some muted chatter MG couldn't hear before Jacob got back to him.

"Okay. Apparently, there's a cargo transport system on this ship that can take your prisoners from the hangar bay up to one of the forward cargo holds where they can be safely stored. The holds are already configured for prisoners. The control panel is near the controls for the outer hatch and has an icon that looks like a train of flatbed cars."

"I see it," MG said. "Looks like it runs underneath the hangar. We can just toss them in, and it will automatically put them in a cargo hold?"

"It's automated. There are built in loaders on the cars," Jacob said.

"We'll figure it out," MG said.

"Hurry up. We've got a location on the surface so as soon as we're done securing the crew we're taking the *Corsair* down," Jacob said.

19

Seeladas Dalton sat numbly in her seat. Her aide squirmed uncomfortably while Ambassador Shapiro waited for some sort of response.

The Terran mission to Syllitr had demanded an audience with the Cridal Premier and, on orders from Earth, dumped the whole thing in her lap. Shapiro had come in guns blazing demanding to know what they knew about Cridal military assets being used to abduct humans. He presented the evidence he'd received from the NIS and a military recon group the president had called Scout Fleet. On the flight out to Syllitr, he had become an expert in galactic quadrant trafficking rings, how they operate, and the specific incidents regarding humans.

"As you will no doubt understand, Madam Prime Minister, our leadership has grave concerns about what appears to be Cridal military assistance in a trafficking operation that is targeting humans," Shapiro said, twisting the knife. He was told to go at her hard, press her and see if she might slip up.

"We are all concerned, honored ambassador," her aide stepped in when it was clear she wasn't going to answer. "You must be reasonable and understand the need for our people to analyze the intel you've brought us and come to our own conclusions."

"We must do nothing of the sort," Shapiro said. "Our interpretation of the data is not open for debate. At least not on our side. The reason I am here is because we hoped you would produce Kobvir Glecsh for an interview by our people. With your own being present, of course."

"That is not something that would be acceptable," the aide said, stiffening.

"Then, let me clarify our position. We know that Cridal personnel and equipment have been used in this atrocity. What we don't know is whether this was a sanctioned action by the Cooperative leadership or if a high-placed official—specifically Chief of Staff Glecsh—was running a rogue operation." Shapiro sat back, completely relaxed. "I must stress that the mood among my people's leadership over this can only be described as outraged. The hard evidence from the Luuxir Border Region is quite provocative."

"Madam Premier?" the aide asked, clearly feeling out of his depth at that point.

"We are unable to produce Kobvir Glecsh," Seeladas Dalton said, her voice clear and strong despite her still staring down at her hands. "He took a leave of absence a short time ago and has failed to check in. All I know for certain is that he is not on Syllitr."

"Madam Prime Minister, the lack of cooperation and urgency we're seeing from the Cridal on this matter is, frankly, disappointing," Shapiro said. "We were given assurances that our concerns were being given the highest priority but, so far, all I'm hearing is you have misplaced a high-level government official we've connected to our missing people, and I'm not hearing any sort of plan to retrieve him."

"A gross oversimplification of the situation, Ambassador," the aide said. "And I would remind you that you're speaking to the Cridal head of state."

"Trust me, I haven't lost sight of that," Shapiro said. "It is why I've been so restrained in this meeting."

The meeting didn't become much more productive after that. He and the aide continued to verbally spar while Seeladas sat numbly in her seat, barely interacting. Her demeanor and mental state seemed to be just as bad as the NIS warned him about. While he continued to goad the aide into fits of indignant anger at his perceived disrespect of Dalton, Shapiro observed her closely and wondered if there was something wrong with her.

After one last round of insults with the now spluttering aide, Shapiro called an end to the meeting and excused himself. He'd seen everything he needed to see to make his report back to his superiors; Seeladas Dalton did not appear to be in control of her own government.

"Mr. Ambassador," a voice said as he walked out of the executive office suite. "How fortunate to run into you here." Shapiro looked over and saw an Eshquarian he recognized from their embassy but wasn't aware of what his function was.

"Indeed," he said carefully. "You have business with the premier today?"

"Not with her personally. I'm meeting with a lesser trade minister." He handed Shapiro a card. "But now that I see you, I can deliver this personally. Have a good day, Ambassador Shapiro."

Once the Eshquarian walked away Shapiro turned the card over in his hand. When his thumb pressed on it slightly it lit up with a confirmation of his identity and an invitation to an informal reception at the Eshquarian Embassy that night. The display went out after a few moments, and he couldn't get it to come back on again.

"Gotta love the cloak and dagger routine," he sighed, putting the card in his pocket and walking toward his waiting aide.

Mark Shapiro made his way quickly through the three security checkpoints leading into the Eshquarian Embassy, a beautiful stonework building that looked both modern and ancient. It was an aesthetic he appreciated. Once he was let into the secure section of the embassy, he was intercepted by a uniformed Eshquarian before he could make it to the reception hall.

"Ambassador Shapiro, if you would please follow me there is a VIP meet and greet before this evening's event begins."

"Lead the way," Shapiro said.

When he was led down into the bowels of the embassy, he knew something was up beyond the mere booze-fueled schmoozing that bureaucrats loved so much. He was brought to a large security door that was already open, his guide gesturing him inside. He hesitated a moment before walking through, wincing as it boomed closed behind him.

"Ambassador," a deep voice said. As his eyes adjusted to the dim light Shapiro could make out four people sitting around a ring-shaped table, two humans and two Eshquarians. "Have a seat, please. My name is—"

"Minister of Imperial Intelligence T'Cali Amon," Shapiro finished. "I wasn't aware you were on Syllitr, sir."

"If I did everything right, neither should the Cridal," Amon said. "I believe you know Admiral Marcus Webb."

"Only by reputation," Shapiro nodded to Webb. "It's good to finally meet you, sir."

"You may think differently in a few minutes," Webb laughed humorlessly. "To get this out of the way, everyone in this room is cleared for the information we'll be discussing. We've brought you into this meeting so we can get your impression of Seeladas Dalton after seeing her today as well as give you a more complete picture of the problem currently facing Earth."

"The abductions?"

"Likely connected to the larger problem," Amon said.

"That being?" Shapiro asked.

"The continued abuse of Earth by the Cridal Cooperative," Webb said. "Have you ever heard of a planet called Galadin Minor?"

"Can't say that I have."

"Hardly surprising. This would have been buried deep. It was a planet where one of my Scout Teams chased a stolen bit of military tech down. It was a mechanized armor unit that was being used as a terrorist weapon. What made the situation interesting was that the theft of the unit, called the Atlas, had actually been a cover for the *real* theft.

"Someone tried to steal critical technology from Earth. It can't be overstated how important and sensitive this thing is. After the dust settled, we traced the theft back to the Cridal."

"How is that possible?" Shapiro asked. "I'd have been notified if the Cridal had pulled such a brazen act of espionage."

"Like I said...buried deep," Webb said. "I'm telling you now so you can see the enormity of what we're dealing with when viewed next to the Cridal involvement of the massive trafficking operation."

"Why are we meeting to talk about it in the Eshquarian embassy?" Shapiro asked. "No offense, Minister."

"None taken," Amon said. "We're here because my agency assisted in the Luuxir Border Region incident. It's where we discovered that Imperial citizens had also been targeted by the cartels and linked them back to Kobvir Glecsh and one of ours, a former intelligence operative named Klytos Finvak. We have the latter in our custody."

"This is both horrifying and fascinating, gentlemen, but why am *I* here?"

"You have more access to the Cridal executive levels than we currently do," Amon said. "Our relationship with the Cooperative has been strained after we confronted them regarding our citizens. They've blocked our ambassador out altogether but, as a member nation, you can't be so easily denied."

"So, you want me to...?"

"Be ready," Webb said. "I'm sure if you're as good as people say you've made more than a few back-channel connections within Dalton's inner circle. Once we get more information to act on, you may need to use them. Needless to say, things are about to get very interesting, very fast."

"To say the least," Shapiro sighed. "And to think I thought this party was going to be a good time."

The next four hours were a brutal slog through the Cridal hierarchy and clearing away the clutter to reveal a picture of the Cooperative's underhanded actions regarding Earth and humanity. What was becoming abundantly clear was that the Syllitr saw humans as an upstart species they could openly prey on, not equals working within a collective economic alliance. Shapiro had left the meeting exhausted, defeated, and humbled by the fact that so much of what he'd been told had happened right under his nose.

"Were you able to get all that, Mr. President?" Webb asked as his shuttle climbed back up to where the *Kentucky* hung in high orbit.

"Unfortunately," President Weinhaus said over the hyperlink unit Webb had been carrying. It had allowed the president to listen in on the meeting and had been brought with the full knowledge and blessing of the Eshquarians. "What did you think of Minister Amon?"

"There's something strangely familiar about him, but I can't put my finger on it, sir," Webb said. "I think he's being honest as far as these things go, but I also detect an ulterior motive."

"As did I," Weinhaus said. "With our relationship with the Cridal looking shaky, he was certainly talking up the benefits of becoming an alliance partner with the empire. To be honest, he might be ahead of the curve on that one. The council will need to be briefed soon on everything we've talked about and there will no doubt be a push to dissolve our partnership with the Cooperative by at least three of the members."

"From where I'm sitting, it's difficult to say that they'd be wrong," Webb said. "The empire will not take the abduction of their people lying down. They need to project strength in their post-occupation state and that probably means military action against a bad actor like Seeladas Dalton's government. I'd personally rather not see Terran warships moving against the Imperial Navy given that our people have been taken as well...and more."

"I understand where you're coming from, Marcus," Weinhaus said, sounding weary. "But you know how these things are. Not everything is so cut and dry."

"Meaning, sir?" Webb frowned.

"They couldn't have done this without help from some of our people," Weinhaus said. "The depleted mining site in particular. This is a bomb that is now ticking and cannot be disarmed."

"Cheery outlook."

"And, on that note, I will end this conversation, Admiral. It's four in the morning here, and I have a lot of peoples' day to ruin in a few hours. Good work...next time try to dig me up some good news."

"I'll do my best to—" The *beep* of the channel closing cut him off.

"I've received word from Obsidian," Weathers said. "That was who I was talking to when I left the room."

"And?" Webb sighed. "No, let me guess...they accidentally declared war on the Saabror Protectorate, but it's okay because they already won, and Brown has been declared emperor, and now he's asking if it's a conflict of interest if he keeps his captain's pay?"

"Not quite so complicated," Weathers said. "They boarded one of the cargo ships from the fleet that took the people away from LOR-773. They're in control of the ship and are getting ready to head down to the surface to check out a few sites the human captain of the vessel gave them. Sergeant Mettler said that there were human and Cridal crew on the ship, but no captives."

"Where are they at?" Webb asked.

"A planet called Dorshone," Weathers said. "Well within the Protectorate's borders."

"My gut is telling me that pretty soon they will need more than the *Corsair* and a captured freighter at their disposal," Webb said. "But asking for a Navy taskforce to violate a no-go zone based on the word of a covert ops team probably won't get me a whole hell of a lot."

"No, sir," Weathers agreed. "But maybe there's another way. Perhaps if Obsidian were to find some Eshquarian captives among the humans."

"That's a dangerous game to play," Webb said.

"That's why you get paid the big bucks, sir."

"For now, we'll shelve that option. The Eshquarians would probably be more than happy to help...as well as have us in a position of owing them and getting the chance to punch the Saabror in the nose." Webb leaned back and rubbed his eyes as the shuttle hummed along on its transfer orbit. "Shelve it, but don't throw it away."

"Understood, sir."

20

"It just goes on and on and on." MG crossed himself as he stared at the main display.

Jacob didn't say anything. He was overwhelmed by what he was seeing. It was a tent city. An internment camp with uniform rows of temporary shelters that went on for as far as the eye could see. The *Corsair* was overflying the southernmost encampment and had so far not been challenged or even hit with a scan. The sensors were programmed to look specifically for human bio signatures and had so far detected far more than could be accounted for just from the Site D abductees. Whoever all these people were, not all of them were asteroid miners.

"There doesn't seem to be much security," Mettler said. "Just some automated towers to keep the prisoners in line."

"Where would they go?" Glenn asked. "Even if they could get to orbit there was only one freighter up there. No point wasting the resources guarding them, just need to keep them alive until they reach their final destination."

"What do you want to do?" Sully asked.

"Head back to the center section and—"

"I think we should turn west," Glenn spoke up. "I saw a more advanced landing zone on our way down from orbit. The most likely place for a centralized control center would be there."

"Captain?"

"What the hell...head west for the LZ there," Jacob said, not breaking eye contact with Glenn. The civilian troubleshooter had an odd, almost manic demeanor about him making him nervous for some reason.

"We have two Cridal combat shuttles and another small ship of indeterminate origin," Sully said as they approached. "Also, a lot of Cridal milling around outside of what looks like an operations center."

"We're being painted," Mettler said.

Jacob had to decide quickly what to do. Once they realized this wasn't a scheduled flight or one of the shuttles from the freighter in orbit, they would either try to raise them on the local net or they would launch ships to intercept. Some things that were absolutely known were that the humans were brought here against their will and that the Cridal were facilitating that somehow. During his last two missions, he'd already been engaged in combat with Cridal special forces units so he would hardly be setting a precedent with the action he was considering.

"Smoke 'em."

"Sir?" Sully asked.

"You heard me. Hit the ops center, and if you detect an engine signature from any of the ships, hit them, too."

"Targeting ops center," Sully said. "Here we go."

The nose of the *Corsair* dipped and took them so low it seemed like they were skimming the tops of the tents they overflew, pulling them up and sending them flying. Jacob winced at the collateral damage, but Sully couldn't let them have an unobstructed shot on the ship while they were approaching over open ground.

"In range," Jacob said. "Guns are hot."

"Firing," Sully said, climbing slightly so the forward plasma cannons had a better angle.

As the first shots slammed into the face of the building Jacob couldn't help but be impressed at the destructive power the *Corsair* carried. The ship had been designed to take on much bigger, heavily shielded ships in space, so a soft target like a hastily built operations center in an internment camp stood little chance. The building was ripped apart, the debris raining down onto the landing pads as the *Corsair* roared over.

"Not a lot of people in there," Mettler said. "Probably. The computer is saying biomass is consistent with six adult Syllitr. The two smaller buildings are intact, but unoccupied."

"Nothing above us, Jake," Sully said. "I'm comfortable putting her down on the tarmac and leaving the engines and dorsal shielding up so you can take a look around."

"Do it," Jacob said. "Everyone else, suit up."

Jacob was in his quarters donning his gear when Mettler knocked on the hatchway. "You want me on the team, boss?"

"You're part of everybody, aren't you?" Jacob asked absently as he checked his weapons.

"It just seems like I've spent a lot of time on the ship lately. Not sure if I'd screwed something up." Jacob stopped and looked up at his medic.

"Sorry, Jeff," he said. "I hadn't realized that's how it might seem to you. But, no, it wasn't a punishment. You and Sully work well together, and you have done an outstanding job at learning new roles by qualifying on some of the bridge positions. Thanks for bringing it to my attention. I'll make sure I spread the love on who has to stay behind and babysit the ship."

"I don't want to be a complainer—"

"Nah," Jacob waved him off. "You've got a legit complaint. Thanks for bringing it up in private. Now, go get your shit on, we'll be landing in a minute."

He arrived in the cargo bay the same time Glenn Mitchell did.

Their passenger was all decked out in full tactical gear rather than just a ballistic vest and sidearm like he'd had before.

"Expecting heavy resistance, bro?" MG asked.

"These people have been held here against their wills for months, some for over a year," Glenn said, hefting his helmet. "Let's just say I'm counting on them being unpredictable."

"Standby," Sully said over the intercom. "Touching down...now." A slight bump and rocking motion announced their arrival on the planet Dorshone. Jacob slipped his helmet on and clipped his weapon onto the single point sling.

"Com check," he said.

"I've got you, Jake. You're all green on the team hyperlink channel minus the civilian and Tin Man," Sully said. "Once you're out, I'll close her up and have ground defense protocols active."

"We're good to go," Jacob said. "Let us out."

The ramp dropped, and they got their first look at Dorshone from the ground. Jacob looked at the leveled operations center and wrote that off as a complete loss. He pointed to the next largest building.

"I'll take this one with MG," he said. "Tin Man, Murph, and Mettler that one."

"I'll clear the ships," Glenn said before pointing out to the rows of tents. After the explosions, the residents were understandably not milling around outside. "How are we going to deal with that?"

"One thing at a time," Jacob said.

He and MG jogged over to the building and saw that it was constructed out of a synthetic fiber board that was popular for cheap, temporary structures. The door was already pushed open, likely from the blast of the building across the ramp, so MG went right in with Jacob covering his blind spot.

"It's a processing center," MG said, lowering his weapon. The large, open area had five distinct lines where people would be shuffled in one side of the building and out the other, getting inoculations, injections, and implants before being sent out the other side. "Probably more of these spread out through the camps."

"Look for any documentation or data cards lying around," Jacob said. "This place hasn't been used in a while."

"Anything interesting over there?" Murph asked over the team channel.

"Not really," Jacob answered. "Looks like medical processing lines that haven't been used in a while. You?"

"Equally useless over here. There's an armory with basic small arms and some parts storage. Probably the only useful stuff was in the building you blew up."

"Technically Sully did that," Jacob said, looking at some of the machines. One in particular caught his eye. "Hey, Murph, are there any handheld tracking scanners in that building?"

"Standby," Murph said. He was gone nearly fifteen minutes before coming back. "There are a handful of scanners with tracking features. That what you're looking for?"

"It is. It looks like they implanted all the abductees with biometric chips that also have a tracking function," Jacob said. "Could be useful. We're heading your way."

By the time they reached the other building, their three companions were already outside milling about. There was still no sign that anybody was coming to investigate them blowing up the landing zone ops center.

"Where's Glenn?" Murph asked.

"Still in the ships?" Jacob asked, turning toward the parked vessels. They all had their boarding ramps down, but there didn't seem to be any activity on any of them. He keyed the standard com. "Glenn, you got me?"

Nothing.

"Maybe the ships are interfering." MG shrugged.

"Fine. Let's go check. We can't stay on the ground here too long," Jacob said.

After checking all three of the small vessels with no sign of Glenn they met back on the landing pad.

"Sully, are you able to track him from up there?" Murph asked.

"His com signature shows he's by the ship you're standing

behind," Sully said. Jacob frowned, walking around the ship again before finally spotting the discarded com unit hidden nearly in the landing gear of the endmost Cridal ship.

"Was he taken?" Jacob asked Murph.

"Hey, guys! Weren't there more of those when we got here?" MG shouted, pointing at a row of small utility vehicles near the gate that led into the interment area. The gate was also unlatched when Jacob knew for certain that it had been locked.

"Son of a bitch," he said. "He's in with the prisoners."

"Seems like he had a plan of some sort," Murph said, pointing to the ground. "Footprints."

Jacob looked and saw there were faint prints in the dry, dusty dirt that led from the ships directly to where the vehicles were parked. Whatever Glenn was up to, he hadn't wasted any time.

"Shit," he swore again. "We have to go in and look for him. Searching from the air would be a waste of time when he can just duck into any tent. Most of them are large enough to hold a tractor trailer."

"Hopefully, the tracks don't blow away," Murph said, pointing to the remaining vehicles. "We better get at it."

21

Glenn Mitchell knew his time was running out. He kept looking over his shoulder expecting to see the *Corsair* blasting into the sky to come for him while simultaneously watching the display projected into his helmet.

"Come on, come on," he muttered, trying to coax any bit of speed he could out of the small vehicle. This wasn't the optimal way he would have wanted to accomplish his primary mission, but he didn't think another opportunity would present itself again. The Scout Fleet team was good enough to get him close, but that meant they were also good enough to eventually figure out he wasn't exactly who he said he was. The battlesynth especially watched him like a hawk since it caught him breaking into an office at that last starport.

The return signal off the passive tracker he was pinging was getting stronger and the resolution on the target's location was becoming more refined. When he looked back, he still didn't see the dusky silver ship rising off the pad. Did they not realize he was gone yet?

As he sped deeper into the encampment, he saw that people were stepping outside to take notice of the commotion at the landing field. Glenn felt a pang of sympathy for the humans he passed, as well as a burning rage on their behalf. He realized there was no way all these people were taken without inside help.

This had the Collective's fingerprints all over it despite the charade they'd put on about sending their fleet to investigate the disappearances. Glenn was disgusted, but in his line of work he was required to remain detached from emotionality. His sanity depended on it. He had one target and only one. The others were on their own.

He slammed on the brakes and slid the small vehicle to the right down another side street and slammed the accelerator back down, the motors whining as the wheels scrabbled on the loose dirt for purchase.

"Almost there," he whispered.

His heart pounded in his chest as the excitement of the hunt overcame him. This wasn't typically what he did, but this job was personal.

"Here we are," he said, sliding to a stop in front of one of the large, beige housing tents. He stepped out of the vehicle and raised his weapon as people began coming toward him. "Get back! Get the fuck back, right now!"

They saw the ugly plasma rifle and melted away into the early evening. Glenn walked with purpose through the doorway of the tent and looked around, his helmet's limited sensors scanning for any threats while he looked for his target.

"Gabrielle Rushton," he said, the harsh voice of his helmet making people flinch. "Where are you?"

"Are you here to kill me?" a voice asked. Glenn turned and saw a small, terrified girl and his heart gave a lurch. He removed his helmet and kneeled down.

"No, sweety, I'm not."

"Daddy?!" the girl screamed, sprinting across the tent and slamming into him, wrapping her arms around his head and squeezing tight. "You came!"

"You knew I would," Glenn said. He disengaged her arms and

stood up, slipping his helmet back on. "Come on, kiddo...we need to get the hell out of here."

"Take us with you!" a woman wailed, looking like she might rush him. He raised his weapon and stopped her in her tracks.

"I'm not here to save everyone, just my daughter," Glenn said. "I'm sorry. Someone else is here, and they *are* here to help you, but I'm not."

He backed out of the tent and put Gabby in the vehicle before climbing in himself and speeding away. He was heading in the wrong direction, but he just needed to put some distance between him and the desperate people who saw him as a way out before a mob formed.

"How did you find me?" Gabby asked.

"Remember the tracker I put in you before you went back to your mother's? I used that to pinpoint your location. The only snag was I had to be on the same planet as you were, so it took me longer than I wanted to track you down."

"You have a ship?"

"Sort of," Glenn admitted. "Don't worry. I'm good at this sort of thing."

"Mom is dead, isn't she?" Gabby asked.

"We'll talk when we're safe, kid," he said. He took the next right and began working his way back toward the landing field. From what he could tell, the *Corsair* still hadn't moved...so what the hell were Brown and his team up to?

"He turned right," Tin Man said, pointing to the clearly visible tire tracks that showed Glenn had taken the turn at high speed.

"Thanks. I noticed," Jacob said. "Murph, I think we're getting close to— Oh, shit!"

"What's happening?" Murph asked over the team channel.

"Looks like the beginning of a riot," Jacob said, sliding to a stop. "How are things where you're at?"

"Quiet," Murph said. "A few people peeking out at us, but that's about it."

The team had split up with Murph, MG, and Mettler taking one of the vehicles and searching the area to the west while Jacob and Tin Man had gone northeast, picking up Glenn's tracks quickly.

"Start heading back to the main road to make sure he can't double back past you," Jacob said. "I don't think he's still here, but it looks like he stirred up a hornet's nest."

"Will do. Sully's got the ship locked up tight, so he's not boarding her without getting smoked from the ground defense guns," Murph said.

"Will you try to question these people?" Tin Man asked.

"That just feels like a guaranteed way for some of them to get hurt," Jacob said, backup up until he came to another side street. "I highly doubt they know anything anyway."

Before Tin Man could answer, a brutally loud alarm blasted through the area and yellow lights atop tall poles flashed on both sides of the street.

"*This is a behavior alert,*" a computerized voice echoed through the street. "*Return to your domiciles and remain passive. Any further aggressive behavior will result in a corrective response.*"

The people reacted in a way indicating they knew just how unpleasant that response really was. They immediately calmed, kept their eyes to the ground, and shuffled slowly back to their tents without so much as a second look at the vehicle. Jacob was incensed at what was obviously a trained response to being abused, but there was little he could do about it at the moment.

"I think we've collected more than enough proof to send uphill so the Navy can bring in the big ships and rescue these people," he said. "You think this is most of them?"

"Not likely given the size of the internment camp," Tin Man said. "But it is not an insignificant amount. An enormous amount of people could be processed through even just a few camps like this in a relatively short amount of time."

Jacob thought about that as he took a few more turns trying to get back to the main road. Was this the main processing center for all the abducted humans in the quadrant? There had been a whole hell of a lot but the temporary nature of the camp they were driving through told him the trafficking ring likely didn't intend to operate once they got to a certain number. It also meant that however many people they weren't able to track down before these people closed up shop would likely be lost forever.

"I believe I just found our wayward troubleshooter," Tin Man said, pointing at a ship lifting off above the tents. It wasn't the *Corsair*. It was the smaller, fast courier ship that had been parked on the tarmac near the Cridal shuttles.

"Son of a bitch!" Jason shouted. "Why is Sully letting him leave?"

"I cannot raise the *Corsair* on standard coms," Tin Man said.

"Hyperlink is down, too. It says the channel is still connected and open, but there's no audio," Jacob said, switching channels. "Murph?"

"We saw," Murph said. "Can't raise Sully either, but the *Corsair*'s transponder is still transmitting and none of the embedded duress codes are flagging."

"Just get back to the ship double time," Jacob said. "Looks like our civilian is finally making his move."

Glenn watched his instruments as the small courier ship zipped up through the atmosphere of Dorshone. He was quickly out of range of the *Corsair*'s dorsal guns, so he let out a breath, finally allowing himself to relax just a bit.

He looked over at his daughter, strapped into the co-pilot seat and already looking sleepy as the lull of the ship's engines and the warm air worked on her exhausted mind and body. He could relate as the cumulative stress of the last month or so began to ebb away, leaving only a weariness he could feel in his bones.

It was still sinking in that he'd actually done it. He had actually found Gabby, rescued her, and made a clean getaway. When the Collective had discovered that something unusual had happened at

LOR-773 they had deployed their fleet to investigate. Glenn had had no desire to ride along with a group of posers and UAES rejects pretending they were still in the military, so he hadn't pushed to be included despite the chance for lucrative performance bonuses. Then, Lydia Shafer got a hold of him.

Lydia had long known that Glenn was Gabby's real father, but she had convinced her daughter that a relationship with someone like him would be *problematic* for her long-term career goals. Janet had listened to her, later regretted it and tried to reconcile, but Glenn's pride got in the way, and he'd rebuffed her. Instead, he'd settled for a secretive visitation scheme that left him mostly outside of his daughter's life...a decision that still hurt his soul.

He'd agreed to it when Gabby had been an infant, not realizing what he was giving up. By the time he figured it out, it was too late. Thankfully, Gabby was a forgiving child and let him build what relationship he could with her.

When Site D was discovered empty, Lydia Shafer had contacted him and told him that both Janet and Gabby had been there. He immediately invited himself onto one of the departing ships and flew out to LOR-773 as fast as they could take him. Once there, he discovered Janet already dead, but Gabby was missing. That's when the Collective allowed him access into certain outside intelligence sources they had access to, and he discovered the widespread trafficking of humans and other species.

After that, it was just a matter of trying to find Gabby. He'd implanted a passive tracking device in her left shoulder that would let him find her, but he had to be within two hundred kilometers for it to work. He picked it thinking that, with Janet's family and their high-profile, Gabby was a target for a blackmail kidnapping and would be within an urban area. When his transceiver picked up the signal as the *Corsair* overflew the internment camp his heart had almost stopped.

"Are we going home, Dad?" Gabby asked.

"Soon enough, kid," Glenn said. "But first, we need to take you somewhere safe and make sure nobody is still trying to find you."

She slurred an answer he didn't understand and promptly fell sound asleep. Once he was sure she was completely out, he took out his com unit and interfaced it with the ship so he could use the encryption modes over the slip-com. He punched in the node address he wanted and waited for an annoyed woman on the other end to answer.

"This better be good, Glenn."

"I found her."

"You-you're kidding?! That's great!"

"I'm coming to you now. Is everything ready?" he asked.

"Ready and waiting," she said. "We'll do the full workup to make sure she's in tip top shape. Are you going to let her grandmother or stepfather know?"

"I'm not sure yet," Glenn said honestly. "I'm playing this by ear. Something about all this stinks to hell and back, and I'm not sure who to trust right now."

"Does that include me?"

"I always trust you. Just have your magic machines ready and I'll see you soon."

He killed the connection and leaned back in his seat. The ship was out of the atmosphere and pushing for a mesh-out point that would take him back to human space. There was something that kept rattling around in his head that Glenn couldn't let go of. Why did someone shoot Janet's already dead body?

It was obviously to cover up the fact they'd clumsily used drugs on her, but what was the point? What did she know that was so important people would try and hide the fact she might have told them even after she was dead?

Just one more fucking mystery in a situation he was just trying to extract himself from.

"What do you mean *on the fritz?*" Jacob demanded.

"I mean, when I tried to target the ship to disable it, everything went crazy up here, and then the engines shut down," Sully said. "The main display went crazy, and then it shut off, too."

"I feel like you let this happen a lot," MG said.

"Pretty obvious Mitchell sabotaged us, but how?" Murph asked. "We've kept an eye on him the entire time."

"Not the entire time, but most of the time," Jacob corrected. "If he uploaded a virus, we're stuck here for hours while we purge and reload all the damn computers."

"You guys see there's a pending slip-com channel request?" Mettler asked, pointing at the com station. "Unknown address."

"What the hell...put it up. We've got nothing else going on apparently," Jacob said. Metter reached over and accepted the request, and Jacob wasn't surprised in the least when Glenn Mitchell's face popped up.

"Hey, guys," he said. "Sorry I had to bail on you."

"It's okay. It gives me time to think about what I'm going to do to you once I track you down," Jacob said.

"If I don't tell you how to restore your systems that won't be anytime soon," Glenn said. "Can we skip the posturing and theatrics so I can explain some things to you?"

"I'm listening."

"Nothing I told you was untrue, but I did leave some parts out. Most important is the fact that Gabby Rushton is my daughter. For her safety, that's not knowledge that's publicly available. I had to use you guys to get her back as I knew you would have a much better shot at it than the amateurs my employers saddled me with."

"So, there really is a Collective?" Murph asked.

"There is," Glenn confirmed. "They're still getting their feet under them, but they are a group you'll want to keep track of in the future."

"Did you get her back?" Jacob asked.

"I did," Glenn said, closing his eyes. "By the grace of God and thanks to you, I did. As a way to pay back just a small part of what I owe you, I'm going to forward you a file that came from a Collective intelligence report that will point you in an interesting direction. The Cridal individual you're looking for is named Kobvir Glecsh. He's

Seeladas Dalton's Chief of Staff, and he was the point man for the trafficking operations tasked with taking humans, Verans, and Eshquarians. If you read it and are quick, you just might snag him."

"And here I was all geared up for a manhunt to come take your ass down," Jacob said. "You know you could have just told me what you were after, right?"

"Possibly. But there was a risk that your mission goals and mine might diverge at some point," Glenn said. "I didn't want to be put in a position of having to hurt any of you."

"I appreciate you not hurting me," Tin Man said from behind Jacob. Glenn paled a bit but managed a strained laugh.

"You know what I mean," he said. "Now...on to current business. If you go down into your forward, port avionics service bay there's a device clamped onto a data bus. It's a nasty little thing but causes no permanent damage. Pop it off and the interference to your systems will go away and the engines will restart. You can keep it. Never know when it might come in handy."

"You got some balls, I'll give you that," Jacob said as Sully left the bridge toward the lower deck access ladder. "Good luck. I'm glad you have your daughter back. Truly."

"Thanks, Captain," Glenn said. He opened his mouth like he was going to say something else but instead just killed the channel. A moment later, the main display snapped back into the proper mode and the rumble of engines in pre-start mode could be heard.

"Yeah, you were watching him so well he put this on my ship," Sully said, storming back onto the bridge and tossing a black cylindrical device at MG.

"I don't know what the fuck that is." MG shrugged, tossing it to Murph.

"Looks like something NIS might cook up, but I've never seen one," Murph said, pocketing it. "Did the file he promised come through?"

"Have it now," Mettler said.

"You guys start going through it. I need to call Webb. There are a lot of humans on this planet who need help."

22

"This is exactly what we needed, Captain. Good work."

"Then the Navy is on the way?" Jacob asked.

"Taskforce will depart immediately to secure the planet, and then a flotilla of ships capable of moving the humans off-world will come next," Webb said. "You'll get the Bronze Star for this."

"We're not done yet," Jacob said. "Mitchell gave us some intel before he skipped town. If we want to rescue all the humans, we need this Kobvir Glecsh."

"The Cridal are hunting him as are the Eshquarians," Webb said. "You going to step into that dogfight?"

"Over something like this? You're damn right I am, sir."

"I'd expect no less," Webb said. There was a distinct note of pride in his voice, a far sight better than the usual mix of scorn and disappointment he had when talking to Jacob. "What's your plan?"

"None yet, sir. We're back in orbit monitoring the site below and parsing through the data Mitchell gave us. Whatever source of intel this Collective has access to, it has a more complete picture of this region of space than the NIS does."

"We'll pass this Collective business up the chain when this is over," Webb promised. "The last fucking thing we need right now is another shadow government popping up as the ConFed collapses and the Cooperative has the stench of death on it. We're still digging up One World sleeper cells every so often."

"You're kidding," Jacob said.

"I wish," Webb sighed. "Anyway, I'm issuing you new orders verbally with paperwork to catch up. Find and capture Kobvir Glecsh using any means necessary. You're clear to violate borders and use deadly force. Just get it done."

"We're on it, sir."

"Stay on site until the taskforce's advance ships at least mesh-in, and then you're clear to haul ass out of there. *Kentucky*, out."

Jacob shut down the hyperlink terminal and walked out of the com room and back onto the bridge. The whole team was there going through the intel while the sensors were trained on the internment camp below. After a couple orbits, they found two more camps, but they weren't able to verify if there were any humans there or not. They'd leave that for the taskforce.

"Kobvir has a few known spots that he might flee to," Murph said as he walked in. "But this looks the most promising. It's called the Shyosi. It's a decommissioned military facility that now operates as a privately owned commerce hub. It's on the Saabror side of the border butting up against Eshquarian space."

"Why's that one jumping out at you?" Jacob asked.

"We actually had to dig back through some information Webb had received from your father's crew to put the pieces together," Murph said. "He has an associate named Klytos Finvak, a former colonel in the Saabror Free Army but, in reality, an Imperial Intelligence asset inserted into Protectorate space before the fall of the empire when the ConFed invaded."

"Okay," Jacob said, making a motion to hurry it up.

"Omega Force confirmed Klytos working for Kobvir on a station called the Gates in the Luuxir Border Region. Klytos was running a trafficking operation for him. They captured Klytos and handed him over to Webb, but Kobvir disappeared as the Eshquarians mounted a hunt for him. He's still in the wind, obviously," Murph said. "With Klytos out of the picture his super-secret evil lair would be available for a new tenant. Any guess where it might be?"

"The Shyosi," Jacob said. "What are the chances anybody else has this additional intel?"

"The Shyosi—I'm pretty sure I'm saying that right—is listed as a place of interest in Mitchell's report without any specifics," Murph said. "They seemed to think it might have been used as a logistics hub for the Saabror-side operation, but I think it was much more given the connection to this Klytos character."

"Is the Shyosi a place like Pinnacle that's open to general traffic and commerce?" Jacob asked. "This knowledge doesn't do us a lot of good if we can't even step foot on the platform."

"It's an open station," Murph said. "But it's a rough place. It would be good to have some sort of cover in place before we dock."

"We've got two or three sets of papers and transponder codes aboard that should fit the bill," Jacob said. "Is The Atlantic Group still a viable entity, or did we blow that one?"

"Still good," Murph said. "Better check what assets are still tied to it, but that should at least give us the appearance of legitimacy to land and do business."

The Atlantic Group was a private security firm that was, on paper at least, based out of Formenos Prime rather than Niceen-3 like most shell corporations mercenaries and smugglers hid behind. That planet was the gateway to the Caspian Reaches, a region of space so wild and lawless that even the ConFed gave up on trying to tame it.

Since their shell corporation came from a respectable planet within the Eshquarian Empire with strong ties to the financial sector it never even got a second glance in most places. They were just looked at as a probable fixer crew running down someone at the behest of the banks.

"You buy everything Mitchell was selling?" he asked Murph after a few minutes. "About all this being about his daughter?"

"I'm inclined to," Murph said. "I can tell when someone finally drops the mask. We got a look at the real Glenn Mitchell. The fact he bothered getting in touch at all tells me he's probably a standup guy. Most operatives will just ditch an asset when it's no longer useful, yet he reached out to help us one last little bit."

"So, where does that leave us?" Jacob asked.

"Grabbing Kobvir and heading home." Murph shrugged. "While we might not do much recon these days in the traditional sense, we're definitely not an investigative unit. Leave running down the loose threads to the pros."

"At least this time we have official authorization," Jacob said. "Normally, when we're this far out on a limb it's an all-or-nothing, succeed or don't bother coming home scenario."

The crew prepped the ship and themselves to assume the role of corporate fixers as the *Corsair* waited for the Navy to show up and take care of the people below on Dorshone. For Jacob, there was a gnawing feeling that Kobvir was getting away and a growing impatience to be on their way, but the safety of the people on the ground trumped everything.

To give himself something to do he watched the live feed from the freighter they'd captured. Sully had put the *Corsair* into formation with the ship so Tin Man could fly over and make certain the crew was still secured and alive so the Navy could collect them as well. The human crew aboard would be handled by NIS agents before being funneled into the legal system. Someone on Earth had brokered the deal for that fleet, which Jacob hoped would lead investigators to the rest of the missing people that weren't being held on Dorshone.

"Get some rest, Cap," MG said from the galley table where he was checking over all the weapons they would be using on the upcoming op. "Squids won't be here for a while."

———

"*Corsair*, this is Captain Zell aboard the flagship, *Cincinnatus*. Are we clear to transit the system?"

"Yes, sir," Jacob said. "There's no opposition to speak of. As per your request, I've not spoken to the locals about the internment camps or the fact a taskforce was on its way in."

"You've done damn good work here, Captain. You and your whole team," Zell said. For some reason, when the starship captain spoke it seemed authentic and not a canned response like so many officers on a steep career track he'd met.

"We've continued to monitor and map out the camps with our sensors, sir. We're sending the raw data to you now," he said.

"Excellent," Zell said. "We relieve you, Captain. I hear there is a pressing matter you need to attend to, so happy hunting. *Cincinnatus*, out."

"Sully, break orbit and get us the hell out of here," Jacob said, walking over to his seat.

"We're out of here," Sully said, shoving the power up and pulling away from the freighter.

"She's resting."

"How bad?" Glenn asked.

"Four trackers total," the woman said. Glenn only knew her as Lia though she made it clear that wasn't her real name. She was a medical doctor with a background in intelligence having worked for both the NIS and NAVSOC. Now, she, like so many, was seeing the money that could be made as a private contractor now that space was opening up for human civilians.

Lia didn't work for the Collective, but Glenn had an open line to her. "There was the one you put in, one her captors put in, and then two of unknown origin other than they clearly come from Earth."

"Inconclusive," Glenn said. "Her mother's family is powerful and important. They may have chipped her as a safety measure."

"I don't think so. These were far more advanced than even the one you implanted. So advanced I had no choice but to destroy them as they appeared to be miniaturized hyperlink trackers," Lia said.

"What?" Glenn snapped. "You're sure?"

"Of course, I'm sure," Lia said. "I know the tech. It's actually how I know it's from Earth."

Glenn leaned back and rubbed his chin. Hyperlink trackers meant that whoever had implanted them could have tracked Gabby down at any time no matter where in the universe she was...but nobody had bothered. Why?

"What else did you find?" he asked.

"She was suffering from the normal things one does when going to an alien planet for the first time, but nothing permanent," Lia said. "She wasn't abused. Just a touch on the side of malnourished but, other than that, completely fine."

"That's something, I guess," Glenn said, taking the tablet she handed him with the quick workup she had done on the hyperlink trackers before destroying them. Thankfully, Lia's lab and workshop were aboard a slip-space capable ship so the last known position of the trackers before they went offline wouldn't do anyone any good. By the time they dispatched someone, they'd both be long gone.

"What will you do next?" she asked.

"I have a safe harbor I can take her to and sit tight until I can get my bearings," Glenn said. "I definitely won't be taking her back to Earth right now if that's what you're asking."

"Your ex's family has a long reach," Lia warned. "Between the Rushton's and the Shafer's, you're looking at a lot of power if they decide to come at you to get her back."

"I'll be ready," Glenn said, not sounding very convincing even to himself. In truth he was terrified of what the Shafer's were capable of. Not for himself. He had already lived far longer than he ever expected given his vocation and reckless youth. It was Gabby he was scared for. A nagging suspicion that they had known she was alive and on Dorshone began to tickle the back of his brain, and if they were willing to leave her there to whatever fate awaited those people, then her *not* being there would suddenly become a liability. Janet was dead so she wouldn't be able to stop them. It was, sadly, entirely in the realm of possibility that they would send a crew to kill them both.

"That's an ugly look on your face," Lia said. "Just now considering how screwed you are?"

"That and wishing I hadn't burned a bridge with a certain Scout Fleet team leader," Glenn said sourly. "It wouldn't have been a bad connection to have in my back pocket."

"You'll think of something. You always do."

23

"High orbit, Captain. Let's stay out of the Navy's way."

"Aye, Admiral," Captain Duncan said.

Captain Duncan had been with the *Kentucky* since he was a commander and assigned to the C&C ship as her captain. When Scout Fleet was peeled away from NAVSOC, Webb had asked for the ship, and Duncan had requested to stay with her. He was now nearing retirement, and Webb was sorry to be losing him.

At the president's request, Webb had flown out to Dorshone to observe the recovery process personally so he could report back. The taskforce commander, Admiral Appleton, had been accommodating in sharing access to the ground feeds with Webb. His team was now down in CIC watching as recovery teams identified captives and directed them to the shuttles that were running up and back to the hospital ships in a continuous loop.

"Has the taskforce received *any* communication from the Protectorate?" Webb asked. "We're here running a major military operation over one of their planets, and they don't even send a scout ship to check it out?"

"Nothing, sir," Weathers said. "An Eshquarian battlegroup is on the way as well to collect their people. So far, they've not been challenged since crossing into Protectorate space either."

"What the hell is going on?" Webb asked, pointing to the main display with its representation of every ship in the system. "And what about all these serviceable ships parked in the outer system? Did the Saabror abandon the entire Orion border region?"

"NIS has—"

"Yeah, I know...they have no credible intel on the region." Webb rolled his eyes.

He watched on one of the auxiliary displays as a long line of terrified people queued up to be processed by the Marines down on the surface. They were then shuffled into heavy-lift passenger shuttles and taken up to one of two hospital ships that were sent out.

Once they were cleared medically, they would go to one of the freighters docked on either side. There were six more freighters stacked up in transfer orbits so that when one was full and departed, another would move in and quickly take its place.

Webb had been away for a time, so he'd not witnessed how skilled and advanced the Navy had become at executing these sorts of complex missions. He felt a sense of pride knowing he'd helped pave the way for where they were now, but also a pang of sorrow knowing that his time was also coming to an end.

He'd been at it a long time, and he was painfully aware these days that he wasn't a near-immortal like his friend, Jason Burke. His career was topped out, and there would be no additional stars added to his boards, and that was okay. Looking back, he didn't think he'd trade any of it for the chance at just one more promotion and a desk to be chained to.

He couldn't complain. He started his career in the United States Navy, became one of the most feared warriors on the planet when he was with the SEALs, and practically built NAVSOC from the ground up with Ezra Mosler. He would hang his spurs up without regrets.

"The *Cincinnatus* just sent word one of their forward scouts is reporting in," Captain Duncan read off a tablet. "This is...interesting."

"Don't keep me in suspense, Captain," Webb said after a moment.

"Oh, sorry, sir," Duncan said. "The scout did a flyby of a planet called Abno, Abnolas-4 on our charts, and found that the planet was abandoned."

"Abandoned," Webb snorted. "What the hell does that even mean? You can't abandon a planet."

"See for yourself, sir," Duncan handed the device over.

Webb cruised through the summary brief at the beginning of the report and had trouble believing what he was reading. The planet appeared to have been depopulated almost completely. There were signs of small settlements still operating, but the large urban centers were all cold, ships drifted through the system on ballistic arcs, all of the heavy industry and power generation on the planet was dormant.

"This didn't *just* happen," Webb said. "Something cataclysmic happened here...how are we just now finding out about it?"

"I'm not sure how to answer—"

"Do we have an NIS liaison in the taskforce?" Webb asked Weathers.

"Yes, sir."

"Get their ass over here on the first shuttle and—" Webb stopped and closed his eyes, taking a deep breath. When he continued, he appeared calm and collected again. "Please, invite the NIS agent attached to the taskforce over to the *Kentucky* for a secure briefing. Tell them I have a team in the field and would like a more complete picture of what's happening here."

"I'll handle it, sir," Weathers said, recognizing the warning signs that his boss was about to blow his top.

Webb, now agitated, began to pace the bridge. The Saabror Protectorate covered an enormous territory, but so much was unknown about them because they were a closed, xenophobic society that didn't like outsiders. They would clash with the Eshquarians every couple hundred years or so, but it almost seemed out of boredom or restlessness than any desire to capture territory. Even after the ConFed attacked and temporarily conquered the empire, the Protectorate never bothered trying to peel off a few border systems for their own.

The Protectorate also served a purpose for the Eshquarian politicians. The omnipresent boogeyman that would help them ram through procurement budgets or enact overreaching legislation from time to time without the citizens making too much of a fuss. Most of their intelligence on the Protectorate came from the Cridal military but all that really meant was that the Cridal were passing them on filtered and redacted reports that came from the Eshquarians.

"Agent Robinson is loading up onto a shuttle now, sir," Weathers said as he walked back up to the admiral. "She'll be here within the next half hour or so."

"Thanks," Webb said.

"Sir...what are you expecting to learn here?" Weathers said quietly, turning so that his back was to the bridge crew. "You don't think the NIS is sitting on intel they've denied us, do you?"

"I don't know," Webb sighed. "Probably not. But they do filter the information we get to see. I want access to the raw intel including unsubstantiated rumors and hearsay. This system of the NIS being the ultimate authority on intel and dolling it out to us per mission isn't working. We've been damn lucky but, eventually, we're going to lose a scout team due to lack of information."

"I don't disagree, sir," Weathers said. "But the raw intel is political power. Without the ability to control it, the NIS loses status. They are no longer the mythical oracles that must be petitioned for information. They become file clerks just filling requests."

"Good God, Reggie," Webb said. "And I thought *I* was a cynic." Weathers just shrugged.

As he waited for the agent to come over for him to verbally spar with, his thoughts turned to Obsidian. They'd been completely let off the leash to try and run down Kobvir Glecsh. He was told the Cridal's capture was of the utmost importance to the Unified Council, which was the president's way of telling Webb that nothing was off the table without having his ass flapping in the breeze, politically speaking.

"Any word from Obsidian?" he asked Weathers.

"None yet, sir."

"I want to know the minute they do, no matter the hour. Understood?"

"Of course, sir."

"So, that's the Shyosi," Jacob said, staring at the rendered image the computer put up on the main display.

"It is actually called Di-Shyosi," Tin Man said. "You sound like yokels saying the first word in your own language."

"To be fair, the captain sounds like a yokel whenever he says anything," MG said. "Ask him what he calls soda."

"It's called pop, and you damn well know it," Jacob said.

"Pop?" Murph turned around. "Like the sound a firecracker makes?"

"We just call it Coke where I'm from," Mettler said.

"What do you mean?" MG asked.

"In restaurants. You know...they ask you what kind of coke you want," Mettler said.

"That's the dumbest thing I've ever heard," MG said. "What about you, Tin Man? Any thoughts?"

"Only that I remain shocked your species has survived long enough to discover interstellar travel," Tin Man said.

The *Corsair* was in a star system loaded on their navigational database as SPR-1209 and flying a standard approach down to where *Di*-Shyosi was built into the side of an enormous asteroid. The irregular-shaped object was made mostly of nickel iron and was a cheap, efficient way of providing the needed mass to put it into a stable heliocentric orbit between the second and third planets.

It seemed like such a simple, elegant solution, but Jacob knew the engineering challenge of moving a forty-million-ton planetoid down from the outer system had to have been immense.

"This is impressive," Mettler said.

"It is. Most of these mega-stations were all built for military use, but then lived on for centuries afterwards in the hands of private owners," Murph said before turning to Tin Man. "Any more information you'd like to volunteer here?"

"I have never been here," Tin Man said.

"Damn, that place is fucking huge," Jacob said. "Trying to find one Cridal hiding in there isn't going to be easy. If it's even possible."

Di-Shyosi's traffic control AI was at least as advanced as the one that controlled ship movements around Pinnacle Station, which impressed and confused Jacob. From what he understood Di-Shyosi was medium-traffic facility owned by a freight consortium that was nothing but a front for the smugglers guild that operated in the region.

Why the expense and hassle of so much traffic management capacity for a station that wasn't built as a hub for starliners or cargo haulers? Had the military left their equipment behind?

"We're granted docking clearance only, no available hangar space for a ship this size," Sully said.

"We're not taking on any cargo so that's actually preferable," Jacob said. "The only downside is that it's tougher to come and go without being noticed from the exterior docking arms."

"Makes it harder for people to sneak aboard and bash me over the head, though," Sully said. "You know, since you guys like to leave me here alone in an unsecured ship all the time."

"Shouldn't happen again," Mettler said. "When she rotated through Olympus for a depot-level overhaul, they added a whole new anti-intrusion system. It's why we had to give Glenn a transponder card so it wouldn't accidentally kill him."

Jacob made a mental note to look into the "double Glenn" anomaly he had seen on the internal sensors. It was pretty obvious that the troubleshooter had found a way to spoof their systems while he attached that bus interrupter to a wiring harness in the avionics bay. At the moment, he was studying the layout drawings that Di-Shyosi's automated system had transmitted to them as a sort of welcome packet for ships that it had no record of having been there before. Their corporate security credentials were accepted without issue as Jacob had expected, and they were allowed a normal approach with no stops for additional security inspections.

The big platforms like Colton Hub, Pinnacle, the Gates, and Di-Shyosi all had mystiques about them and personas that grew over the centuries. Some were revered like Pinnacle, others were feared like the Hub, but one thing Jacob had discovered in his travels was that above all they were chained to commerce.

No matter how dangerous they were said to be, if you had enough money and claimed you were there to spend it, the people in charge would make sure you were given that chance. Thanks to the mercy of former crime lord Saditava Mok, Obsidian had a lot of money to flash to get them access.

Over the next four hours as the *Corsair* transited the system, the team went over their cover and made sure it was airtight. It had been some time since they had bothered with actual covert tactics on an op given how kinetic their recent recent missions had been. Obsidian had been used more as a traditional spec ops unit than a scout team.

Most of the preparatory work centered around trying to get MG to act and present himself as someone who was in executive protection. Murph and Mettler were naturals, and Tin Man never needed any extra prep. By the time Sully swung the ship around the planetoid Di-Shyosi was built into and lined up for his final approach, the team was as ready as they were going to be.

"Show time, boys," he said.

24

"The trackers all went dead within seconds of each other, but she was definitely back in human space when they did, sir."

Senator Douglas Rushton glared at the man in front of him as if the whole debacle was his fault. He was just coming from his office where he had received a briefing from some UEAS lackey that the UEN had mounted a rescue mission in Saabror space and that nearly three hundred thousand humans were being brought back to home.

He'd feigned shock at the abductions and enthusiasm at the noble heroes of the United Earth Navy saving the day but, inside, he was seething. Years of work possibly ruined and his own neck on the chopping block.

"She wasn't rescued with the others by the Navy's efforts?" Lydia Shafer asked from where she sat on the couch.

"No, ma'am. The trackers were away from Dorshone well before the taskforce would have arrived."

"Get out," Rushton said. The man nodded and scurried from the office, closing it with a soft *click*. The light above the door glowed purple to indicate the locks were engaged and the anti-eavesdropping countermeasures were active. "Fuck!"

"She likely knows nothing," Shafer said.

"We don't even know who has her or why," Rushton said.

"Of course, we do," Shafer scoffed. "Glenn Mitchell somehow tracked her down. Our fleet commander said he left with a Navy special forces unit they found poking around the site. He likely surmised his best chance at getting the girl back was by latching onto a smaller, specialized military unit."

"We have any way of tracking Mitchell?"

"He's too slippery. He never submits to medical procedures or exams...nothing that would allow us to put a tracker in him."

"What does the Collective leadership think?" Rushton asked.

"They're still unaware of our deal with Glecsh," Shafer said. "But they are not stupid. A few have suspicions, which will cause them to start digging. I won't sugarcoat it for you, Douglas...Gabrielle was a risky loose end. Letting her be taken instead of leaving her to be found with her mother gave Mitchell the motivation he needed to track the missing site workers, which can lead back to us."

"How close are they?"

"They're not," Shafer said. "But that won't last long. At this point, we need to minimize the damage, make it look like we thought Glecsh was speaking of a legitimate contract offered for McMillian-Shafer to fill. Our best weapon is ignorance, but there's a fine edge to balance on there. We mustn't look incompetent or stupid or the other members will pounce. Which brings us to the child. She's the wild-card here. If Gabrielle does have incriminating information, however...let's just say the situation is fluid."

"Look, I'm sorry," Rushton said, tossing his arms up in a shrug. "We have a count we're trying to fill, and she was one more on the tally. How the hell could I know it would cause this sort of trouble? Why the hell did you keep Mitchell around anyway?"

"I like him," Shafer said, a strange smile on her face. "Back when he was just Janet's bodyguard, I recognized something in him. A potential to be an enormous asset. We put considerable resources into his training and enhancements but, in the end, he was simply too stubborn. Too latched onto a code of honor that limited his use to us."

"Well, I'm glad we might be taken down because you *like* your daughter's ex-fling," Rushton snorted.

"There is no *we* here, Douglas," she chuckled. "I am isolated. Kobvir Glecsh came to us through you...you are the intermediary that this will get pinned on. But take heart, Douglas. Nothing they'll find at Dorshone will do anything but raise more questions with no answers. It certainly won't lead them directly to us."

Rushton wasn't so sure, but he wisely kept his mouth shut. When his marriage to Janet had been all but arranged prior to his run for the Senate he'd just assumed the Shafer family would be a financial backer in exchange for the usual favors. After meeting Lydia, however, he'd had second thoughts. He thought her reptilian at first. Looking back, he realized he was being too kind with those early impressions.

"I assume you have a team looking for Mitchell?" he asked.

"Don't worry about these things, Douglas," Shafer said, getting to her feet. "We'll be in touch. Janet's memorial service will need to be planned once she is returned by the NIS, and you will need to be suitably distraught, so please practice having human emotions. The cameras will be there."

Once she was gone, Rushton sat in his chair, furiously thinking of a way out of his current predicament. When he'd been approached by Kobvir Glecsh about an opportunity to expand humanity's influence while lining his own pockets, he had eagerly accepted without fully knowing the details. Glecsh needed a powerful facilitator, so he had naturally introduced him to Lydia Shafer as someone who could handle the logistics of what he needed.

Once he'd realized what they were dealing with, it was too late to back out. So, as he tended to do, he began to justify his actions in his own mind. He even thought that the people they were diverting from the frontier to meet the quotas would come to thank him...eventually. But there was a built-in period of extraordinarily high risk that they were still smack dead in the middle of. Now was not the time for something to go this spectacularly wrong.

Douglas was no idiot. Lydia had already made it clear that he was at least one of her scapegoats if their deal was discovered too early, something he'd fully expected from the beginning. It was why he had made his own contingency plans. She was too powerful to take head-on. Even recorded conversations of her dirty dealings would do little more than inconvenience her for a week or two. He'd had to get creative to make sure he was protected.

Was now time to put one of those plans in motion? Was Lydia Shafer just trying to rattle his cage? Or was the snake so confident that she felt there was no risk in giving him fair warning he was about to be railroaded?

All this trouble for the little brat Janet had before they were even married. Damn the luck. He pulled up a section of the hardwood floor and opened a hidden floor safe to retrieve an unregistered hyperlink com unit and a small notebook. No harm in at least getting his dead-man switches armed in case she decided early he would make a good patsy.

"If that bitch wants to play...we'll play."

"Mr. Brown, what a pleasure to meet you. While we're a major trade hub that matches providers of unique and specialized services to our exclusive clientele, your company stood out as exceptionally rare. There aren't many battlesynths working in protection throughout the entire quadrant."

"You have a discerning eye, Dar Barrin," Jacob said, using the proper salutation for that region of Saabror space. Barrin was a lemit, a sub-caste species within the Protectorate. "Their species is so rare that not many people recognize them at first."

"You are too kind," Barrin said. "I also note that your cybernetic upgrades have the distinctive look of Khepri about them. Very high quality. Tell me, Mr. Brown, how can Di-Shyosi help you and your company?"

"My team finished a job earlier than expected so we decided to take the opportunity to branch out and see what might be available in Protectorate space," Jacob said. "We understand the difficult legal circumstances, but we've heard from other companies based out of the Caspian Reaches that things are different these days."

"Indeed, they are, Mr. Brown," Barrin said enthusiastically. "The Protectorate is going through a...transitory period, let's say. There is opportunity in abundance. What might you be looking for specifically?"

"We specialize in VIP protection, but we have been known to execute precise interdictions when called upon. Like the Protectorate, we also find ourselves in a transitory period as we would like to expand our offered services. While here on Di-Shyosi we would like to not only connect with potential clients but with potential employees as well."

"Delightful!" Barrin said. Despite his goofy personality, Jacob couldn't help but like the guy. "As you settle into your complimentary suite and workspace, is there a particular specialty you would be interested in adding to your team?"

"Now that you mention it..." Jacob pretended to think it over. "We could really use a good tracker."

"Say no more, sir," Barrin bowed and walked toward the door. "We will speak again soon!"

Once the door closed, Mettler and Murph went to work scanning the provided suite while Tin Man and MG went behind them, neutralizing any monitoring devices they found. There were surprisingly few. Three audio-only bugs that looked like they'd been installed decades ago and one camera in one of the bedrooms that was offline. What shocked Jacob was that there were only two audio monitors that looked like they were part of the station's security.

"You were laying it on a little thick, weren't you?" Murph asked once they were certain every device had been found and dealt with.

"It felt expected," Jacob said. "Remember, we're a high-profile

corporate protection company not a crew of blood and guts mercenaries like we usually play."

"Fair enough," Murph said. "What now?"

"I don't expect Barrin to be back for some time," Jacob said. "Tin
Man and I are going to do a walk-around. You guys get setup and
establish our link with the Zadra Network."

The residential section of Di-Shyosi where they had been given a
suite of rooms and workspace looked as nice as anything you'd find in
Mid-Section on Pinnacle Station. It was also a hell of a walk to get to
the first moving walkway that would take them into the Galleria
Adonti, an enormous market space that was on what Jacob thought of
as the port side of the station. The starboard side had a smaller
public area called the Bann Promenade.

"This is not how I envisioned it would be," Tin Man admitted.

"Me either, but it makes sense," Jacob said. "Klytos Finvak would
need a place with stability and order to operate out of. A place like
Colton Hub isn't somewhere you can leave something and think that
it will still be there when you return."

"True," Tin Man conceded.

They'd made it almost to the arching entrance into the Galleria
Adonti when a large, blue hand seemed to materialize out of
nowhere and grabbed Jacob by the jacket, flinging him down a side
passage.

"Jason Burke, you piece of shit!" a harsh voice barked. "I told you
I'd kill you if I ever saw you again!"

Jacob tried to roll over, but he was kicked in the gut, and then
again in the back, unable to get his bearings. He focused on the attack
in front of him, grabbing the boot with his cybernetic left hand and
commanding it to full power as he squeezed, eliciting a scream of
pain. Someone grabbed him from behind, but then those hands were
yanked away, followed by another startled yelp.

"That will be quiet enough," Tin Man said loudly, throwing the
attacker he was holding down the corridor where it landed in a heap.

"You stay out of this, Lucky! This bastard owes me, and you know
it!" the one in Jacob's grasp snarled.

"I am not Lucky. He is not Jason Burke. You have made a potentially deadly mistake," Tin Man said calmly. "If my companion releases you, do you promise to allow us to discuss this calmly?"

"What are you on about!? I know what you two look like!" the assailant insisted. "Don't think you can stall me until Crusher gets here!"

"You cannot win here. I think, if you will permit us to explain who we are, we might find a mutually beneficial arrangement," Tin Man said.

"Like what?"

"You help us with local intel, we allow you to live."

"Take the deal, Boss," the second attacker wheezed from where Tin Man had thrown him. "Please."

"Sure...why not? Let's grab us a drink and you can tell me what game this is you're playing," the first one said.

"Captain, release him. I will ensure he does not go back on his word."

Jacob released his grip and rolled up onto his feet, looking at his attackers clearly. They were both Taukkir, likely from the same brood by the look of them. The squatty, powerful aliens stared at him with naked hatred, and he could only sigh, wondering what his father had done to piss them off so badly.

They found an open-air bar and sat, everyone stiffly glaring at each other while they waited for their drinks. Once the serving bot dropped the bottles and scurried away the lead Taukkir leaned in heavily on the table.

"So...who are you two?" he asked. "I can see now that he looks like someone I know, but not exactly. But what are the odds a human looking similar to the one I'm after is walking around with a battlesynth?"

"Your information is well out of date," Tin Man said. "Lucky is dead. He was killed in the battlesynth uprising on Khepri, the one that took out the Central Banking AI. The human sitting before you is related to Jason Burke but has no contact with him. They are essentially strangers."

"Lucky isn't dead," the second Taukkir said. "We'd have heard."

"I assure you, he is," Tin Man said.

Lucky, the battlesynth on the Omega Force crew, *had* been killed in the battle on Khepri as Tin Man said, but Jacob knew he hadn't stayed dead. Members of his father's team had found a way to resurrect their friend by putting his mind into a new prototype body supposed to be part of the second generation battlesynth program. The whole thing was illegal, so those who knew about Lucky's real identity were sworn to secrecy.

"Is Burke dead?" the first asked eagerly. "And that bastard, Crusher?"

"As far as I know, they are still in good health," Tin Man said. "Might I ask what they have done to earn your hatred?"

"Burke tricked us into killing an ambassador from Oocard-4," the leader of the pair said.

"Oh, for fuck's sake," Jacob sighed, putting his head down.

"Why would he do that?" Tin Man asked.

"He and that nasty little Veran of his needed to get aboard the ambassador's ship to steal something. It was docked at Pinnacle Station, and the security was especially tight, so he needed a distraction. He came down to the lower levels and told us that Oocard-4 was there for talks to buy the station and that they were going to move it to their home system and evict everyone first."

"That doesn't even make sense," Jacob muttered.

"He got us all wound up and set to protest during a presentation the ambassador was giving. Some of our brood are the excitable types, and we've lived aboard Pinnacle for many years so they might have brought some heavy weapons to the protest."

"How heavy?" Tin Man asked.

"Some explosives and an anti-material plasma launcher."

"To cut this short, the ambassador was accidentally killed, we had to flee," the second Taukkir said. "There is a bounty out for us, so we dare not return to ConFed space."

"You know the ConFed is gone, right?" Jacob asked. "Smaller systems like Oocard will not be worrying about you guys anymore."

"You lie!" the first Taukkir accused.

"He is not," Tin Man said. "You can probably find the news even on the nexus within the Saabror Protectorate. The ConFed has dissolved its widespread protection treaties and has withdrawn its influence to the Core Worlds for now."

"What of Taukk?" the second asked. "It is no longer protected by the ConFed?"

"I'm afraid not," Jacob said. "I believe they have a mutual protection pact with Ver, but it's not something I keep up with."

"Nasty Verans," the first growled before turning to his partner. "We must prepare to return home. We will be needed."

Taukkir were somewhat of an enigma to Jacob. They were widespread throughout the quadrant with family groups living on damn near every populous world, even Pillar Worlds like Miressa Prime and Khepri. What made that interesting is that they were widely considered to not be especially bright, usually relegated to low-skill labor jobs or the thing they were most suited for: military service. Case in point would be his father trying to use them to create a simple distraction for whatever stupid thing he was up to at the time and the Taukkir blowing up a diplomatic delegation.

Perhaps it wasn't that they were less intelligent than other beings, they'd integrated into the galactic community with notable success after all. It was their lack of nuance that seemed to get them into trouble. They were the embodiment of the "when you're a hammer, everything looks like a nail" approach to problem solving.

"We apologize for our attack," the first went on. "But if you see your broodmate, Burke, tell him we will still want to kill him."

"I'll definitely pass that on," Jacob said. "But maybe you can do me a favor in the meantime...in exchange for having attacked me earlier."

"Perhaps," the first said suspiciously.

"We're looking for a...friend," Jacob said. "He's supposed to operate out of here from time to time. Ever heard of someone called Klytos Finvak? He would have been known as a former officer in the Saabror Free Army."

"It does not sound familiar," the second one said. "But there are many officers of the paramilitary group you describe that reside in the Eyrolie District."

"That's helpful," Jacob said.

"Perhaps not. It is a secured section of the station, very difficult to get into if you were thinking of paying your *friend* a surprise visit."

"Have either of you heard any rumors about operatives from the Cridal Cooperative on the station?" Tin Man asked. The pair looked at each other and shrugged.

"Not that we've heard."

"Thanks for the time," Jacob said. "I encourage you to find out what you can about the current state of things on Taukk. As the galaxy begins to realize the ConFed is really gone, it will become a much more dangerous place."

"Our thanks, friend," the first Taukkir said. "No hard feelings for kicking you in the torso multiple times?"

"Nah. I like that sort of thing," Jacob said, wincing as he stood. "Stay safe, fellas."

They walked back toward the entrance to the residential section they'd come from, deciding to cut their tour short after the encounter. The little bit of intel they'd collected gave them a starting point to begin their search, which was far more than Jacob had hoped for.

"That was productive," Tin Man said.

"Yeah," Jacob said. "Thanks for letting him use my rib cage for soccer practice, by the way."

"You suffered no permanent damage."

"You really are an asshole, you know that?"

25

Glenn Mitchell watched Gabby sleep from the doorway as he contemplated his next move.

He debriefed his daughter as best he could, pushing gently around the edges without dragging her back down into despair as she was just starting to show signs that she was processing her ordeal. The loss of her mother, Janet, was a brutal shock to her. Glenn's feelings about Janet were a bit more complicated.

He still loved her in the way that any father would love the mother of his child, but he still harbored a lot of resentment and anger at how she'd dismissed him without a moment's remorse when her family needed her to be attached to someone more politically useful. He'd foolishly thought anyone raised around the Shafer family could be capable of unconditional love.

What she'd told him disturbed him greatly. She'd seen Janet fighting with executives from McMillian-Shafer so he'd surmised it must have been Percy Walker. Their responsibilities didn't overlap or touch in any way, so he couldn't imagine what Percy and Janet would have to fight about, but Gabby was insistent that it was lengthy and heated. She said that it had to do with someone named Saber, but that made little sense and he'd been forced to back off before he lost her.

Glenn softly closed the door and walked back into the main living area. The small house was in a remote area of the Raleigh Province on Terranovus. The small community wasn't far from the commune where the battlesynths of Lot 700 used to live. Glenn made arrangements to secure the place for his personal use well after they'd already left, but he'd always wanted to see them. In that regard, meeting Tin Man had been a profound honor even if he had punched him in the face once.

He sighed, dreading what he had to do next, and slid behind the slip-com terminal and powered up the node. The other end picked up almost immediately.

"Glenn Mitchell," Jacob Brown said. He stood in a room somewhere that definitely wasn't the *Corsair*. "What the hell do you want?"

"Hello, Captain," Glenn said. Jacob bounced the slip-com channel through their hyperlink relay in the *Corsair* to their portable com system they'd taken aboard Di-Shyosi.

"How's Gabby?" he asked.

"Good. Shaken, but...good."

"I'm glad. So. What's up?"

"I tried to get a little information from Gabby about what might have preceded the attack on Site D. Does the name Saber mean anything to you?" Glenn asked.

"Oh, shit! I forgot to give it to you," Jacob said.

"What?"

"I found Gabby's journal on that shuttle the Navy was holding on Breaker's World. I read in there that Janet Rushton was arguing with Percy Davis over someone called Saber, but I thought she probably just misheard Saabror. My guess is that Davis was working for the

Cridal at the behest of someone within the Protectorate. Still no idea why, though."

"This is starting to make more sense," Glenn said, leaning back in his chair. "Maybe. Without more information on what the hell the Saabror are up to, holding these people for the Cridal it's all just pointless speculation. Where are you now?"

"Deep in Saabror territory," Jacob said, careful about how much he divulged. "We think we're onto a high-value target that is key to this whole operation. We snag him, we start getting answers."

"I can be on my way in—"

"You're over a week away at max slip," Jacob said. "If we're still here by then, we already failed. Stay where you're at, keep your head down, and take care of your daughter. Take it from me, you'll look back and wish you'd stayed."

"You have kids waiting for you at your secret base?" Glenn asked sarcastically.

"No...I *was* the kid," Jacob said, not sure why he was opening up to a total stranger who had already taken advantage of him once. "My father left me behind to go flying off and be the hero. He had no choice, if I'm being fair about it, but it didn't make it any easier for a boy who just wanted his dad."

"Sorry, I had no idea," Glenn said, rubbing his hair.

"I'll let you know what happens here. Now that I know how you're tied in, you might need the intel depending on how deeply McMillian-Shafer is involved," Jacob said. "Get some rest, bro."

"That dickhead have anything interesting that might help us?" MG called from where he was lounging on a couch.

"Nothing," Jacob said. He was interrupted from saying anything further by the door chime.

"It's that doofus that met us at the ship," Mettler said from the door.

"His name is Barrin. Please don't call him doofus to his face," Jacob said. "And let him in."

MG adjusted his position on the couch, holding a weapon down by his side in a way that would allow him to cover the door. Mettler keyed it open and Barrin came walking in with four beings in tow.

"Mr. Brown! As I have promised, I deliver," Barrin said with a flourish as he waved to the four stone-faced aliens. "The best trackers for hire on the station."

"Mind if I talk to them one on one in private?" Jacob asked, nodding his head toward the separate office where Tin Man waited out of sight.

"Of course," Barrin said, his high-wattage smile never faltering.

"You," Jacob pointed at the Veran in the group. "Follow me."

He'd picked him partly out of nostalgia because he reminded Jacob of one of his father's crewmates and partly because he was the only species he knew out of the group. Verans were one of the very few sentient species in the quadrant that evolved with a different configuration than bipedal with bilateral symmetry arranged with two arms, two legs. Verans had four arms, the upper arms being the stronger, larger pair.

"What's your name?" Jacob asked once the office door closed.

"Jatto," he said, looking calmly at Tin Man. "You're a real battlesynth?"

"I am," Tin Man said.

"I've never even seen one of your kind before. It's a pleasure to meet you," Jatto said. Tin Man looked taken aback by the Veran's open, friendly demeanor.

"Thank you."

"This will be a temporary position. You okay with that?" Jacob asked.

"No problem. You guys look like you live on a ship and I'm more of a dirtside, large station type of guy," Jatto said. "Is this really a tryout or you need me to find someone for you?"

"You're really that good?" Jacob asked.

"I am, but that's not the relevant point," Jatto said. "I'm the only actual tracker. The others Barrin brought are just to pad the numbers so he can earn his fee. They'd take your money and do a local nexus search, maybe ask around a bit, and then tell you that whoever you're looking for isn't here."

"And you?" Tin Man asked.

"I'm guessing you picked me because you know what Verans are good at. I can get into any security system, standalone or station, and find your target. I have some conditions to protect me from reprisals if you're looking for one of our more dangerous and connected residents, of course."

"Of course," Jacob said, looking at Tin Man, who just nodded imperceptibly. "How well do you know the Eyrolie District?"

"I've heard of it. Never actually been there," Jatto said. "Mostly high-end mercenaries and assassins back in there. Some of the lunatics and butchers from the Free Army as well. Your target there?"

"It gets complicated, but yes...to start with we'll need to locate a specific holding in that area, and then we can narrow our focus to the individual and how best to dig them out. You interested?"

"What's the pay?"

"What's your fee?"

"Sixty thousand plus expenses and a performance bonus if I beat your deadline."

"I'll give you seventy-five plus your bonus if you do the job and forget you ever met us."

"You understand how negotiations like this work, do you not?" Jatto asked, laughing.

"Money I've got lots of. Time? Not so much," Jacob said. "I also don't need someone coming after us once we leave here."

"For the extra scratch, I'll delete all record of you from Di-Shyosi's system logs and the backup archives. It will be like you were never here. Don't worry about Barrin, either. He's a pro. He knows how the game is played."

"We have a deal?"

"Let's get started." Jatto smiled.

After Jacob had dismissed Barrin and the other trackers he'd brought, he sent Jatto, Tin Man, and MG out to retrieve the Veran's gear he would need to begin the search. Much of the work would be done in the suite but Jatto warned them that some of the security systems had to be directly accessed, which meant getting into sensitive areas and splicing into a data bus.

"Feeling lucky here?" Murph asked.

"Maybe," Jacob said. "My gut tells me that you're still right, and Kobvir is here hiding on this station. The more I see of how large it is and how it's structured, the more I'm certain of it. It's too bad we can't directly contact the Eshquarian intel folks and see if they could get the location from Klytos himself."

"Now there's an interesting thought," Murph said. "There is someone we know who has probably been to this station *and* might have well-placed sources within the Imperial Intelligence."

"You can't mean—"

"Oh, but I can. He's an exploitable resource right now. I'm not saying you need to ask him to come riding to the rescue—again—but just a little information would probably help the healing process along."

"You're shamelessly full of shit," Jacob said.

"Still doesn't mean I'm wrong." Murph shrugged. "Make the call."

"Damn, I can't wait until you transfer out of my unit."

26

"That doesn't look like the inside of the *Corsair*. Where're you at, kid?"

"A place called Di-Shyosi," Jacob said, wincing as his father spit his drink out, spraying the camera with droplets of whatever he'd been swilling.

"What in the fuck are you doing in Saabror space?" Jason Burke asked, wiping the camera lens with his sleeve.

"We're running down the leadership behind the trafficking ring you guys stumbled onto in the Luuxir Border Region," Jacob said. "Webb has us chasing the Cridal Executive Chief of Staff."

"Kobvir Glecsh? I'm surprised the Cridal haven't killed him yet," Jason said. "You think he's hiding on that station?"

"Murph found that Klytos Finvak has a holding here," Jacob said. "Now that the Eshquarians have him, we're thinking Kobvir might have fled here to hide from Seeladas Dalton and her Red Strike teams."

"Not a bad theory," Jason conceded. "What do you need from me? I assume this isn't just a social call."

"It's both," Jacob said defensively, feeling a twinge of shame at exploiting his father's desire for a stronger relationship to get access to his network. "I'm hoping you have some connections within Imperial Intelligence that we could use and see if they got any information from Finvak on his holdings aboard Di-Shyosi. I know it's a long shot."

"Maybe not as much as you think," Jason muttered, suddenly looking conflicted.

"Huh?"

"I can't give you direct access to the person I know. It's...complicated. What I can do is have someone contact you directly if they agree to share what intel they have."

"That works," Jacob said. "Not looking to poach a source, just need a little bit of a boost getting this investigation back on track."

"Is that what you guys are now? Investigators?" Jason asked. "Every time I talk to you it seems you're doing everything *but* recon missions. The last time, Admiral Fuckstick had you operating undermanned on a mission, and you lost an arm *and* an eye for it."

"We're scouts in name only," Jacob said. "What are you up to? Is that the SX-5 you're on?"

"Yeah...the *Phoenix* is undergoing a major rebuild. Got her shot out from under me on the last mission," Jason said. "Actually had to stash her in a cave on a hostile planet when a surface-to-orbit cannon blew half the right wing off."

"Holy shit!"

"All good now. Twingo is super excited to re-design the engine management system or some shit. I stopped listening after a while to be honest."

"Then, you're on your own right now?" Jacob frowned.

"I've got 701 with me." Jason rolled his eyes and looked back over his shoulder. "Twingo is with the ship, Crusher is out of commission in a way that requires Doc's help, and Lucky has managed to get himself *and* Kage captured again, so I'm heading back out to the frontier to get them."

"Dad...this sounds really reckless. Even by your standards," Jacob said, concerned.

"I'll be fine," Jason waved him off. "Watch your back on Di-Shyosi. It may seem a lot more civilized than Colton Hub, but there are some real predators there."

"Tell me about it. I got jumped by a pair of Taukkir who thought I was you. Did you actually convince them to blow up an ambassador on Pinnacle Station?" Jason started laughing uproariously at that.

"I only told them I needed a distraction. It was the Taukkir's unwholesome love of explosives that killed the Oocard ambassador. Seriously...you wouldn't believe how much they love blowing shit up. They used enough explosives to take out a frigate. Put two decks completely out of commission on Pinnacle," he said, still laughing. "I can't believe they're still pissed about that."

"They thought Tin Man was Lucky, so that's how out of date their information is," Jacob said. "I owe you for the bruised ribs, though."

"I'll keep that in mind," Jason said. "Let me reach out to some people and see what I can do. If you don't hear anything by tomorrow, assume it was a bust."

"Will do. Appreciate it."

"No worries. Stay safe out there."

"You too, Dad."

The slip-com channel closed, and Jacob slid back from the desk. His relationship with his father had been slow building and was beginning to hit its stride with both of them being comfortable speaking to the other without their guards up.

He walked out of the room he and Murph were sharing and saw that Jatto had already set up in one of the office areas and was busy unpacking his gear. Like his father's crewmate, Kage, most of what Jatto would need to do his job was already in his head.

Veran code slicers were always in high demand throughout the quadrant. Their unique brains had some evolutionary quirks that gave them the ability to merge with computer networks on a level that couldn't be rivaled. The Kheprians had made some impressive AI systems that could rival even the best Veran, but they were rare, expensive, and unwieldy. For now, the flighty, high-strung little aliens still dominated the market.

"You have everything you need?" he asked.

"All set," Jatto said. "I already have a few automated search strings running looking for your Klytos Finvak, but I'm almost ready to start the real work."

"Just let us know if you need anything," Jacob said.

Most of their missions came with long periods of waiting or observing so he was well-accustomed to the art of doing nothing but, this time, he was having trouble calming his mind and waiting for some intel he could act on. The longer they were there, the more risk they had of being outed as a Terran military unit operating in Saabror space.

"Anything we can be doing right now?" MG asked.

"Just make sure the gear is prepped and you guys are all rested and ready," Jacob said. "If Kobvir is aboard this station, he'll have a protection detail with him."

"Madam Premier."

"Zuchari," Seeladas Dalton greeted her chief of intelligence. "What news do you bring me?"

"Kobvir Glecsh remains elusive, ma'am," Zuchari said. "We've had assets trying to locate him, as well as having Eshquarian and Terran intelligence operatives tracked as they try to find him. So far, it seems as if none have had any luck. The humans have nearly finished their recovery operation on Dorshone and are now scouting other planets to begin hunting for their other missing people. We expect the Eshquarian Imperial Navy to mirror their efforts."

"This news is no different than yesterday," Seeladas sighed. "Is there nothing new you have to report?"

"My sources tell me the humans are getting ready to evacuate their embassy here. They will pull everyone out and expel our diplomats on Earth."

"A move that would precipitate them withdrawing from the Cooperative," Seeladas hissed, showing more emotion than she had in months. "When did you learn of this?"

"Only this morning, Madam Premier," Zuchari said carefully.

"Have your people observed the Eshquarians meeting with dignitaries on Earth?"

"Nothing beyond the contract negotiations for four new classes of cruisers we already approved."

"Still...something is off about this. A joint operation between their two fleets is something we should actively discourage right now."

"I...am not a political adviser, Madam Premier, but given Chief of Staff Glecsh's suspected involvement in the trafficking rings perhaps it would be indelicate for us to insist that—"

"What else?"

"Earth's Navy is mustering into four taskforces. We assume they're to be deployed into Saabror space if their scouts find more captive humans."

"I don't have to tell you how important it is that we find Kobvir first, do I?" Seeladas asked. "If the humans or the Eshquarians get a hold of him first and make him talk..."

"Madam Premier, is there something I should know about these trafficking operations?" Zuchari asked pointedly. "I can't do my job properly without having all the information I need at hand."

"Just find Kobvir. Whatever it takes."

"Of course, ma'am." Zuchari recognized a dismissal when he heard one, so he rose smoothly and bowed before walking out of the office.

Once out of the office, he collected his aide and left the executive suite as quickly as he could. They walked in silence until they were safely within the confines of his air shuttle and heading back to the Ministry of Intelligence.

"She's cracking," he said after a moment. "Losing touch with reality."

"She has pulled ruses like this before to flush out traitors in her inner circle," the aide argued.

"This isn't that. She's been prone to obsession lately and has been erratic to the point of her staff needing to keep her isolated. They're trying to keep her from interacting too much with her own government."

"To what end?"

"I'm not certain. I caught a hint that she might know more about what Kobvir Glecsh has been up to than she has let on. There seems to be a genuine panic that the humans will find him first."

"Maybe they already did. They are preparing to abandon their embassy, after all. Maybe those taskforces on the edge of their space aren't going into Saabror space after all."

"I thought of this as well," Zuchari said. "The unfortunate reality is that while they may not fully realize it, the Terran military would wipe us out in short order. They have a real knack for violence and have built warships that are second to none."

"Might be a good time to have the family visit family off Syllitr for a while," the aide said as the shuttle flared and began its final approach.

"Probably not a bad idea," Zuchari said. "I assume you have an exit plan of your own?"

"Place on Aracoria."

"Not bad."

"You, sir?"

"I have a few options," Zuchari said.

The truth was that his family had been off Syllitr for nearly a year already. As soon as he found out Cridal military units had clashed with Terran special forces involving the theft of an ultra-secret human asset, he knew the alliance was crumbling. He had taken his time and moved them around using falsified identities and private transports to put them on a new world that was well outside Seeladas Dalton's grasp. Now, he just had to make sure he could get himself away as well.

The fact they were so openly discussing the pending collapse of the Cooperative didn't even seem all that unusual these days.

The ConFed was gone.

The Cridal Cooperative was collapsing.

Something huge was happening within the Saabror Protectorate.

All the old nations, some of which had stood for over ten thou-sand years, were either imploding or forced to restructure like the Eshquarians. It was all happening within an improbably small window of time which made Zuchari skeptical that this was all just coincidence. His instincts were screaming that there was an external force tearing down all the old castles...but what could do that and make it look like a collection of unrelated, random events?

More pressing, however, was the complete chaos they were in for when all the worlds that had lived under the umbrella of these larger nations for hundreds or even thousands of years began to realize they were on their own. No more protection from the mighty ConFed battlefleet. No more trade treaties. Regional wars would erupt, and everyone would be scrambling to make powerful allies as quickly as they could.

He looked over at his aide, who was obviously proud of his hold-ings on Aracoria and just shook his head. High profile, high value worlds like Aracoria with her extensive shipyards would be the worst place to hunker down to stay safe and anonymous. The trick was to find a place that offered nothing so valuable someone would be willing to take on a planetary defense system to get to it.

"Yeah," he said. "Aracoria is definitely nice."

27

"I'm sorry...but Klytos Finvak isn't appearing anywhere."

"That's impossible," Murph said. "I thought you said you were the best."

"I am the best! At least the best on this station," Jatto said. "I'm telling you, this person is not here."

"Son of a bitch!" Jacob groaned. "This was our best shot at getting this guy."

"It makes sense he wouldn't use his real name, doesn't it?" MG asked.

"I even went outside of Di-Shyosi," Jatto said. "Under the parameters you gave me, I can't find any evidence he ever existed."

Well, why don't you—"

"Cap, your terminal," Mettler said, pointing at the light on the device flashing green indicating an incoming slip-com channel request on the *Corsair*."

"To be continued." Jacob pointed at Jatto and walked into the other office and closed the door. He accepted the channel request and sat down at the desk, blinking at who he saw on the other end of the channel. "Similan?"

"You're my father's source," Jacob guessed.

"I was asked if I might pass on some intel we had regarding a former asset of ours," Similan said. "I'm surprised you didn't contact us directly."

"Propriety," Jacob said. "I appreciate the help and kindness you and your boss have shown us, but I don't want to abuse the relationship and treat it like an open door for whenever I get myself into a bind."

"This answer impresses me," Similan said.

"How's Minister Amon?"

"He is well. He will appreciate that you asked."

"I guess you got the rundown on our problem already?"

"Yes, and I think I can provide you with the nudge you need," Similan said. "You are searching for Klytos Finvak, are you not?"

"Unsuccessfully...but, yes," Jacob said. "Our intel shows he was a colonel in the Saabror Free Army and that he had operated out of Di-Shyosi, but we're slamming into a wall."

"Intelligence sources can become...hazy. Cross-contaminated," Similan said, leaning back and steepling his fingers. "It is important when you are compiling your data and pulling from different sources to not assume all those sources will have the same degree of accuracy."

"Okay. I'm with you," Jacob said. "Our intel came from both the NIS and the Zadra Network."

"Neither of which have deep roots into Saabror space," Similan pointed out.

"Fair enough."

"Okay, young Captain...lecture over," Similan said, actually smiling ever so slightly. "Klytos Finvak was an alias for the operative you're tracking down, but that was his alias within *Eshquarian* space. When he was with the Free Army he was known as Colonel Axi Sigato."

"You mean we're stuck because we're tracking the wrong name?" Jacob could only laugh. "Holy shit."

"I'm transmitting you the relevant intel I can share on Axi Sigato and his misadventures in Saabror space," Similan said.

"I can't thank you enough, Similan," Jacob said. "I know it's highly unlikely, but I hope one day that I can return the favor for all the help you and Minister Amon have sent our way."

"Good luck in your hunt, Jacob Brown," Similan nodded his head in what was almost a bow. "I hope to see you in person again soon."

"Likewise, my friend," Jacob said. "Thanks again."

The files Similan sent were short, redacted, but loaded with usable intel. He took a quick read through what Axi Sigato had been up to before he'd broken contact with his handler and went rogue. The parallels between Sigato and Elton Hollick, a rogue human intelligence asset, jumped out at him right away. "Better keep an eye on Murph," he muttered as he scanned the rest of the info.

"Something useful, I hope?" Mettler asked when Jacob walked back into the main common area.

"The target goes by the name Axi Sigato," Jacob said. "That's what he was known by in the Free Army, so there should be official record of him there at least."

"I can just plug it in and go with what I have," Jatto said. "You have the Jenovian Standard spelling?"

"Here," Jacob let him see the tablet he was holding with the name highlighted with the unique spellings for regional languages.

"Standby...this won't take long."

The Veran's eyes fluttered as he dove deep into his nexus connection. Jacob watched the monitors as the data scrolled across at blinding speed. No matter how much he was exposed to the species, their capabilities always left him awestruck.

"We should be ready to move," Jacob said. "Everybody, suit up."

While his team got their gear together, Jacob alerted Sully, still aboard the *Corsair*, that the operation would be going hot soon and to have the ship ready to move. Moving armed aboard Di-Shyosi wasn't as difficult as Pinnacle Station, but Jatto had still suggested some discretion. They would wear a thin, tearaway garment over their tactical gear similar to an Arab thobe. It was something that wouldn't attract a lot of attention and could easily conceal their equipment if it was rigged carefully to not present an oddly shaped profile.

"Your target is very clever, Mr. Brown," Jatto said. "But I'm better. He's hidden his identity behind layers of security, but I found him. He's here."

"Wait, what?" Jacob asked. "Sigato is here?"

"That's who you're looking for…right?" Jatto looked confused.

"We're looking for any holdings he has here on the station," Murph said. "Specifically, any residential or operational spaces. It's extremely unlikely he's here."

"Ah, I see the confusion, Jatto said. "What I'm saying is that his digital passkey has been used as recently as an hour ago. It's possible to have a passkey not bio-coded, meaning it can be given to someone else to use and that person would gain all rights and access that you yourself would have aboard the station."

"What's our passkey been doing?" Jacob asked.

"There have been three trips out of a secure area near the Vadron District to a private hangar that's operated by the Free Army…or at least used to be. Now, it's controlled by the gang that took over this territory. Anyway, that's where it's been."

"Did Sigato have anything in that area?" Murph asked.

"It's listed as storage," Jatto said. "He has four different places in that area, but it doesn't look like any of them have been accessed in over a year using this passkey."

"A hangar indicates our buddy might be getting ready to make a run for it," MG said. "We should probably come up with some sort of plan."

"Pulling data on layout and security measures now," Jatto said. "Most of this stuff is heavily restricted. These quasi-governmental military types show up, buy entire sections of the station, and then rebuild it to purpose. Whatever I find is likely to be horribly out of date."

"A word," Murph said to Jacob, nodding to the other office.

"What's on your mind?" Jacob asked once they were out of earshot.

"Even if our little friend out there gets us the most current schematics of the security layout, you realize a frontal assault is out, right?"

"I'd never even considered that approach. What did you have in mind?"

"I'm not sure," Murph admitted. "Should probably bring Tin Man in on the planning session here."

"He's probably listening right now," Jacob said. "Come on in, Tin Man."

A moment later, the battlesynth walked into the room, not at all looking embarrassed at having been caught listening.

"Eavesdropping is a disgusting habit, you know that?" Murph asked.

"It is not my fault my hearing is acute and you speak loudly enough to be heard three rooms away," Tin Man said. "I believe you both are correct that a frontal assault on the security chokepoints is not advisable. Probably suicidal, to be honest."

"Alternative?"

"These stations tolerate modification of spaces up to a certain point, but there are always vulnerabilities. The decks directly above and below will still just be standard decking, for example."

"Cutting through is hardly practical," Jacob said. "They'll have sealed up any access panels."

"There are other ways," Tin Man insisted. "But we will need to take Jatto with us to provide a service interruption or two on critical systems. He will not be able to do more than a short-interval outage, but it should be enough."

"What've you got in mind?" Jacob asked.

"We're almost done moving everything, Kobvir. You're certain the big boss said this was okay?"

"He gave me full access," Kobvir Glecsh said. "We're restructuring our organization and moving assets around."

For the last three days, Kobvir had been moving all of Klytos Finvak's hard wealth, mostly certified precious metals encoded currency chits backed by the Eshquarian Empire. He was having it all transferred into a medium-duty freighter that Finvak had at the station along with an impressive haul of rare art and a case of blackmail material on various officials throughout the quadrant.

He figured Klytos would never breathe free air again—the Eshquarians would see to that—so there was no point in the ex-operative's massive hoard sitting and going to waste. Or at least until his employees finally got bored and began cracking cases open to help themselves. Klytos had given Kobvir the hard-coded passkey as an emergency failsafe.

What Klytos likely hadn't realized was that the passkey would give Kobvir access to his private quarters and all the credentials he would need to open the vaults containing his personal fortune. Now, it was his. He would need it if he was to get away and survive, for he had no doubt Seeladas would send everything she had after him soon.

"That's the last from vaults two and three," the worker told him as the generic, black transit crates were hauled up into the freighter. "We'll let the loadmasters arrange the cargo, and then we'll be ready for vaults one, four, and five. You should be ready to go by early tomorrow."

"Excellent. Please, have the ship provisioned and fueled for an extended duration flight," Kobvir said. "You'll be rewarded for your discretion, of course."

"It is a pleasure to serve," the worker said, bowing before walking off to supervise his people aboard the freighter as they arranged the rows of crates.

"We killing them all before we leave?" a harsh voice asked from behind him. He turned and was looking into the black, faceless visor of a Red Strike helmet. He had a team loyal to him personally along as his private security, although their loyalty was contingent on being paid so it would be more accurate to call them mercenaries.

"Too memorable," Kobvir said. "We will pay them and leave. Eventually, they'll wander off and someone will reclaim this space, nobody remembering we were ever here."

"Suit yourself," the voice growled.

As the ex-Red Strike merc walked away, Kobvir realized they were also a threat. It was one thing to pay them, it was another to ask them aboard a ship full of untraceable treasure and expect them not to just kill him and toss his corpse out of the airlock.

"This is getting complicated," he grumbled as he walked off to make further arrangements to guarantee his safety.

28

"I'm becoming uncomfortable with the amount of explosives you're bringing with you."

"Why?" MG asked.

"Because you probably plan on using them, and I live here," Jatto said. "You'll fly off, and then I'll be stuck in an ISC detention center answering questions about who you were and what you were doing."

"We're just preparing for all contingencies," Jacob said. "If all goes to plan, we'll be gone before anyone knows it. Let's get the gear packed up and back on the *Corsair*. I want Tin Man and Murph on sanitation duty. No trace left behind that can link any of this to home. Let's move!"

All of their mobile systems were modular and quickly broken down into wheeled cases, so Jacob and MG were able to get it all packed up and out of the suite by themselves, leaving Mettler to help Jatto pack his own gear up while the other two cleaned. They made certain they weren't being observed, and then rolled the transit crates through the automated security checks of the docking arm complex and up to where the *Corsair* hung suspended in space with a bright red, flexible cofferdam attached to her portside airlock.

"How much longer you think this team will be together, Cap?" MG asked.

"Why? You wanting out of here?" Jacob asked.

"Not me. I love this shit, but I have a feeling Sully will promote out of being our pilot soon and Murph will probably be tapped for something that better uses his brain," MG said. "Tin Man won't stick around much longer after Murph leaves I don't think. We've had a hell of a run, though."

"You're acting like this is our last mission," Jacob said.

"I know we've got a few more good ones left before the team starts to split up," MG said. "Just thinking back on how far we've come since you came aboard."

Jacob didn't say anything more as they lugged the cases up the shallow ramp. What MG was saying was true. Units like Scout Teams didn't stick together for a long time. People died, people quit, people gained so much knowledge and experience they were too valuable to use in the field anymore.

Two members of Obsidian were on loan from other services anyway. NIS could call Murph back at any time they wanted and Tin Man was there under his own volition. He could very well decide he was bored slumming with humans and head back to rejoin his cohort. It was quite the depressing line of thought to be honest.

"This is all that's coming back?" Sully asked as he looked at the two crates.

"We packed light," Jacob said. "You want it in the cargo bay?"

"I'll take it," Sully waved him off. "You guys go. By the time you leave the suite, I'll have this stuff locked down, and she'll be ready to go."

"You're okay doing this solo? I can send Mettler up to help."

"I'll be fine. You'll need every person you have. I got the upload from Jatto, so I know exactly where I'm going. Good luck."

"You, too," Jacob said. The hatch of the *Corsair* closed with a *boom* and a series of loud *thunks* as the main locks engaged.

"Party time," MG said, rubbing his hands together.

———

"Broodmate of Jason Burke!"

"What the fuck," Jacob sighed, recognizing the voice. He turned and, sure enough, saw one of the Taukkir that had attacked him earlier approaching quickly.

The team had finished clearing out of the suite and was moving through the lower levels of Galleria Adonti heading toward the rapid transit system when the shout came. They'd been trying to keep a low profile, moving in pairs randomly through the public spaces at random intervals. Now, people were stopping to look as the Taukkir continued to shout and wave his arms.

"What can I do for you?" Jacob asked, struggling to maintain control of his temper.

"This is fortuitous we have run into each other as I was just about to begin searching for you and your powerful friend," the Taukkir said, gesturing to Tin Man. "I have discovered a way I might make amends for attacking you earlier."

"I assure you it's not necessary—"

"I insist! Trust me, this will be the easiest money you have ever made. We simply need to ambush and kill a team of Cridal mercs."

"Cridal?" Jacob asked. "You're certain?"

"Quite. The one who hired us was Syllitr himself and claims he is being hunted by a crew from his home planet. He's paying in four thousand units of refined gold."

Jacob almost choked on that. Doing the math in his head, that was nearly two-hundred and fifty kilos worth over eighteen million credits in most exchanges.

"Does he want you to kill an entire battalion?" Jacob asked.

"He assured us it would only be ten individuals."

"Red Strike team," Tin Man said quietly in English. "Likely his security detail."

"Tying up loose ends," Jacob agreed before switching back to Jenovian Standard. "How many do you have?"

"Counting you two? Four."

"Oh, dear Christ..." Jason pinched the bridge of his nose. "Is your partner around?"

"Yes."

"Please, retrieve him. You'll have five minutes to convince us to join. What are your names?"

"I am Syzo, my partner is Sath. Our mother was—"

"Just you two, that's enough," Jacob cut him off. "Go grab him. Remember...five minutes."

"Calling an audible?" Tin Man asked, using one of the human idioms he had taken a liking to.

"Maybe," Jacob said, keying in the team channel. "Everybody, hold up and loiter. We might be changing plans. Don't clump up or acknowledge each other."

It was only a few minutes before Syzo and Sath came back, both in a much more gracious mood toward a *Burke Broodmate* now that there was a huge pile of money on the table.

"Who hired you to do this job?" Tin Man asked, cutting off any time-wasting pleasantries.

"Contract was anonymous, but our point of contact is some stuffy-looking Cridal," Syzo said. "It was brokered through the Vizan Guild. They control all the hit contracts and merc hirings out of Bann Promenade, so this is all legitimate."

"You talked directly with this Cridal?" Jacob asked.

"We did. It's required by guild law. He was there when the contract was offered. We have another six hours to confirm we'd take it, or it will go back to open status. That's why we were looking for you," Sath said. Jacob thumbed through his com unit until he found what he was looking for.

"Was this him?" Jacob said, holding the screen toward the Taukkir.

"That's him. Who is he?" Syzo asked.

"Someone I want to have a chat with," Jacob said. "Okay, here's the deal. We'll join you. We'll let you keep all the pay, we just want to talk to this particular Cridal."

"You might not get that chance. Payment has already been given to the guild to hold in third party escrow. We fulfill the contract, we get paid. We won't see this one again," Syzo said, sounding distressed.

"Leave that to me," Jacob said. "We'll help you take these guys out, you take all the pay, and we do our thing alone so you're not in violation of guild laws."

The pair looked overcome by emotion as they whispered to each other in a language Jacob's implant was having difficulty translating. Tin Man took the opportunity to do the same, talking to him in English again.

"Why let them keep all the pay? That will seem suspicious."

"I need a quick, knee-jerk, emotional answer," Jacob answered. "Kobvir is almost gone. We still need to hit this Red Strike team and hope they have something on them that will give us direct access to him."

"Your offer is beyond generous," Syzo said, interrupting whatever Tin Man had been about to say. "You are a man of quality and breeding. We accept this proposal, and please tell Jason Burke we consider the matter between he and our family now closed. With this money, we will afford passage to Taukk and return as proud warriors again."

"Then, we all are getting what we want." Jacob smiled. "Go gear up. Meet here in..."

"Thirty minutes?"

"Perfect."

"This is hardly a lock," Mettler argued. "Ten Red Strike operatives aren't going to just roll over for us."

"Yeah, they put a pretty good beating on us when we were looking for that steel chicken," MG said.

"We still won, though," Jacob argued. "Look, we need a way in. This could be it."

"What do you need me for?" Jatto asked. "I'm not a soldier."

"We'll pay you to just stay on standby well out of harm's way," Jacob said. "We may still have to go back to Plan A, which I was never in love with to be honest, and you're key to that. Don't worry, though...no shooting or running for you."

"Appreciate it."

"Here they come," Murph said.

The Taukkir had abandoned subtlety and were in full armor, both carrying heavy plasma rifles. There was a confident strut to their walk that hadn't been there before, and Jacob wondered if this pair had been exiled to Di-Shyosi after the Pinnacle Station debacle and were forced to earn their way back into the family.

"There are more of you," Syzo said suspiciously.

"The rest of my team," Jacob explained. "Our deal remains the same."

"Acceptable," Syzo said. "We have confirmed the contract with the guild and have received our target intel package from the Cridal who hired us."

"Don't keep us in suspense...where are they going to be?" Jacob asked.

"There is a storage complex near the public hangars in the Bann Major district," Sath said. "We will set our ambush up there. The team will be wearing black armor and is going to be going to a specific unit within the next five hours to retrieve something. We will hit them hard and fast and be gone before security can mount a response."

"Simple and clean given we've never worked together before," Jacob said. "Let's go."

"Do you wish to gather your weapons and equipment?" Syzo asked.

"Already have it with us," Jacob said, patting his chest so his combat harness rattled beneath the billowing robe. "This is just a little concealment before we get into the area of operation."

"Ah!" the Taukkir said at once, as if the concept had never occurred to them.

"You guys don't do a lot of covert type missions, do you?" MG asked.

"It is not our specialty," Sath admitted.

The mismatched group, now led by a pair of Taukkir, made their way to the rapid transit terminal while Jatto discreetly peeled off on his own and disappeared into the crowd. Jacob caught him out of the corner of his eye and could only shake his head. For being such unusual-looking little creatures, Verans had the ability to disappear at will and thrive in some of the most dangerous places in the galaxy.

He remembered how tough and ready Weef Zadra was. She lived alone on Niceen-3 of all Godforsaken places, and nobody dared touch her. Kage, a Veran he knew better than he wished to, had escaped from at least four maximum security prisons they knew of and had cons actively running across the entire quadrant.

"You know what to do if this is a double-cross," Jacob said quietly to Tin Man.

"I will handle it," Tin Man said, never taking his eyes off the Taukkir.

29

"What is this thing the little shit can't live without now?"

"Who cares?" Hen Kiatheu said. "Just grab it, give it to him, and we're one step closer to ending this job."

Hen was the squad leader of Kobvir Glecsh's personal security detail. They'd been doing the little twerp's dirty deeds for so long he almost didn't remember when they'd been Red Strike, members of the most elite special operations units in the Cridal military. They'd balked when High Command had permanently assigned them to the chief of staff's office, but once they saw how dirty Kobvir was, they saw an opportunity for themselves.

By the third time the team had been used as Kobvir's personal hit squad, Hen had approached the bureaucrat and told him they wanted in. They'd fought on dozens of planets to protect his corrupt schemes with the promise of profit sharing, but now they were looking at the endgame. They were well-aware of what had been loaded up on the freighter they were taking out of Saabror space: enough money to set them all up for twenty lifetimes of complete luxury on whatever planet they wanted.

Why take a sliver of a percentage when you could have the whole thing? All they had to do was wait until they were underway, and then shove Kobvir Glecsh out of an airlock. When he'd approached his team about the idea, they were beyond enthusiastic.

"Why did we all come?" one of the troopers asked.

"This gives us a chance to go over the final planning without being overheard by any of the staff in Finvak's operation," Hen said, pausing before a locked door in the storage complex. "I don't want any mistakes on this. If he just disappears, we can disappear. If he's found, they'll come for us."

He exchanged a look with his two mates standing at the back of the group. In truth, Hen had no intention of splitting that treasure ship ten ways. Not because he didn't think it would be enough, but because he didn't trust most of his team to not grow a conscience and go crawling back to Syllitr begging forgiveness and selling the rest out. He singled out two he knew he could trust no matter what and sold them on the idea that they only needed three for a clean getaway.

"Damn, this lock is jammed up with something," he said, giving the go-code phrase. "Uupe, take a look at this."

He backed away to let their most tech-savvy operator move up. As expected, the others kept their attention on him rather than the three members of their team who had backed away and drawn their weapons.

"I don't—" Uupe never finished his sentence as the three opened fire, mowing down their comrades. It was a short, ugly bit of business. At such close range, the Red Strike armor couldn't withstand the concentrated plasma fire for very long. One managed to get his weapon up but never got a shot off before he went down.

"Sorry, my friends," Hen said when it was over. "But I have no intention of spending the rest of my life inside one of Seeladas's prisons. I'll get the door open. Let's get them inside, and then we can hit them with the decomp inhibitor and be on our way."

Han was full of regret and shame as he worked the lock and let the door to the storage unit rise. He was so preoccupied with his feelings that he almost didn't notice the two glowing red eyes waiting for him on the other side. He couldn't be sure he uttered any warning to his compatriots before an armored fist smashed into his face, turning everything black.

"Damn, we're good," Jacob said, looking around.

"Yeah, this job is a lot easier when they kill each other first," MG said. "Downright courteous of them."

"Is the leader still alive?" Jacob asked.

"He is," Tin Man said, standing over the other two he'd killed. Mettler and Murph were dragging the bodies into the storage unit while the Taukkir stood watch.

Jacob knelt and pulled the helmet off the Cridal, wincing at how damaged his face was from the brutal hit Tin Man had delivered. He turned the helmet over and saw it hadn't been secured for combat like it should have been. Overconfidence and complacency had teamed up to deliver him a shattered jaw and crushed right eye socket.

"Mettler! Wake him up."

"MG, take over here so I can— Ugh!"

Jacob snapped his head over and saw that one of the Taukkir had stabbed Mettler in the side while his partner was lining up with his weapon on MG. Before he could react, Tin Man raised his arm and fired, blowing the head clean off the one attacking Mettler. This distracted the other one just long enough for MG to react.

"No!" Sath screamed as Syzo's headless body sank to the deck. "No!"

MG wasted no time and pulled his own blade, closing the distance and ramming it home between the joints in the torso armor and twisting. Sath screamed, and his legs gave out, so MG let go of the handle and backed away, raising his weapon.

Murph rushed to Mettler's side and began taking readings from his neural link to assess the injury. Jacob walked over to Sath, kicking him over onto his back.

"What the fuck was that?!"

"We...we had orders. From home," Sath wheezed. "Our Brood Sire wanted you...alive."

"Me? Why?"

"R-r-revenge. On...your father."

Jacob leaned down into his face, staring into his eyes.

"That was a mistake," he whispered. "Attacking my friend? Worse mistake. How did you know he was my father?"

"The...the brood...the brood kept—" Sath's eyes rolled back, and he let out a last, raspy breath before going limp.

"Murph?" Jacob asked.

"It's bad, but his armor has stabilized him. He needs to get back to the *Corsair* ASAP, though," Murph said.

Jacob looked around the large storage unit and saw a trio of powered carts used for moving cargo to and from the hangar area nearby. He pointed at one of them, and Murph nodded, walking to grab it so they could load Mettler up onto it.

"Wake our survivor up," Jacob told Tin Man, pulling his knife. "Still need to get the hangar access."

"He is awake already," Tin Man said, stepping between Jacob and the injured Cridal. "Perhaps I should handle this."

"Excuse me?" Jacob demanded.

"You are emotionally compromised, and I feel a more practical solution is in our best interests."

"Whatever," Jacob said after a beat. "Just get what we need."

Tin Man knelt in front of the surviving Red Strike member, looking him over without speaking for a moment.

"There is no point in you dying here today," he said. "We are after your boss, whom you were about to betray anyway. Give us access to Finvak's sanctum, and we will leave you. Alive. You will be medically treated by the people here, and you are free to take whatever you wish after we leave. We will not pursue you."

"Ughhh," the Cridal rasped, pointing to his left hip pocket. Jacob could see the cold rage and calculating in the remaining eye. Tin Man reached into the pocket and fished out a small, black device and tossed it to Jacob.

"Encrypted passkey," Jacob said, turning it over in his hands. "Rolling codes that change every time it's used so it can't have its signal intercepted and copied."

"I'm ready," Murph said. "I can take him by myself. You guys get to that hangar."

Jacob walked over and looked Mettler over. His medic was unconscious with a look of intense pain etched on his features. Seeing him like that made Jacob's blood boil again, and he wished he could kill the Taukkir all over again.

"Be careful," he told Murph before keying the hyperlink channel to the *Corsair*. "Sully, we have one wounded coming back with Murph. Hold fast until you have them aboard."

"Copy," Sully said. "Holding fast."

Murph nodded and partially closed the lid on the cart before wheeling Mettler out of the area. Jacob looked around and saw the area had been policed and, thus far, nobody seemed to be paying them any close attention. The fight had been quick and brutal but contained. It also helped that security in the area was notoriously, almost institutionally, lax so that the smugglers had an easier time of it.

With one last middle finger to the wounded Cridal, who was lying on the ground and breathing shallowly, Jacob pulled the door closed just enough to leave a noticeable gap. Someone would be along to find him and, by then, they'd either be long gone or dead.

"Jake, incoming signal from the big boss," Sully said over a private channel to Jacob. "Patching it through now."

"Captain Brown," Admiral Webb said. "The political situation is deteriorating rapidly. How close are you?"

"We're close, sir," Jacob said carefully, trying to make sure Webb could maintain plausible deniability.

"Better give me the rundown."

Kobvir wasn't prone to panic, but the longer he went without hearing back from the two Taukkir brothers that had taken his contract, the more he approached a truly panicked state. The pair had convinced him they'd dealt with elite soldiers before and that they could put together a team that would easily overwhelm the Red Strike operators, but they were long overdue to report in and claim payment and provide proof of death.

Hen Kiatheu had been hand-picked to lead his personal security detail for a reason. He was ruthless to the point of almost being a sadist as well as cunning and utterly fearless. Perhaps he'd been foolish to think the local thugs on some backwater station would be able to handle them at all.

Back when Seeladas Dalton had reluctantly authorized him to pull personnel from the military, he'd actually been warned that Hen would likely be ill-suited to the task of personal protection and better used for direct kinetic action instead. Kobvir chose to ignore them, and then, once he'd revealed to Hen just how lucrative his side operations could be, the pair had developed a strong working relationship.

But Kobvir wasn't stupid. He knew Hen would eventually try to supplant him. It had been a delicate balance giving Hen enough to do his job but not divulge so much that he made himself redundant. Men like Klytos Finvak didn't care who they dealt with, just that they were getting paid. The sound of footsteps jostled him from his thoughts, and he looked in time to see one of Finvak's local administrators approaching.

"Sir, reports are coming in over nexus about a security action in the storage complex near the hangars."

"And?" Kobvir asked, his breath catching in his throat.

"They report a team of black-clad soldiers all dead, as well as two Taukkir outside of a storage unit that was left open. There wasn't anything inside of importance, was there?"

"Of course not," Kobvir said. "It can't even be traced back to us. So, all the Red Strike troopers were dead?"

"The initial reports specify no survivors."

"This is...excellent news. Thank you." Kobvir smiled, feeling the tension flow from his body.

"Will you need further assistance?" The question was pointed.

"I will not. Please, collect your payment with my thanks and be on your way."

"You think you'll ever see Finvak again?"

"Highly doubtful."

"The miserable excrement was Eshquarian the entire time," the administrator snorted in disgust before walking away. He paused and turned back.

It hadn't been hard to get the full cooperation of Klytos Finvak's—*Axi Sigato's*—former staff aboard Di-Shyosi. All he'd had to do was reveal to them that he had been given permission to be there, and then let it slip that Sigato had actually been a high-placed Eshquarian intelligence operative the entire time along with presenting them the evidence he'd brought with him.

They'd been enraged. Most walked off immediately, a few had been a bit more pragmatic and had agreed to help Kobvir in exchange for a healthy severance package. Fortunately for him, none of the permanent staff in Finvak's hideout knew what had been stored in the vaults. They'd been loyal out of fear as their employer had a reputation for brutality and a short temper.

Once he was alone, he closed and locked the door to the spacious office and fired up the slip-com terminal he'd brought with him from Syllitr. It was one of the newest models, and it still felt and looked like an antique compared to the new hyperlink units the humans were flashing as they walked around on his homeworld.

They were stingy with their new tech so access to the amazing superluminal com network had become a status symbol for connected Syllitr that were lucky enough to be offered access. Kobvir had not been one of them.

The system hummed as the slip-space field built in the antenna chamber and Kobvir took a moment to reflect on why he'd agreed to the trafficking operation to begin with. It had been lucrative, certainly. But so had all his other side ventures he'd pursued selling access to his office.

He'd had high hopes for a partnership with a human named Margaret Jansen, but she was too aggressive and reckless and ended up getting herself killed and her entire network purged from the human government. His new partners on Earth were certainly more controlled but perhaps overly cautious.

Kobvir didn't like humans. At all. He'd despised the one that Crisstof Dalton had entertained himself with mentoring for years only to have the ungrateful bastard get him killed in the Avarian Empire. He'd never forgiven Jason Burke for the death of Crisstof, and he admitted that had poisoned his feelings toward the species, so much so that he took a perverse pleasure in having used a few hundred thousand of them to fill his contract quotas.

"Is this important?" a voice said as the slip-com node connected and there was actually someone on the other end of the channel.

"I didn't expect you to answer," Kobvir said.

"So, that's why you called me? Because you didn't think I'd answer?"

"You've become less pleasant over the years, Carolyn...and that's saying a lot."

"I'm killing this channel."

"Wait! Okay, calm down," Kobvir said. "You're still on Syllitr?"

"Obviously."

Kobvir steadied his nerves for what he was about to do. There would be no coming back from this, and it would be the ultimate betrayal of Crisstof Dalton's memory. Was his miserable life worth that?

"You're a go," he finally said, answering his own question. "Do it. Soon."

"Consider it done...just as soon as the remainder of the payment hits my account," the Viper said.

"I will initiate the transfer, although I feel your fee this time is...exorbitant."

"Killing a head of state is never cheap, my dear," she said. "You want to play in the big leagues, you need to cough up the big bucks."

"I never know what the hell you're saying," Kobvir grumbled as he executed a pre-programmed funds transfer from his accounts on Miressa Prime to the Viper. The assassin was idiosyncratic, almost unstable, but she got results, and that's what Kobvir needed right now. "Transfers initiated."

"Good. I'll check in an hour, and then I'll get to work," the woman known as the Viper said, sounding pleased. "You want this subtle or dramatic? You paid enough, I'll give it to you either way."

"Just do it," Kobvir ground out, hoping she didn't survive the mission.

"Within the next two days, Seeladas Dalton will be dead," Carolyn said. "Now, what about the contract on Kellea Colleran?"

Kobvir had forgotten all about that. He'd put deposits down with the Viper on both Seeladas and Kellea but for different reasons and at different times. He'd put a hold on both but was now activating the Dalton contract to save his own skin. Was there in point in killing Kellea? Other than he'd never much liked her and thought the Dalton family had given her far too much trust and power, but what would be the practical reason for killing her?

"Cancel the Colleran hit," he said finally. Kellea was a highly placed officer within the Eshquarian Imperial Navy and killing her in a way that could lead to him would be reckless. He might dodge the Cridal, but the Eshquarians would hunt him down and make an example of him. "And, yes...I know the deposit is non-refundable."

"Pleasure doing business with you. I always have had a strong level of respect for your money," she said, killing the channel.

"I hate that woman," Kobvir said, shutting down his terminal.

He checked the time and saw he had less than five hours before the flight crew for the ship showed up, and he would start his new life as a new person.

"Nothing to do now but relax and wait," he said, leaning back with his eyes closed and forcing himself to think about anything except for the fact he had just taken a contract out on the head of someone he swore to protect.

30

"Captain, we have Mettler strapped down in the infirmary and the machines are doing their thing. Prognosis is ninety-seven percent for a full recovery."

"Thanks, Murph," Jacob said. "Sully, you ready?"

"Engines are up and hot," Sully said. "Calling for decouple now. You're clear to start."

"We're a go," Jacob said aloud for the benefit of the team members not tied into the hyperlink net.

"Why am I here again?" Jatto asked.

"We needed you to find the super-secret backdoor," MG said.

"I could have done that over a com call."

"We like your company," Jacob said. "Also, we need you to make sure no alarms trigger when we use this passkey."

"Yeah...let me do that," Jatto said, pulling out an interface box and digging into the panel MG and Tin Man had already opened.

They were crouched down in a dim, narrow corridor that looked to be nothing more than a maintenance access for some machinery down near where the row of private hangars started. Rather than

march up to the main entrance, which was inside a secondary security barricade, Jacob had reached out to Jatto about finding another
way into where they assumed Kobvir was hiding.

The engineering prints that had been filed with the district's head
office weren't easy to get a hold of and had cost the Obsidian crew a
healthy amount of bribe cash, but they showed there was a hidden
entry way into Finvak's private hangar that was far more accessible
than fighting through two layers of heavily armed station troopers.

"There was a single proximity sensor on the door itself that is
discreetly wired to somewhere inside the complex, but there's
nothing tied into the main security systems," Jatto said. "They're
counting on controlled access it looks like. The door is heavily
armored, and that rolling encryption lock is not something even I
could easily slice into."

"So, we're clear?" Jacob asked.

"Clear," Jatto said. "Good luck."

"Thanks," Jacob said, pressing the key to the black square pad on
the wall near the door.

At first, nothing happened, so Jacob kept the device pressed
against the pad and waited. It was a long few seconds before a short
trilling tone sounded from the panel and the door shook with
heavy thumps as the locks disengaged. Apparently, Finvak really
didn't want any uninvited guests. The final lock gave way with a
reluctant *clunk*, and Jacob raised his weapon as he pushed the door
open with his boot. He really had to lean into it as it was a heavy
bastard.

The room beyond was dimly lit. It was also occupied.

"Is that Atemo?" a voice slurred. "We're not supposed to ever open
that door. Close it before the alarm goes off."

Jacob stepped all the way in and, through his helmet's optics, saw
three aliens sprawled around the room and discarded orbs strewn
around them.

"Buzzballs," MG said, kicking one as he walked in.

"No," Jacob said, watching them try unsuccessfully to stand and
get away from the terrifying armored beings walking among them.

"These idiots are on something else. They must have just re-used the vaporizers. You and Tin Man secure the corridor, I'll handle them."

"Don't kill us," one of them said to Jacob. "We're sorry."

"For what?" Jacob asked, his modulated voice making them flinch.

"For...whatever we did. To you?"

"Damn...you morons are too fucked up to give me anything useful, aren't you?" Jacob muttered. "How many people are left in this complex?"

"What? Oh...lots? Maybe. Or maybe they left?"

"Whatever, doesn't matter," Jacob said, pulling out three sets of restraints. He quickly zipped their arms behind their backs and dragged them into the corner before kicking all the spent buzzball vaporizers near them to clear the floor. He pushed the door closed and latched it before disabling the lock so nobody could come in behind them unannounced.

"Cap, we've got an issue up here," MG said.

"On my way," Jacob said, moving up quickly and quietly.

Tin Man and MG were crouched in the shadows and looking out through an open door into the hangar beyond. Jacob quickly spotted Kobvir Glecsh standing near the ramp of a light-duty freighter. He had his hands up, and his eyes were wide and full of fear.

"Three dead aliens near the ship," MG said. "All wearing the same uniform, probably the flight crew."

"Who is attacking?" Jacob asked. "I can't get a better angle with the door partially closed."

"I dunno," MG said. "But they sound pissed."

Jacob moved up closer, risking being spotted so he could see what the hell was going on. He also boosted the audio gain on his helmet's sensors.

"...think we're stupid?! We know what's on that ship!"

"We had a deal!" Kobvir said, trying to project strength. "You've been paid for the work you did."

"This isn't a negotiation. We're taking this ship and everything you stole out of the vaults. If you want us to leave you here alive, then step aside."

Jacob moved and could see there was the one speaking along with nine other aliens, all armed and agitated. He could see they weren't trained fighters but, with ten guns at short range, it wouldn't matter. Kobvir would be hamburger before they could get to him.

"I'm not giving you this ship," Kobvir was saying. "I suggest you all turn around and leave this hangar before my Red Strike team returns and kills each and every one of you, then kills your families, neighbors, and anybody who you even waved to in the commons. You've seen what they do, you know I'm not lying."

Jacob had a burst of hope as the mob seemed to waver at the mention of the Red Strike team. He wondered if Kobvir wasn't aware they weren't coming back or if he was just bluffing.

"He's lying," a new voice shouted as a new player walked from the office area toward the group. "His Red Strike team is dead. He had them killed by Taukkir mercenaries. I know this for a fact."

The mob turned back to Kobvir, their rage renewed, and began to advance. Jacob knew he had seconds to do something but most of his usual moves would only result in at least one dead Cridal and likely taking a few hits himself.

"Damn, damn," he whispered. "You guys come up here. We're going to have to do something crazy."

"Sweet!" MG said.

Kobvir had backed as far as he dared near the ship. Not that it mattered. He wasn't a pilot, and they'd killed his flight crew already.

He had just been about to leave when one of the locals came up to him and asked him to check over one more thing. When he let the bastard get close enough, he ended up looking down the business end of a plasma blaster. The rest of the mob showed up, demanded the flight crew disembark, and then killed them without warning.

After that it devolved into a tense stalemate that he was losing.

They still weren't too sure about killing a high-ranking Cridal official, but they really wanted what was in those crates.

Any minute the dam would break, and they'd rush him, probably just beat him to death with their hands and feet. Just when it seemed like they were ready to pounce, a loud bang echoed across the hangar near the back wall.

"Everybody! Look out! They're behind you!" a voice boomed from an open door, pointing frantically behind the mob.

The group, already high-strung and fearful, spun around with yelps of terror and weapons raised. Kobvir was no different, hoping irrationally that the figure was pointing to his Red Strike team coming to save him. As soon as they had all turned, Kobvir vaguely registered hearing something like a maneuvering jet fire but, when he turned back, his view was blocked by a battlesynth that had suddenly materialized in front of him.

It grabbed him by the front of his clothes, spun him about, and *flew* up the ramp into the ship, slapping the controls to close the ship just as the mob turned around and screamed in rage. Kobvir huddled on the deck as he heard weapons fire erupt, but none of it made its way into the ship before the ramp closed and locked. His sense of relief was short-lived as he was roughly grabbed by the battlesynth and put into restraints, then dragged over and lashed to the bulkhead with a cargo strap.

"Do not move," it said before running disappearing in the direction of the bridge.

"What the..."

As soon as Jacob shouted, Tin Man fired his repulsors and arced across the hangar bay, slamming down right by Kobvir and grabbing the startled bureaucrat. As soon as he was turned and Tin Man had his body between him and the mob, Jacob and MG opened fire. Five of the mob went down immediately before they all scattered, screaming in fear and firing wildly. Since they had shit for cover near them, Jacob and MG had to reposition as well and sprinted for some substantial looking machinery used for ship maintenance.

"So far, so good!" MG smiled as the freighter lifted from the deck and moved toward the open bay doors.

The remaining locals understood they were outmatched and hit the general alarm. This would bring all the station security at the checkpoints they bypassed running into the area, likely far more than they were set to handle.

"Sully?" Jacob asked over the hyperlink channel as MG hammered at a group of three aliens with his dual-barrel plasma cannon.

"I'm here. A freighter just left the hangar and is moving out at high speed. That you guys?"

"One of us. Tin Man grabbed Kobvir and left in that ship. MG and I are in the hanger still under fire."

"Coming in."

"Negative! Hold fast. They sounded a general alarm, so we need to seal the front entrance to make sure they don't bring in something big enough to hurt the *Corsair*. Standby...this will be quick either way."

"I can be quick, Cap," Sully said.

"Just hang on until— Fuck!" Jacob flinched as the machine he was crouched behind took a hit from something big and molten metal sprayed all over his armor and the exposed skin of his right wrist.

"Shall we?" MG asked, holding out a grenade to him and pulling another off his harness for himself.

"No affirmations on your grenades anymore?" Jacob asked.

"That was just while I was deep in therapy discovering myself," MG said. "I'm all better now."

"Really?"

"The doc said she never wanted to see me again." MG shrugged. "Sounded pretty clear that I'm cured."

"That's not— Fuck it. Which target?" Jacob asked.

"Our buddy with the cannon," MG said. "Thirty meters, two o'clock. He's behind that spare engine cradle."

"Ready...throw," Jacob said. Both grenades arced up and over the obstructions, bouncing off the far bulkhead and landing a second before they exploded.

"Ha! Twofer," MG said as two mangled bodies were flung out from behind the cradle. "Looks like we're clear."

"There's four more, two injured, I think, but still mobile," Jacob said. "Come on. We need to seal that main entrance."

The main entrance to the hangar was wide open. It was also mangled to the point that they couldn't close the doors, much less seal them off. The next reachable chokepoint was all the way at the main entrance, but there would be no way they could make it there before station security swarmed them.

"What now?" MG asked.

"Hold the entrance here as best you can, but don't take any chances," Jacob said. "If they're coming, retreat, and we'll backtrack through the secret entrance and try to make it out another— Shit, we can't do that. I smashed the lock."

"As usual, sir, I stand in awe of your foresight and planning."

"Shut up," Jacob said, unable to think of a better comeback. "You know what? I changed my mind. Hold the entrance even if it means blocking it with your perforated corpse."

"Will do, Cap."

Jacob sprinted back into the hangar bay and looked around until he found what he was looking for: a universal load lifter. The boxy, heavy vehicle was found in nearly every hangar and could do damn near everything. It had powerful hydraulic arms, extendable conveyor ramps, and enough power to be used to tow smaller ships around if needed. More importantly, however, was that it was big enough to jam into the entrance opening and too heavy to easily dislodge.

He leapt up onto the driver's platform and powered up the loader, spinning it around so he was backing toward the entrance. The sound of weapons fire told Jacob that MG had been engaged so he pushed up the throttle to full speed, which wasn't much.

MG turned and saw him coming, flashing a huge smile and a

thumbs up before laying down withering suppressive fire with his dual-cannon, smoke coming off the weapon as he pushed it to the limit.

After maneuvering to the right side of the short passage, Jacob swung sharply to the left so he could jam the vehicle into the opening at an angle. The back of the loader went through with a *screech* of metal on metal before the protruding arm booms slammed into the bulkhead, stopping his progress. He deployed the stabilizer arms, further jamming it into the entrance and killed the power before shooting up the control panel with his pistol.

"Not bad, Cap," MG said with a nod.

"You're about to be on fire," Jacob told him as he hopped down, pointing to wear the searingly hot weapon had set his tactical harness to smoldering. MG tossed the weapon away.

"She was ruined anyway," he said. "One of my favorites, too."

"Sully, the hangar is secure. Come get us," Jacob called over the hyperlink.

"Yeah...that's going to be tricky. The station alert extended to the surrounding space. They're deploying starfighters and blocking off all hangar entrances, yours included," Sully said. "Is there anything you can get out in?"

"Putting aside the obvious issue that neither of us are pilots, no," Jacob said. "There's some antique looking Eshquarian fighter in half a million pieces and some spare engines for a ship that wasn't even here, and that's it. Tin Man took the only flyable ship."

"Hang on, let me think of something," Sully said. "Can you hold out for a few minutes."

"Guess we'll find out," Jacob said.

31

"What've you got in mind?" Murph asked.

"Something I shouldn't even be considering," Sully said. "It's dangerous as hell. For them *and* us."

"Sounds like our sort of plan."

"We can shoot the gap in the coverage easy enough, but the usual landing cycle for getting into a hangar, and then back out is long," Sully explained. "What I can do is come in hotter and not actually land."

"You mean just get into the hangar and hover?" Murph asked.

"Too dangerous to Jake and MG with the main engines in normal flight mode." Sully shook his head. "I can try to put the forward part of the ship through the barrier, let them get on through a forward airlock, and then back us out before the defending ships can get a shot at us."

"You can do that?" Murph asked skeptically.

"I said I can try," Sully corrected. "This isn't something we train for, and there's not much margin for error."

"You're in command right now, but my vote is we try it," Murph said. "If not, they'll be captured or killed. If they're caught, there will be no diplomatic solution to get them back."

"Okay, then," Sully said, taking a deep breath. "I guess I'll try not to kill us all."

"That's the best we ever hope for."

"You want to *what?*"

"As soon as you see the starboard airlock, you go for it," Sully said. "I won't be able to come to a full stop or hold her completely stationary. You might need to use your Superman shit to throw MG up since I need to keep her nose off the deck. Got it?"

"No," Jacob said. "But what the hell, let's do it anyway."

The pair had still been working to make sure the station security couldn't find a way in, as well as having to kill one more of Finvak's people they found hiding in a side office. So far, the assault on their improvised barricade had been ineffectual, but it was only a matter of time before they brought in their own machine that could dislodge the loader. At least they had enough sense to not just use explosives and blast half the section into space.

"What's that crazy bastard about to do?" MG asked.

"It's better if you don't know," Jacob said. "Just stay back from the bay opening."

They didn't have to wait long. The *Corsair* seemed to just appear out of the blackness beyond the barrier, coming in so fast that Jacob and MG both flinched and ducked, certain Sully had miscalculated and that they were about to die.

"Holy shit!" MG screamed as the *Corsair* jerked to a halt with her aft section still out in space. As soon as the airlock popped open, Jacob grabbed MG and shoved him.

"Go!"

Jacob discarded his own weapon and put everything he had into covering the distance, streaking past MG and skidding to a halt underneath the bobbing nose of his ship that was almost five meters off the deck still. He turned and waved MG to pick up the pace.

"I can't jump that—" Jacob grabbed him by the harness and swung him around in a full circle before launching him up into the hatchway. He made it through the opening, but the ship bobbed right as he was thrown. As it dipped, MG slammed into the ceiling, and then into the deck, Then, the ship rose again.

Jacob didn't stop to see if he'd cleared the airlock before leaping, but the nose pitched up just enough that instead of easily clearing the hatchway, he slammed into the hull. Right before he would have slid off, his left hand snagged the lip, the powerful actuators grabbing so hard that he stuck.

"Your other hand!" MG appeared in the hatchway and outstretched his arm. Jacob swung around and clapped his right hand into the other, and MG easily hauled him into the ship and pushed him out of the way so he could close the hatch.

"Sully! We're in!"

The only response Jacob got was the engines roaring, and both he and MG pitched forward into the bulkhead as the *Corsair* reversed out of the hangar. Jacob ripped his helmet off and bolted for the bridge.

"What's happening?" he asked as he ran to his station Murph had just vacated.

"We're running," Murph said since Sully was concentrating on flying. "We're being pursued by six, no...eight Di-Shyosi fighters. What the hell did you do in there?"

"We just tossed a couple grenades," Jacob said. "Nothing to get too bent up about. Are they making any demands?"

"Nope," Sully said. "Just coming after us. To be honest, this might just be a pack of dogs chasing the first thing that moved. We're faster, but they were close when the chase started."

"You hear from Tin Man?" Jacob asked Murph quietly.

"We're tracking him," Murph said, pointing to the main display where a blinking green icon named *Obsidian 02* was already into the mid-system and pushing hard. The ship was alone and being ignored by everybody else in the system.

"Who the hell are these guys?" Jacob asked, pointing at a cluster of capital ships moving downhill flying generic beacons.

"No idea," Murph said. "Three ships. Smallest one could be a frigate."

"I don't like it," Jacob said.

"More ships joining the pursuit," Sully said. "You sure you didn't steal anything?"

"Well, yeah," Jacob said. "But it's all on the ship Tin Man is flying. What's our risk?"

"Moderate, but climbing," Sully said. "We're free of Di-Shyosi's interference so we're about to pour on the speed. So long as they have no true interceptors, we should be home free."

"New contact," Murph said. "Meshed-in ahead of the unknowns. Resolving beacon...Saabror cruiser."

"Think they're here for us?" Jacob asked.

"They're turning to intercept," Sully said. "Gave away the game a little early, but they're definitely turning into us."

The computer didn't have much on the Saabror ship classes, but it did let him know that the *Corsair* would have trouble going head-to-head with it. But they could mesh-out well before the ship was in range, so what the hell was their strategy? You can't box someone in with a single ship.

"There have to be more ships on the way," Jacob said.

"Agreed," Sully said. "They send that one in to get us to react, then feed course data to their incoming taskforce. They're going to pin us down."

"Ship is yours, Sully," Jacob said. "Just let me know what you need, but all tactical decisions are up to you."

"Copy," Sully said, sounding calm and confident as always, but Jacob could see the sheen of sweat on his forehead.

"Mettler?" Jacob asked. Murph.

"Stable. Resting. Punctured one lung but the nanobots are stitching him back up."

"I'll go sit with him," MG said from the back of the bridge. "I'm useless up here right now."

They flew on for another hour with not much happening. The cruiser continued to move on a direct intercept and, interestingly, the unknown capital ships accelerated and were now racing toward the inner system, ostensibly to Di-Shyosi. The thing that made Jacob take note was their acceleration profile of the two larger ships. Even the newest ConFed cruisers couldn't match it.

His ruminations over the unknowns were cut short when the pursuing ships began decelerating and turned sharply off-course, taking them back to Di-Shyosi. That could mean only one thing.

"Here they come," he said. "Fighters just broke off pursuit, blockade ships will be moving in next."

"Mesh-out?" Sully asked.

"Give it a minute longer," Jacob said. "They won't coordinate this to be instantaneous. I don't want to leave Tin Man until we're absolutely sure we can't escape."

"I think he's waiting for the same before he leaves, but he's already out of normal com range. We're waiting for him to get a hold of us over slip-com," Murph said.

"We really need to get him fitted with hyperlink," Jacob said.

"Unknowns changing course," Sully said. "Turning in on us."

"Damn," Jacob sighed. "Their blockade was here the whole time, just stupidly deployed. Keep us here as long as possible, Sully, and then mesh-out heading back to Dorshone."

"Copy."

"New mesh-in signatures," Murph called out. "Two. Behind us and splitting apart, same class as the ship ahead of us."

"That's six capital ships after us?" Jacob asked. "What the hell do they think we have?"

"No!" Sully said, sounding excited. "Only three. The unknowns just activated their ident beacons. Two UEN destroyers, the *Essex* and *Hampton*. Also, one frigate...the UES *Kentucky*."

"What the hell?" Murph asked. "The old man came out here?"

"Incoming hyperlink channel request," Jacob said, grimacing as he accepted it. "Go for *Corsair*."

"Captain," Webb's voice came over the bridge speakers. "You have him?"

"He's on the light-freighter you see crossing into the outer system with Tin Man, sir," Jacob said. "We had to split up to get him out alive."

"He *is* alive?"

"Alive and well, sir."

"Out-fucking-standing, gentleman," Webb said, the relief in his voice obvious. "I knew you'd come through. I want the *Corsair* heading back to Dorshone, and get Tin Man to follow. We have a beachhead there and, at the moment, the package is too hot to take back through Cridal space. We'll make sure your new friends don't try to pursue."

"Understood, sir," Jacob said. "*Corsair*, out."

"Getting a hold of Tin Man now using the address he last used to contact us," Murph said.

"Course set for Dorshone," Sully said. "On your command, Captain."

"Hold," Jacob said. "Murph?"

"He was already anticipating this order," Murph said, pointing at the screen. The icon labeled *Obsidian 02* stopped and started blinking with a blue halo around it indicating it had meshed-out. "He'll meet us over Dorshone."

"Get us out of here, Sully," Jacob said.

"We're gone."

32

Jacob sat in the officer's lounge with the rest of his team aboard the UES Kentucky watching the broadcast from Earth, hardly believing what he was seeing.

"This is real, sir?" he asked.

"Now you see why it was absolutely critical you succeeded," Webb said somberly.

The space around Dorshone had turned into a base of operations for the Navy and the CIS to continue scouring Saabror space for human abductees. The problem was that nobody had kept records of individuals when they took them, only the raw numbers. Families had been split up, people had died without being recorded, and the captives themselves were so disoriented they knew very little except for their day-to-day existence in the camps.

It had been just over a month since Obsidian had fled Di-Shyosi, not knowing the outcome of their mission would be the political equivalent of a neutron bomb going off. The ripples propagating out were carrying profound ramifications throughout the entire Orion

Arm Region that shocked and frightened Jacob, both for the safety of himself and his team as well as for all of humanity.

"I am speaking to you now after an emergency session of the Unified Council," President Weinhaus said after stepping up to the lectern. The previous two hours had been a government spokesperson giving a briefing on the scope of the trafficking rings that had targeted human colonists.

"Here we go," Webb muttered.

"As you've just heard, we have been investigating a massive trafficking operation that spanned much of the quadrant. While thousands upon thousands of humans were caught up in their snare, so were many other peoples of different species," Weinhaus said, seeming unsure of his footing as the speech lurched on.

"The United Earth Navy and the Naval Intelligence Service have done excellent work in tracking down our missing people and even locating most of them. They are being rescued and processed for return to Earth as I speak. They have also discovered who was behind this atrocity and, unfortunately, it hits close to home.

"Corrupt elements with the Cridal Cooperative were actively working with underworld organizations to capture and transport human captives to the Saabror Protectorate. This is in addition to the Cridal being implicated in an attempted theft of one of our most sensitive military assets and—" the president was drowned out by the shocked cries from the audience and shouted questions from the press pool. He gamely kept talking for a few more seconds until he gave up and stepped back, waiting with his hands clasped behind his back until they quieted.

"I understand your shock and outrage," he said. "I share in it. I assure you, steps are being taken to prevent this from ever happening again. This brings us to the most important aspect of this press conference.

"In accordance with the Untied Earth charter, the Unified Council has exercised its right to a simple majority vote on exo-planetary treaties and alliances. Our decision is that Earth, and her vassal worlds, will no longer be a member of the Cridal Cooperative."

This announcement was met with stunned silence. The cameras were panning the crowd, and everyone simply stood there with their mouths hanging open.

"The Cooperative government has already been notified of our decision and that it is irreversible. Cooperative diplomats have been expelled and, for the time being, we are cutting all ties, both economic and diplomatic, with Syllitr. The breach of trust is simply too vast for this to be considered politics as usual. I want to assure you, however, that we are not considering any retaliatory action, military or otherwise. There will be no questions taken at this time, and information will be forthcoming through official channels. Thank you."

Weinhaus walked from the stage to shouted questions and, oddly, a smattering of applause. Jacob wasn't sure what they were cheering about, or if they were just so overwhelmed it was an automatic response to someone concluding a speech.

"Holy shit," Mettler whispered. He was ambulatory but still not one hundred percent after being stabbed in the chest.

"This is half the reason I called you guys over," Webb said, gesturing to Reggie Weathers to kill the monitor. "The decision to leave the Cooperative was based entirely on the information we gained from a strangely compliant Kobvir Glecsh. If you guys hadn't grabbed him alive, the council would have likely not had the balls to pull the trigger on secession. For going above and beyond as you always do, I salute you."

"Did Seeladas Dalton know about it, sir?" Murph asked.

"We don't think so. She was aware Kobvir had some side enterprises going on that he was using Cridal military assets on, but word we're getting is the prime minister is beginning to suffer what could be a break with reality. Her advisors tell us they're having difficulty making her understand things these days."

"So, why the hell were they taking people?" MG asked. "That's never made sense."

"That's the other part you're here to learn," Webb said. "Reggie?"

"The Saabror Protectorate is dying," Weathers said. "I mean that literally. They've had a series of events that has caused a population collapse on an unprecedented level. Within the last fifty-five years, they've lost nearly eighty-three percent of their total population."

"That's impossible!" Jacob said.

"So, it would seem, but I assure you it's true," Weathers said. "Entire planets were abandoned as the surviving groups kept consolidating. They tried to hide it from outsiders as their scientists tried to figure out a way to reverse their implosion, but once they reached a tipping point, it seemed that the three major species within the Protectorate could go extinct."

"What the hell happened?" Sully asked.

"A combination of things. The first was a fast-acting plague that wasn't caught in time before it could spread across multiple systems. Centuries of genetic tampering in one species ended up causing a massive decline in birthrates. There is also some suspicion of external influence, but that's not been verified by our people."

"So, they needed a worker caste?" Murph asked. "Slaves?"

"Not slaves. New citizens," Weathers corrected. "They were going to repopulate their planets with species they knew to be productive, intelligent, and prolific breeders. Humans were identified as one such species, and the Saabror approached the Cridal Cooperative about facilitating it. Kobvir knew that Seeladas would not entertain such a proposal, so he seized the opportunity to go into business with the Saabror himself. His rationale was that by taking colonists who were looking to start a new life on another planet already, he wasn't really doing anything all that wrong."

"They would control travel and communications on and off the planets for a time and let the populations adapt and flourish," Webb said. "Within a few generations, you would have young, growing, healthy populations on planets you'd already colonized and industrialized. Given enough time, the people on those planets would never even know they weren't originally from there."

"Diabolical," MG said. "Are we getting ready to mount up and kick the shit out of them now, Admiral?"

"No," Webb said.

"No?!"

"We see an opportunity," Webb shrugged. "They have the planets, we have the people. You do the math."

"And the miners from Site D?" Jacob asked.

"The Saabror desperately need certain types of skilled labor, resource mining being one of them," Weathers said.

"Seems like there was more to it than that," Murph said. "Those ships were crewed by humans and—"

"And as far as you're concerned, Agent Murphy, that's the end of it," Webb said. "Some things are above your paygrade."

"But—"

"I said that's the end of it," Webb said firmly.

"Copy that, sir."

"You don't have to like it, you just have to follow orders. And now the last thing," Webb said, glaring at his Scout Team. "We looked through that ship you stole. Are you aware of what it's carrying?"

"We didn't have time to read the manifest when we were under fire, sir," Jacob said. "Tin Man?"

"I explored during the slip-space flight," Tin Man said. "The ship is carrying a veritable fortune."

"That's a bit of an understatement," Webb said. "I asked Kobvir about it, and it turns out it was the accumulated hoard of Klytos Finvak. Since he's now a permanent guest of the Eshquarians, it seems like we have a bit of a dilemma."

"We turned the ship over, and none of us were on it to steal anything and not declare it, sir," Jacob shrugged. "And Tin Man doesn't have any pockets."

"I want you to get rid of that ship," Webb said.

"Sure thing, sir. Just let us know when it's unloaded and—"

"Nobody said anything about unloading anything. I just said get rid of it," Webb said, standing to leave. "Immediately."

"That was fucking weird," MG said once he was gone.

"Plausible deniability," Weathers said. "All I'll say is that politics change. Scout Fleet might not exist as an independent force, it might not exist at all at some point, and running a private military operation takes a lot of money. Wouldn't you say so, Captain?"

"I...guess it does," Jacob said, looking at Murph and shrugging. The agent, however, seemed to understand the subtext.

"We'll take care of it," he told Weathers.

"See that you do," Weathers said, walking out.

"What the hell did that mean?" Mettler asked.

"It means we need to fly that ship up to the Eshquarian Empire and make some more deposits," Murph said. "Then ghost the ship. The admiral wants independent sources of funding for this operation if the political climate goes sour on us."

"We should leave immediately," Tin Man said, gesturing to the black monitor where the president had been speaking. "I have a hunch we are going to become a lot busier soon."

"Yeah," Jacob agreed. "Bad times are coming."

EPILOGUE

"Have a good evening, Senator."

Douglas Rushton ignored his driver and stepped out into the rain for the short walk to his front door.

The last few months had been nothing short of a nightmare. All the work, preparation, and risk...all for nothing. He'd heard through a friend in the UEAS that the NIS had Kobvir Glecsh at a black site on Olympus, still questioning him. Douglas now lived in constant fear that his involvement in the trafficking operation would be disclosed. Given the current mood on the planet, he would never make it to trial. They'd come and tear him limb from limb.

The absolute kick in the balls was that he just heard the Unified Council and the Saabror were working out a deal to let any colonists who wanted to remain on the worlds they'd been taken to would be allowed to. So, after all the Collective's scheming and plotting, the council was just going to give it away for free. Un-fucking-believable.

Lydia Shafer hadn't been much help. Her indifferent attitude had come with two clear messages. "You win some, you lose some," and, "You are no longer of any use to us, good day." She'd even had the unmitigated gall to have him escorted out of the house like a common beggar. At least she had taken care of Mitchell. She said he'd been on Terranovus but still no sign of Gabrielle.

"Carlos! Where the fuck are you?" he shouted after the front door clicked shut. "Why are all the damn lights off in here?"

Douglas stomped through the house looking for his butler. The man was normally at the ready for him, the house prepared for the evening. The place felt abandoned. It even had cold chill like the heat had been turned off. When he came around the corner toward the kitchen, he saw that the light was on, so he made his way toward it.

"Carlos! Why aren't you answering me?"

"Carlos has been given the evening off," a voice said from behind his right ear. "That was very generous of you." Then, Douglas was shoved so hard he went flying into the kitchen, sprawling onto the marble floor.

He turned and saw who it was, his mouth dropping open.

"But...you're dead!"

"No," Glenn Mitchell said. "You're dead, Douglas. You died the minute you decided to let Gabby be taken and Janet killed."

"I-I don't know what you're talking about," Douglas blustered.

"That's okay," Glenn said pleasantly as he walked into the kitchen. "I already know the truth. Your admission of guilt is not required."

"It was Lydia and her friends who—"

"Oh, I already know all about their role in this. Don't worry. They'll all be getting visited. I just wanted to do this one myself. Give it that personal touch, you know?"

"What are you going to do to me?" Douglas was nearly in tears now, his heart hammering in his chest so hard he thought he was having an attack.

"I already told you...I'm going to kill you," Glenn said, pulling a hypodermic needle out of a plastic case. "Don't worry...not gonna torture you. I can't have your friends getting spooked and locking down. If it makes you feel any better, I'm going to kill Lydia next."

"It does, actually," Douglas said.

"See! No worries. Now that you've accepted it, you can be a man about it and not a blubbering infant."

"Can't we just—" Glenn lunged so quickly that Douglas almost didn't see it. He flinched and, when he looked up, the other man was still holding the hypodermic needle. It was empty.

"It's peaceful," Glenn said, putting the needle back in the case. "Which is more than you deserve, and more than Lydia Shafer will get."

"Is...Gabby... Is—"

"She's alive," Glenn said. "Safe and hidden."

"That's...good." Douglas couldn't keep his eyes open and felt himself drifting off into a deep, peaceful sleep he so desperately needed. "This...isn't so bad."

His heart stopped fifteen seconds later, triggering a signal through his neural implant that would bring emergency crews within the next twelve to fifteen minutes.

"No, Douglas," Glenn said, "not bad at all."

ALSO BY JOSHUA DALZELLE

Thank you for reading *Aftershock.*

If you enjoyed the story, Lieutenant Brown and the guys will be back in:

Blackheart

Terran Scout Fleet, Book 6.

Subscribe to my newsletter for the latest updates on new releases, exclusive content, and special offers:

Connect with me on Facebook and Twitter:

www.facebook.com/Joshua.Dalzelle

@JoshuaDalzelle

Check out my Amazon page to see my other works including the #1 bestselling military science fiction series: *The Black Fleet Saga* along with the international bestselling *Omega Force* series:

Printed in Great Britain
by Amazon

22873468R00158